BROOD

ALSO BY CHASE NOVAK

Breed

BROOD

CHASE NOVAK

MULHOLLAND BOOKS

Little, Brown and Company

New York Boston London

The characters and events in this book are fictional. Any similarity to real persons, living or dead, is coincidental and not intended by the author.

Mulholland Books/Little, Brown and Company
Hachette Book Group
1290 Avenue of the Americas, New York, NY 10104
mulhollandbooks.com

First Edition: October 2014

Mulholland Books is an imprint of Little, Brown and Company, a division of Hachette Book Group, Inc. The Mulholland Books name and logo are trademarks of Hachette Book Group, Inc.

The publisher is not responsible for websites (or their content) that are not owned by the publisher.

The Hachette Speakers Bureau provides a wide range of authors for speaking events. To find out more, go to www.hachettespeakersbureau.com or call (866) 376-6591.

Library of Congress Cataloging-in-Publication Data
Novak, Chase.
  Brood / Chase Novak. — First edition.
     pages cm
  ISBN 978-0-316-22800-8 (hardback)
1. Parenthood—Fiction. 2. Twins—Fiction. 3. Horror fiction. I. Title.
PS3569.P455B77 2014
813'.6—dc23   2014018984

10 9 8 7 6 5 4 3 2 1

RRD-C

Printed in the United States of America

For Celeste

BROOD

PROLOGUE

They were not here to clean up a crime scene. That grisly work had been accomplished two years ago by RestorePro, when the town house on Sixty-Ninth Street was closer to hell's ninth circle than it was to its former incarnation—a stylish, impeccable, historically correct Upper East Side town house, one of the few left in New York City that had remained in the same family since its construction. Its last owner had been Alex Twisden, who had lived there his entire life, first as a child, then as a playboy, then as a corporate lawyer obsessed with his work, then as a somewhat reclusive bachelor, then as the newly wed husband of a beautiful younger woman named Leslie Kramer, then as the father of twins, and, finally, stemming from the fertility treatments he and Leslie endured in order to procreate, as a kind of beast for which neither science nor folklore has a name.

RestorePro's workers, decked out in muck boots, respirators, and HAZMAT suits, had swooped in. Of course, the worst thing about the cleanup was the blood, the hair, the fur, the bones, and the teeth, the parts of bodies for which neither Alex nor Leslie had a taste—they both eschewed ears, and found feet as a rule inedible. But there was a lot more to do than simply remove the evidence showing that for a time the elegant

3

old house had been an abattoir. There was disinfecting to be done. There were odors to be dispelled and others that could only be covered up. There were scratches in the plaster, claw marks deeply grooved into the wooden floors. There were piles of smashed furniture—it looked as if crazed vandals had gotten into the storeroom of Sotheby's before an antiques auction. Once-precious Blackthorn wallpaper, brought into the house by William Morris himself, hung in long drooping curls. Sconces had been torn from the walls; sofas had become public housing for all manner of rodents. RestorePro's motto was No One Will Know, but though the workers did their job diligently, and did not stint on labor or time, the house they left behind when they finally got to the end of their contract still bore the ineffable marks of a place where something hideous had happened. You did not have to believe in the spirit world to sense that an aura of misery and doom hung over the place, even after it had been scrubbed clean.

Two years passed. If the house was haunted, the ghosts had it to themselves. The doors were locked. The shutters were closed. The electricity and the gas were disconnected. Alex's estate paid the taxes on the place, though his once-sizable fortune had been severely compromised in the ten years between the fertility treatments in Slovenia and his sudden bone-crunching death in front of the Metropolitan Museum of Art, where he was struck down by a Fifth Avenue bus. (Leslie's violent death—more clearly by her own design—came shortly after, on a tarmac at the Ljubljana Airport.) Alex Twisden's sister wanted nothing to do with the place, and though Leslie's sister, Cynthia Kramer, an antiques dealer herself, had always had a love for the house that bordered on lust, she was not in line to inherit it. It really belonged to Alex and Leslie's twins, Adam and Alice, but they were only ten years old when their parents died and had been left to float unhappily through the troubled, murky waters of New York's foster-care system.

Their mother's will had been quite clear on the subject: the twins were to go to her sister, Cynthia. But the law moved slowly, following its own maddening path, and two years passed before Cynthia had a date in Surrogate Court to finalize her adoption of the children. She would move from San Francisco to New York, and the twins would be restored to their old home—a site of countless terrifying nights, but nevertheless the only real home they had ever known.

Cynthia did not know these children very well, but she was thrilled to suddenly have an opportunity to be a mother, a chance she would have said, even recently, was as remote as her becoming secretary of state or a rock star. She granted that, once upon a time, Alex and her sister had been loving parents to the twins, but the last year or two with their parents had been terror-filled, and the time in foster care, well, who knew what damage that had done to them? Cynthia accepted the fact that the twins would need rehabilitation, a lot of it. Therapy perhaps. Tons of love, for sure.

She had tons of love.

And more where that came from. She had never been more certain of anything in her entire life. She could and would love these children back to health. She would return to them their birthright—to be well educated, to be safe, to be cared for, and to live in their beautiful house.

And so, as the wheels of the legal system slowly turned, Cynthia presided over the final renovations of the house on Sixty-Ninth Street from the opposite coast, organizing the whole thing via e-mails, phone calls, and Skype from her shop in

Pacific Heights. There were light fixtures to be torn out and replaced, a kitchen to be modernized, nine bathrooms to be redone, some in need of a little twenty-first-century touch-up, some needing…everything. There was furniture to purchase, windows to be replaced and curtained or shuttered; there was flooring so brutally scarred that it needed to be torn up and replaced, and there were sixteen rooms that needed repainting.

The most pressing job, however, was the cellar. It was here that Alex and Leslie kept their tragic menagerie, the cats and dogs, some bought at pet shops, some "rescued" from various shelters in the tristate area. The cages and cramped runs in which these doomed beasts were once confined had to be removed, and all evidence of their ever having existed had to be completely erased. The cages were heavy and had been bolted into the cellar's stone walls. Mack Flaherty, the contractor overseeing the entire job, had saved the cellar for last, and to make certain it was finished on time—Cynthia was due in New York in a week—he hired more men. They worked fourteen-hour days to get the job done. A few of the workers heard the squeak and scratch of rodents in the walls, but it was in nobody's best interest to admit to it. The finish line was in sight. Cynthia was on her way. Let's get 'er done, was the mantra; all the guys were saying it. Let's get 'er done.

CHAPTER 1

"Y ou know what I always say?" Arthur Glassman announces to Cynthia as he elbow-guides her through the echoing halls of the Surrogate Court in downtown Manhattan. "If life gives you lemons, what you have to say is 'Hey, life! Enough with the fucking lemons already.' " He is a stout man with an expansive smile and an expensive smell—the smile cost him about $100K and the smell was $315 an ounce. He can be a fool for a beautiful woman—and Cynthia is quite his type. She has shiny dark hair parted in the middle, a generous mouth, a long neck, broad shoulders, long legs. When he attends parties with his wife, and a woman of Cynthia's type walks in, Mrs. Glassman pokes Arthur in the ribs and says, "Hey, there's one for you." Once upon a time, Arthur had been Alex and Leslie Twisden's attorney, and now he has become Cynthia's, without exactly being asked to. He has worked without compensation helping Cynthia to get the poor twins out of the foster-care system and into her custody once and for all, and now they are at the finish line and he is happy—if *happy* can be used to describe anything that arose from his relationship with the twins' late parents.

"Will I be able to take them home with me?" Cynthia asks.

"I believe that today's your day, Cynthia. My hope is that

7

with all the time that's passed, this town's morbid curiosity about the children will have faded and they can lead a normal life—if teenagers can ever be called normal." He winks to show he is more or less joking.

"They've been through a lot," Arthur says. "Psychologically, of course. The loss of their parents. And both of them, as you know, have severe eating disorders. They've been hospitalized many times."

"I'm an excellent cook, Mr. Glassman," Cynthia says. "I have to believe that with some stability in their lives, they'll eat normally."

"My theory too," Arthur says, patting her arm. "I think refusing to eat has been the only control they've been able to exert, since everything else in their lives was out of their hands."

"Well, I've cooked for all kinds of people. I know kids can be picky eaters, but I'm pretty comfortable in the kitchen. I actually love to cook."

Arthur glances over his shoulder and suddenly steers her into an empty courtroom, which seems to be all but waiting for them. The door closes behind them with a breathy *ooomph*.

"It's a very complicated situation, Cynthia. I want you to be fully cognizant of that. These terrible treatments Alex and your sister went through—they weren't the only couple to do it, you understand? Many people of means availed themselves of those treatments. Sometimes it worked out well, and sometimes…" He spreads his soft hands, as if to make room for the unspeakable. "Funny, isn't it? How money can put wings on your feet, but you can end up flying to places you never should have gone."

"So other children had to live with the terrors that Adam and Alice lived with, is that what you're saying?"

"And some of them are still out there. That's what I'm saying. Not many, but some. Not just here—a lot of places. But with a concentration here in New York because…" He smiled his pricey smile. "We have more than our share of one-percenters. Frankly, I wish you'd take Adam and Alice away from here. But at least you plan to drop the Twisden name—wise decision, and one that the court intends to uphold."

"You speak as if everything's already been decided."

"Oh, it has, it has. Your sister's will stated quite explicitly that the children were to go to you, and there was nothing in Alex's will one way or the other regarding permanent custody of Adam and Alice. No one has stepped forward to contest the will and the City of New York is more than happy to be released from its financial obligations to these little orphans. As far as the court is concerned, there could be no better resolution of this matter. The twins will be with their aunt, and the foster-care system can cease paying for their upkeep, beginning today. And, just between you and me and the lamppost, there are people in city government—shall we say, at the highest reaches?—who have a special interest in seeing that justice is done for those children."

"And what about the house?" Cynthia asks. "Has that been decided too?" She clears her throat, glances away. She does not want to appear overly interested in the Twisden town house on East Sixty-Ninth Street. She was not sure what the appraised value of the place was, but it had to be a fortune, even with its recently acquired reputation as a site where monstrous acts were committed.

"Ah, yes. The house. Of course. The social workers have given it the A-OK," Arthur says. "You did an admirable job putting that place back together again."

"Have you been there? Have you seen it?"

Arthur shakes his head no. He cannot imagine ever stepping foot in that house again.

"It must have cost a lot," he says.

"Yes. There are services that specialize in that sort of thing. Just the cleaning was nearly a hundred thousand dollars. I had to sell some of their things to cover the costs."

Arthur looks shocked, as if she has just confessed to something that strains the boundaries of attorney-client privilege.

"I don't want to hear anything about that, Cynthia."

"What choice did I have? The place was uninhabitable." She shudders, shakes her head, remembering how she used to lust after that classic Manhattan town house, with its graceful staircases, the sconces, the tables, the paintings, the rugs. Much of it had disappeared as Leslie and Alex's life spiraled out of control; they had sold off a lot of it (often at shockingly low prices), and most of what was left had not survived daily life in the house.

"I worry about the kids going back to that place," says Arthur. "But on the other hand, it's the only home they've ever known."

"They won't be living there as Twisdens," Cynthia reminds him. "They'll be Kramers. And they won't be attending their old school."

"Well, we'll wait and see," says Arthur.

As they make their way through the courthouse corridors, it seems there's no one Arthur does not know, or at least no one whom he does not feel obligated to acknowledge, either with a nod or with his standby verbal greeting: Well, look at you!

Cynthia is overdressed; she looks as if she should be strolling through the lobby of some chic hotel rather than down the scuffed, chaotic corridors of municipal justice. She is wearing four-inch heels, a pencil skirt, her most expensive satin blouse. Yesterday, on the phone, she'd asked Arthur how she should dress for her court date, but he'd made light of her concerns.

"Just don't wear a cape," he'd said. "Or one of those bracelets shaped like snakes, with little ruby chips that look like shining red snake eyes. But honestly? I wouldn't worry too much. You should see some of the people the court sees fit to send children home with. Mothers with tattoos! Whoever thought we'd come to a time when Mommy's got a tarantula tattooed on the small of her back and Daddy's wearing eyeliner? It's a whole new ball game out there, Cynthia."

Arthur pushes open the swinging door of courtroom 4 with all the swagger of a sheriff walking into a saloon.

"You're late, Mr. Glassman," the presiding judge calls out as soon as she sees him. She is a tall, weathered woman with a voice that sounds like a chain-smoking Canada goose. "My docket is full full full, and I can't be wasting time, not today."

As the two approach the bench, Cynthia glances at the people in the gallery. Many of them—actually most—appear to be staring at their shoes; it takes Cynthia a moment to realize they are all surreptitiously staring at the screens of their hopefully named smartphones, despite the widespread notices throughout the courtroom prohibiting the use of cell phones. Here, the supplicants before the law come in all the shades and sizes of a great city, seated on pews in a church whose bible is the Constitution, waiting to contest a will or further an adoption. Somehow, Arthur used the influence he gathered in the course of his long career and jumped Cynthia's petition for custody to the top of the docket. It makes her feel a bit queasy. Where she comes from, this kind of line-jumping is considered bad manners. She decides to make it easier on herself by avoiding all eye contact. She fixes her stare straight ahead as she and Glassman approach the judge, who is swiveling back and forth on her high-backed leather chair while satisfying an itch on her scalp with a long bright yellow pencil.

And that is when Cynthia lays eyes on her niece and nephew for the first time in years. They are seated front left, their knees touching, holding hands. Even though she knows they have been resisting food, refusing it, possibly even throwing it up, their thinness stops her in her tracks for a moment. They have nothing extra. Each one's skin fits like a wet suit, like paint on a wall. And yet, there is a beauty, the beauty of youth, unvanquished even by the madness of self-starvation. They are both gracefully tall, with quiet, shy demeanors. Ethereal. They have their mother's reddish-blond hair, their father's stubborn chin and slight underbite. The sight of them breaks something that has been frozen inside of Cynthia. She lets out a gasp, holds on to Arthur's arm for balance, and begins to weep.

Arthur has considerately arranged for a car to take Cynthia and the twins home, and as soon as the three emerge from the courthouse, they see a dark blue Lincoln Town Car at the curb with a liveried driver holding a hand-lettered sign bearing Cynthia's surname—Kramer. She glances over her shoulder, looking for Arthur, but he is nowhere in sight. Probably one of the innumerable people he knows has detained him in the corridor. *I'll call him later,* she thinks as she shepherds the twins into the backseat of the car and then gets in herself.

They are off without delay, pulling quickly away from the curb. A moment before they blend with the northbound traffic, a hand pounds angrily on the passenger-side window.

The sound of it fills the car like gunshots. Startled, Cynthia grasps the children's hands. She sees a tall, long-faced man in a chauffeur's uniform shaking his fist at their car as it begins its journey to the Upper East Side. As the car moves, she twists around for another look at him—his sneering mouth, his furious eyes. He pulls a phone out of his jacket quickly, as if he were drawing a gun.

Dennis Keswick, in a chauffeur's uniform, watches the Town Car with Cynthia and the twins pull away. Those kids have no idea how close they came to getting themselves snatched. Not only today—today, Dennis must admit, was a long shot, a sudden inspiration on his part when he learned that they were going to be in Surrogate Court—but over the past year, while they were both in foster care. If there was someone who cared to listen, Dennis could fill his ears with the ins and outs of drugging and capturing a child; it is simply not as easy, not as straightforward nor as foolproof, as the average person assumes. It is a very difficult job. And very underappreciated. Oh, well…they were not the only fish in the sea. Dennis's superiors (whom he hated, as a matter of fact) had a special interest in Adam and Alice, but meanwhile, there were other similar little beasts for Dennis to deliver.

"You folks comfortable back there?" the driver asks. His face is difficult to make out. He has a full beard, though there is something oddly childlike about him too. The visor of his chauffeur's cap is yanked low; he wears a scarf—in summer!

"We're okay," Cynthia answers. "Right, kids? Are you cool enough?" She worries they might be cold, without any fat on their bodies to insulate them. She feels enormous next to them, filled with hundreds of rich meals, oceans of tortellini and crème brûlée.

A thought presents itself: What if she were still drinking? Her breath catches for a moment. She closes her eyes and thanks the Higher Power for her sobriety.

"Hey," she says to the twins. "I have a little present for you, no big deal." She'd been counseled by friends and books that kids recoil if they think you're making a big deal out of something. She opens her purse and takes out two wristwatches. As soon as she touches them, however, she thinks she has made a mistake. They are ridiculously gender-specific: an American Girl watch for Alice, a Swiss Army watch for Adam.

She decides to let them choose which watch they want— both will fit their slender wrists.

"Funny," Adam says, choosing the American Girl.

"Alpine," says Alice, choosing the Swiss Army.

"I know kids don't really use watches anymore," Cynthia says. "What with phones and all."

"No, this is amazing," Adam says, strapping on the green-and-yellow watch with its face splashed with stars and daisies.

Cynthia also read that *amazing* is what kids say now instead of *cool*. Things are clicking into place; this might not be as difficult as she was afraid it would be. Afraid? Forget it. Try *petrified*. Try *sick with dread and uncertainty*. Try *hourly confrontations with her own inexperience*. Becoming a parent at her age is like suddenly moving lock, stock, and barrel to a new country, knowing only a few rudimentary phrases of the language.

"More AC?" the driver asks. His voice is foggy, strange, off. It occurs to Cynthia that he might be transgendered. What a brave new world!

14

"We're fine back here," she says.

She glances down at her hands and notices they are shaking. As much as she has looked forward to having custody of her sister's children, she feels right now that the whole thing has been sprung on her as a huge surprise. No amount of thinking and wishing and planning has prepared her for this sudden and overwhelming sense she has that two helpless children have been entrusted to her. They have been through hell, and now Cynthia must remind herself that she has within her the power to restore them to some semblance of the carefree happiness and safety that she believes to be the birthright of every child.

After accepting her gifts, they are paying no attention to her whatsoever. They are holding hands and gazing at each other. Their silent, cellular communication has not lessened in the many months they have been apart. Cynthia feels a small pang of exclusion, but mainly she is happy they have reconnected. Overjoyed, really. Overjoyed. No one will ever understand Alice the way Adam does, and no one will understand Adam like Alice, and thank God they are back together. May they never be separated again!

"Did you have sisters where you were?" Alice asks Adam.

"I guess. They had two girls, two boys, and me."

"Were they nice?"

"The last ones? Which ones do you mean? I had four different families."

"Yeah. The last ones."

"They were pretty old. They worried a lot about money. You had to choose if you wanted one of the heated rooms or a real lunch."

"I bet you took the heated room," Alice says.

"Definitely!"

"Eating's weird."

"My Staten Island family served goose on Christmas Day," Adam says.

"Ick. Let's be vegetarian."

"Okay," Adam says. "How many calories do you do?"

Alice frowns, looks away. "So I guess you're all mature and everything now, right?" she murmurs.

"No way!" Adam says, as if it were a matter of honor.

And then, after a few moments of silence, Alice says, "Did you do okay in school?"

"No."

"Me neither."

The ringtone on Cynthia's phone is chapel bells, and they are chiming now in her purse. She glances at the screen: *Arthur Glassman.*

"Hello, Arthur," she says.

"Where are you?" he asks. He sounds furious.

"In the car. Thank you for arranging it for us." She sees the driver's eyes glancing back at her in the rearview mirror.

"Your car is here, Cynthia. Waiting for you."

Chug-chug. The driver uses his controls to lock the doors.

CHAPTER 2

In a long, narrow apartment overlooking Gramercy Park, Ezra Blackstone and his sixth wife, Annabelle Davies, are fighting over air-conditioning. Ezra is seventy-one years old and has circulation problems and feels clammy and cold even on a hot day like this. Annabelle is twenty-eight; she spent the first twenty-seven years of her life in Monroe, Louisiana, and then, as she frequently says, she "came north to get out of the fucking heat." They'd had a rather nice courtship, particularly refreshing to Annabelle, who'd come to believe that gallantry, seduction, roses, and romance were a thing of the past. The touch of her young flesh, the lemon-and-spearmint tang of her kisses, were like a time machine to Ezra, restoring him to a youthful vigor. But the rituals of courtship soon gave way to dailiness, and the excitement of her young flesh soon stopped working its decade-dissolving magic on Ezra. Since marrying five months ago, they have fallen into squabbling about any number of things, including where to eat, which candleholders to use, how to get to Amagansett, how much to pay their house-keeper, and whose turn it was to feed the piranha. But today's confrontation over whether or not to air-condition their apart-ment is one of the most bitter fights they've had in weeks—

well, if not weeks, then at least days. Or, at the very least, the worst fight they've had today. So far.

For now, peace has been restored. The air-conditioning remains off, but the windows overlooking the park are wide open, letting in a soft summer breeze, barely strong enough to stir the gauzy white curtains.

Their nerves are unusually taut because they are expecting the doorman to ring them any minute to announce a visitor, a young boy named Boy-Boy. Boy-Boy did not give—and perhaps does not even have!—a last name. He was that kind of visitor. Ezra's connection to Boy-Boy is through Bill Parkhurst, who worked for Ezra back in the day, when Ezra was producing three daytime game shows, one on each of the major networks. Bill had been a loyal lieutenant but was, in Ezra's view, weak of character, always chasing after the newest revolutionary therapy, the most enlightened guru, the next can't-miss self-help regimen and, even as a young man, consuming a fistful of vitamins and supplements with every meal. And drugs too, of course, he had a contemptible weakness for drugs and the attendant softheaded beliefs—peace through pot, enlightenment through LSD, ecstasy through Ecstasy. Bill's latest enthusiasm is something called Zoom, a drug so new to the New York underground that it is not even illegal.

"A few years ago," Bill had explained to Ezra during lunch at the Carnegie Deli, peering over a pastrami sandwich that was nearly as tall as he was, "a few very desperate people went over to some cockamamie place in Europe for fertility treatments."

"I remember," Ezra said. "I remember the story well. Don't tell me you're taking that."

"No, no. Some of those people went crazy, and I think a few of them died. I like shtupping, but I'm not meshuga." Bill had been raised in a bleak wintry village in New Hampshire by a Congregationalist minister and a descendant of Betsy Ross, but someone had told him when he was starting off in the entertainment business that it would be helpful to his career if he sprinkled a few Yiddish words into his conversation, and though there was no reason to believe the advice had any value, he had taken it to heart anyhow, and now it was an integral part of who he was.

Bill took a modest bite out of his sandwich and chewed in silence twenty-six times before swallowing.

"It's their kids, they carry just enough of whatever that doctor gave those poor schmucks. It's in their blood, you know? Just a *bissel*. But the kids are supercharged. And a few drops of their blood? Whew. It's like *havah nagilah,* and then have another *nagilah*."

"What the fuck are you talking about, Bill? Children's blood?"

"Hey, they're not such children. They're a lot bigger than me. Some of them have beards. I mean, come on. And believe me, they're doing very well for themselves. They may be a bunch of shmendriks living who knows where, but they are first-class *hondlers*."

Ezra felt Bill's eager little hand touching his leg under the table. Knowing the drill, Ezra put his hand under the table and accepted what Bill had brought—it felt smooth and cool when Ezra closed his hand around it.

"What did you just give me," Ezra murmured.

"A vial of blood. You just drink it."

"Yeah? And get ass AIDS? What the fuck, Bill? Really, man. What the fuck."

"Best shtupping I've had since Haifa," Bill said, referencing, as he so often did, a trip he made to Israel in 1973.

The elderly Korean waiter approached their table, limping badly. "You want I should wrap that up for you, maybe have it for a nosh later on?" he said, indicating the elderly men's half-eaten lunches.

Later that week, Ezra was worried and bored enough to try the elixir Bill had given him, and, just as promised, he made love to his wife that night for the first time in weeks. It was not the best sex he had ever *ever* had, but it was without question the most pleasure he'd felt in months. And there was something wonderfully...ferocious about it too. He wasn't shy about sharing with Annabelle the source of his vigor, and she agreed with him that it might be even more fun if she took some too. (She didn't want to make waves and fully intended to stay married to Ezra until he died, but her body felt sluggish and thick with sexual boredom, so if there was something that could get her hobbled hubby humping away like a sailor on leave, she had every intention of getting in on the action.)

The delivery is due at ten, and, right on time, the doorman calls up and says, "There is a Mr. Boy-Boy to see you, Mr. Blackstone."

A couple of minutes later—Ezra and Annabelle are on the nineteenth floor—there is a startling *boom-boom-boom* cop-like knock at the door. Ezra is the one who goes to answer. He carries an envelope with three hundred dollars in twenties in it. He's already been told the cost is two hundred and fifty dollars, but his plan is to treat the kid right and maybe become a favorite customer, just as he used to regularly tuck a twenty into the headwaiter's tunic at the old Russian Tea Room. Back in the day.

Ezra opens the door to Boy-Boy. He is younger than Ezra

had expected. Fifteen? Sixteen, tops. Dark luxurious eyebrows, with another set of eyebrows tattooed over them. He has hair down to his shoulders, a wide mouth, a small nose, green eyes, and the air of a wild boy living without protectors or rules. He wears blue jeans and a dirty T-shirt and carries a backpack with decals of flags of all nations plastered over it.

"Ah, you must be Boy-Boy," Ezra says. He gestures the boy in and closes the door behind him.

Boy-Boy walks through the apartment's long hall, and Ezra must hurry to keep up. Now they are in the living room, where Annabelle sits on the sofa fanning herself with a copy of *Vogue*. Boy-Boy looks appraisingly at Annabelle and then back at Ezra. "Don't yous two worry. Everything's going to be money. Dr. Boy-Boy is here."

He sits and wriggles free of his backpack, which he then places on his bony lap. He opens the backpack and takes from it a small vial of blood, so dark it looks almost black.

"Weird color," Ezra says.

"You's want it or you's not?" Boy-Boy puts his hand out, waiting for the envelope.

"I want it, but I want it to work."

"It's going to work. All me's customers come through other customers. Folks ain't money, me's fucked." He holds the vial up, cocks his head. "You don't like the way it tastes, put it in a soup or something. Little garlic, maybe some red pepper flakes. Some of me's customers use cilantro. Drink some water. You should be hydrating anyhow. Peeps don't drink enough water. Wait maybe fifteen minutes and you's money."

Ezra feigns a toss of the envelope but holds on to it. "I've got a question."

Boy-Boy looks at Annabelle. "Your old man always like this?"

"Always."

"How does this even work?" Ezra asks. "And why?"

"First of all, it's none of your fucking business," Boy-Boy says, his voice oddly reasonable. His smile is fierce, a bright white knife. "You want it, here it is. You don't—me's taking your little envelope anyhow because me's came all the way over here and Boy-Boy don't do nothing for nothing."

Annabelle has seen more violence in her life than Ezra has, and she thinks of him, despite his age, as naive. She cautions him, using one of Ezra's stock phrases. "Moving right along now, Ezra. Moving right along."

"I heard it was a lot better if it was fresh," Ezra said, his voice a sneer. "What do you say you draw the blood right here, right in front of us? Word on the street is that's the way to go."

Boy-Boy shakes his head. "Word on the street? Listen, old man, you don't know shit about anything that goes on in the streets of this city. Word on the street. You's got to be out of you's mind." He stands up, wriggles his backpack on again. "You's want what I got? Want to do the wicked dance? You's want to make this lady forget she married some dude with one foot in the grave?"

"Listen here, you little punk—"

Boy-Boy turns his gaze toward Ezra with the suddenness of an animal in the wild. There is no expression at all on his face except total absorption. His eyes are without emotion. They are only for seeing. And seeing and seeing.

In a heartbeat, he pounces on Ezra and runs him back toward the open windows.

Do it, Annabelle thinks, though at the same time she has never felt such terror in all her life. She hears her own screams as if they were coming from another room.

Ezra is not a small man, but he can offer no resistance to Boy-Boy. Boy-Boy scoots him across the living room as if the old man weighed no more than a pillow. The next thing Ezra knows, he is half out the window. The upside-down world, with its taxicabs honking and nannies pushing strollers and a dog walker with eight dogs straining at their leashes, looks so distant and so sad…

A few moments later, the crazy kid pulls him back into the apartment, sets him on his feet, straightens his clothes, and dusts him off, like some valet from hell.

"We's good?" Boy-Boy asks.

"Yeah, yeah, we're good." Ezra is still holding the envelope, and he hands it to Boy-Boy, wishing there weren't an extra fifty in there.

Boy-Boy winks at Annabelle. "Have fun," he says, and he tosses the vial of blood to her.

Just like back home, where nothing was ever simply passed. Her brothers used to toss everything, from saltshakers to car keys to hammers. She snatches the vial out of the air and closes her hot little hand around it.

CHAPTER 3

Stopping the car in the middle of Center Street, impervious to the honks and furious shouts his blocking traffic has caused, the driver reaches into the back of the car and wrests Cynthia's cell phone from her. His beard is bright with perspiration. A thick aroma of sweat and anxiety comes off him like heat off a highway.

Cynthia gathers the twins close to her. They neither resist nor welcome her touch.

"Who are you?"

"Friends of Alice and Adam sent me. Me's not hurting anyone and we's not doing anything wrong." It's clear now: he is no more than sixteen years old.

"What's your name?" Alice asks. Her voice is steady, soothing.

"Toby," the boy says. "Toby's a money name, yeah? You like that name?" He starts to drive again. New York is filled with people who don't want to go where they are going but who are also frantic to get there. His finally moving the Town Car and freeing the frozen traffic seems to do nothing to soothe the furious drivers who have been honking and cursing at him and who continue to do so. "Going to take you to us's place. People are waiting for you."

The twins exchange worried looks.

BROOD

"You're going to take us home, Toby," Cynthia says. "And if you don't, you're going to get in more trouble than you'll know what to do with."

"Fuck you, lady. Okay? You's in Toby's car, and you's on Toby's ticktock. And this poor creature named me will fuck yous up." He suddenly pulls into a bus stop, then turns around, glowering. "This being none of your business," he says.

"Where you taking us, Toby?" Alice asks in a calm, friendly voice.

"Rodolfo is waiting for you," Toby says. "You and you can live with us. We's got a sick place way up on Riverside, yous won't believe it. Bedrooms and bathtubs and all the foods we's want. We's kind of rich now, we's in business."

"Sounds great," Alice says. "What do you think, Adam?"

"Rodolfo," Adam says. "He always liked you."

"Oh yeah," Toby says with a laugh. "Big-time."

"What about the lady?" Alice asks. "We don't even know her." She touches Toby's shoulder with her fingertip. "She's like our aunt or something."

"Yeah, let's dump her," Adam says. "Put her out right here."

"So how is old Rodolfo anyhow?" Alice asks. Just saying his name gives her a strange feeling. Of all the wild children she knew when she was running from her parents, Rodolfo was the one she liked the best. The last time she'd seen him, he was leaning out of a window and saying, "I love you." To her. To her!

"Rodolfo is king," Toby says. "He runs the whole bidness, capiche? Back in the day, we's all crashing here and there and we's sleeping in the park and shit, but now we's all carrying a knot of fifties and hunnerts and living in a bee-you-tiful place, wait till you see it. We's making some mad money." He pulls out of the bus stop, merges with the traffic.

"Let's dump her and go," Adam says, a little more urgently this time.

"Adam!" Cynthia says. "I'm your mother now."

"My mother's dead," Adam says, thumping himself in the chest. "You're no one's mother."

"She got us out of foster," Alice says, her voice soothing, as if she is trying to talk a cat down out of a tree. "And now we're free." Then, almost as an afterthought, she adds, "But she's okay. Let's not hurt her. Okay?" She touches Toby's shoulder again.

Adam tries the back door. "Open it up and let's get her out of here. And go."

Toby hits the master switch, and the locks pop up.

"Stop here," Adam says.

"Or wherever," says Alice.

They are on Canal Street now. The owners of the shops selling headphones, old DVDs, Crocs, pot holders, plumbing supplies, household cleaners, plastic flowers, and weirdly deranged-looking baby dolls with red hair and mad eyes have dragged their wares onto the sidewalk and now guard them anxiously as thousands of pedestrians stream by. Toby pulls into a loading zone behind a feeble little truck from which two sad-looking, overworked Chinese women are unloading open cartons of shower slippers.

"All right, get her out of here," Toby says.

"I'm not leaving," Cynthia says. She jams her feet against the back of the front seat, locking herself into place.

"She probably wants her phone," Alice says.

Toby glances at the phone on the empty seat next to him. "Fuck it," he says, tossing it back.

Alice catches it, puts it in Cynthia's purse.

"Go," Alice whispers.

"Absolutely not," Cynthia says. So this is what it's like, parenting. Jesus Christ Almighty, it's a nightmare…

"Flush her," Toby growls. "Come on, we gotta bounce."

The twins close their small but shockingly strong hands on Cynthia's arms, and, despite her efforts and in spite of her cries and threats, they pull her out of the car. Will she ever see them again? Her mind is chaos, an explosion of words, terrors, and impulses. They have overwhelmed her, and the world throbs and spins.

The next thing she knows, she is standing on the street with the twins beside her.

"Let's go, get in," Toby calls out to Alice and Adam.

But the kids take Cynthia by the hand, Adam on the right, Alice on the left, and, holding on to her, they break into a fast walk, a trot, a run.

They hear Toby's furious shouts.

The screech of tires as he guns the car into reverse.

"Subway," Alice says.

"On the corner," says Adam.

"Oh, kids, kids," Cynthia manages to say. Her feelings are symphonic—strings, brass, pounding timpani—and she feels a love beyond any measure.

As they run toward the subway entrance, the children lift her hands and bring them to their lips and kiss the backs of them. One of them—she is too rattled, too confused, to say which—also licks her hand.

Rodolfo sits on the window seat of the rambling old apartment on Riverside Drive. He is trying to keep his mind occupied—there is so much to take care of, orders to keep track of, money to stash; his business has a hundred moving parts—but he cannot keep himself from continually checking the street below for signs of Toby and the twins, and now he has succumbed to his own preoccupation and simply sits there, waiting.

Alice.

Oh, Alice…

In the time Alice was out of the city, he thought of her often. And when he learned she was returning, his desire to see her became a kind of mania. To hear her voice. To touch her. He has waited patiently for this day. And now the day has come and he has no more patience. His mind races. He has so much to show her. The apartment. The money. The Sub-Zero Pro 48 fridge, perfect for keeping blood market-fresh.

Rodolfo hears footsteps behind him, *click-click* on the bare hardwood floors. He doesn't want to be bothered and does not turn around. He sees from the reflection in the glass that it is Polly, just about the smartest and the least wild of all the cast-off boys and girls of Rodolfo's crew—a crew that includes not only the nine people living here on Riverside but about a hundred others, spread around the city in squats, shelters, and parks.

Polly waits for Rodolfo to acknowledge her presence. A minute passes. Silently. Finally, she speaks.

"Maybe there's a lot of traffic."

"Maybe," Rodolfo whispers.

She waits for him to turn around. She has always known she is not pretty enough for him.

"You can't do her, you know," Polly says. She is aware of the sneer in her tone, regrets it.

Rodolfo doesn't respond and gives no evidence that he is even aware of Polly's presence.

"Just saying…" Polly says. She turns to leave—but can't.

She still believes that misunderstandings can be cleared up with a sentence or two. "I hear she's really sweet," Polly says. "Alice. But, you know, all I'm saying is if you had an accident, the baby might be really...you know. Weird."

"Well, here we are, kids," Cynthia says, putting the long shiny key into the lock of the twins' ancestral home on East Sixty-Ninth Street.

Because she has been supervising the cleanup of the house, Cynthia can now see it without being flooded with memories of Leslie and Alex and the life that once took place in these stately rooms. She can see it without recalling the museum-quality antiques, the profusion of heirlooms, the gloomy old oil paintings of long-deceased Twisdens. And she can also finally see the place without nauseating memories of the depths to which it had sunk—the clawed walls, the mildewed upholstery, the locked doors, the cellar filled with kennels that were also abattoirs.

She wonders, How does the house look to Adam and Alice? This is their home. But it is also the place where they were imprisoned at night, the place they risked their lives to run away from. As she opens the door and ushers them in, she is very glad that the air inside is cool and that the first thing they see is a vase full of white roses.

Yet something is wrong. She feels a presence in the house. She does not pause to think it over. She pushes past it, but the thought clings to her, like the smell of tobacco after you've walked across a smoky room.

"Well, kids," she says, but that's all she has time for. The twins have burst into the house, and now they race madly into its interior, their feet pounding on the newly varnished floors, their excited voices echoing against the high plaster ceilings.

This is the moment she has been waiting for, and she stands in the foyer clutching her purse to her breast and letting their joy infuse her. She breathes deeply. Though the house is nearly 170 years old, it smells new: untold hours of scrubbing, disinfecting, sanitizing; fresh paint, new plaster, sanded and varnished floors. This is going to be their home. This is where the healing will be done, and where they will be a family. A family! The word has never meant more to her than it does right now.

"Up here, up here!" Alice is calling.

"I'm coming!" Adam answers.

Cynthia listens to the crazy drumbeat of his feet racing up the stairs. Oh, to be young. To be able to recover so quickly, to seize happiness the moment it appears.

Cynthia's eyes fill with tears. Like a fever finally breaking, her misgivings have disappeared.

And in their place is a joy like none she has ever experienced. She is not a religious woman, but the warmth filling her right now feels holy. Holy is the love of a defenseless child, holy is putting others before yourself, holy is the memory of her poor sister, holy is tomorrow, tomorrow, oh, beautiful tomorrow — the greatest of God's consolations: time untouched, ours to make the world more perfect.

CHAPTER 4

Toby has parked the Town Car in an underground garage a couple of blocks from the apartment where he and his crew are living, and now, as he walks slowly up Riverside Drive, he tears up the parking stub—it's a stolen car, after all, and he has no intention of reclaiming it. What is he, stupid? He is in no hurry to return to the apartment and face Rodolfo's fury over his failure to deliver the twins. (Everyone in the crew knows that Rodolfo is fucking obsessed with little Alice, though Toby for the life of him can't figure what he sees in her—she basically looks like her brother, chest and butt included.) There is no question that Rodolfo is going to be mad. The only real question is what he will do to Toby. You never knew with R. Sometimes he was totally cool about things and did not hold himself above you, did not judge, and just went with the flow. And then other times he was totally insane and you'd end up getting shoved against a wall or slapped in the face, and once two guys had even been kicked out of the apartment, kicked out of the crew, and were left to make it on their own, and no one knows what happened to either Ulysses or Menachem; maybe they were dead, maybe they were somewhere in Central Park or upstate or—you never knew—living large in the Hamptons, sleeping in the scrub oak forests during the high season and maybe squatting in some mansion when summer was over and all the princes and princesses were back in Manhattan.

The sky is full of little clouds, like sailboats in a harbor. Toby stops to look. Usually the New York sky didn't have those puffy little clouds; usually it was just one color or another. A long alligator-shaped cloud was chasing a bunch of lamb-shaped clouds due north, straight up the Hudson. *Come on, guys, book,* thought Toby, urging on the little clouds.

When he lowers his eyes, he sees a man walking toward him. Tall. Mushroom-colored. Maybe thirty years old. Lonely-loser type. Short dark hair spiked out in all directions, greased up and shiny in the sunlight. He wears black pants, belted high, and a Yankees T-shirt that looks as if it were being worn for the first time. He carries a beat-up black book—maybe a Bible?

Toby can tell by the way the guy moves he isn't just out for a stroll. He looks as if he is walking right over to Toby—and in this, Toby is right.

"Good morning," the man says. He stands on the sidewalk close to Toby.

A couple of child-care workers walk by, pushing strollers and speaking to each other in Spanish. Toby and the man make room for them, stepping off the sidewalk for a moment.

"May I show you something?" the man asks.

"If it's you's junk, me kill you," promises Toby.

The man smiles. His teeth are small and lusterless, perhaps from a vitamin deficiency.

"Something much more interesting," the man says. He seems to have some kind of accent, and then a moment later he seems not to. The man holds up the black book.

It's not a Bible after all. Thank God for that! But on closer inspection, Toby sees that it's a photo album, chock-full of plastic pages. Is this guy going to show him some gross picture?

"Me's not interested," Toby says. He pushes past him.

"Oh, you will be," the man says. "I promise you that." He stops Toby, grabs his upper arm.

Toby wonders: *Does this guy even have a clue that I could tear him to shreds?* He yanks his arm away and is surprised at the strength of the man's grip—not strong enough to hold Toby still but a lot stronger than Toby would have guessed.

"What kind of pictures?" Toby asks. The guy's got him curious. And Toby is in no hurry to get back to the apartment.

"Family photos," the man says. He pronounces it strangely—"pho-toes," with a long pause between syllables. "Here, look, just this one." He opens the book, pages through it while humming softly. "Yes. Here. This is interesting."

Still holding the book, the man shows Toby a page of slightly faded snapshots, the colors gone soft and blurry, a world of melted crayons. They are pictures of a man and a woman in an office of some sort—a medical office, judging by the poster of a skinless figure illustrating the human circulatory system. The man has a widow's peak, sunken eyes, a long nose. He looks supremely uncomfortable. The woman has a young, rather melancholy face and a graying ponytail. She is shapeless, as are her clothes.

"How'd you get these?" Toby asks. He clears his throat.

"You are recognizing them?" the man asks.

"Yeah. Me's mommy and daddy." Toby reaches out as if to touch them but thinks better of it, withdraws his hand.

"And what about this?" the man asks, turning the page. Here there is a photo of the couple, the man with a beard, the woman exhausted and leaning on a cane, both of them looking very much the worse for wear, standing in front of the Museum of Modern Art with a four-year-old boy between them, holding their hands.

For a moment, Toby is unable to speak. His eyes mist over. He clears his throat again, dries the corners of his mouth with his knuckle. "Little man cub," he whispers. "Taken back in the day when me's not scared yet." The look of pain on his face suddenly turns to suspicion and anger. "Who's you? Why you's going around with snaps of me's old folks at home?"

"Would you like to have it? For a memento, a keepsake?"

Toby would like to have that picture of him standing between his parents, but he is reluctant to say so. It's been four years since he's seen them. He's not even certain they are alive. They were living on the edge last he knew; they could be anywhere, in California, six feet under, or just across town. Yet he cannot altogether refuse the man's offer. His hand remains suspended, hovering over the photo album.

"Would you like to know how I have this?"

"Because you's a fucking pervert?"

"No. I'm a man of science who works with other men and women of science. Come. We'll find a bench across the road in Riverside Park. We'll sit and you'll hear the story."

He pats Toby on the back, rather hard, between the shoulder blades, as they cross Riverside Drive.

Toby feels a stinging, a nasty little pinch, where the man patted him. He reacts for a moment, but as quickly as the little twizzle of pain appeared, it vanishes. He looks over his shoulder, making certain they are not too close to his apartment. The last thing he needs is for Rodolfo or any of the crew to look out the window of their rambling nineteenth-floor apartment, with its views of Riverside Park and the Hudson River, and see him sitting on a bench with some stranger when everyone has been waiting for Toby to deliver Alice and her brother.

"Let's walk a little bit this way," Toby says, turning south and indicating a bench a hundred feet away.

The noise from the West Side Highway sounds like a gigantic angry hornet.

They pass a chubby old man in shorts walking a dog that strains at the leash and visually checks each tree for squirrels. That little painful spot between Toby's shoulder blades starts to act up again. It is devilishly placed so he can't reach it no matter what angle he comes at it from. At last, with much straining and twisting, he manages to touch the sore spot with one fingertip. It's wet! He quickly pulls his hand out of his shirt and checks his finger, wondering if he'll find blood. But no. The wetness is like tears, devoid of color.

Maybe me's popped a pimple, he thinks. He sniffs his fingertip. Weird smell, a bit like burning rubber. Oh, well. The pain has subsided...

They sit on a bench, their backs to the Hudson, the apartment houses of Riverside Drive lined up like massive gravestones in front of them, and the man makes himself comfortable, laces his fingers behind his neck, crosses his ankles.

"First, Toby, Toby Whitaker, let me tell you my name. My name is Dennis Keswick. I work for a company called Borman and Davis. We are a bioengineering company and we are very, very interested in special young men and women like yourself."

"Weird," notes Toby. He tells himself, *Get up,* but his brain seems to be speaking a different language than his legs.

"There is—or was—a doctor in Europe, in Slovenia, actually, who made it possible for you to be born."

"Me's know this," Toby says. His voice is muffled, as if it must make its way through layers of gauze.

"Good for you, Toby. You're a smart lad."

"Me's not smart," Toby says, lowering his eyes.

"Of course you are. You're just…unique. And we want to find out just how unique. You understand? That doctor used a formula to help your parents conceive. His fee was very high, and the procedure was painful, so we must assume that your parents tried every known fertility treatment in the world before seeing him." Keswick pauses, pats Toby's leg. "It must be quite wonderful to be so wanted. In my little life, it was not the case. My father never wanted a child; in other words, he did not want me." Keswick's laugh has all the merriment of gravel being shaken in a tin can. "But my mother resisted his entreaties to abort. She was a good Catholic girl. And a punching bag for an ignorant baboon."

"Me's can't get up," Toby murmurs.

"Yes, I am sorry about that."

"What did you do to me?" He twists his arm and reaches to touch his back, but the movement is awkward, exhausting, and he gives up after a couple of tries. "You stuck me."

Keswick smiles, nods approvingly. "Smart boy; you don't take all day to put two and two together."

Again, Toby tries in vain to stand up.

"Don't be upset," Keswick says, almost crooning. "You're about to make a great contribution to science."

"Me's not liking science," Toby says, barely audible.

"Oh, it's good to make a contribution." Keswick lowers his hand to his book of photographs, as if he is being sworn in before testifying in court. "My rocky beginnings—well, they prevented me from excelling in school, and by the time I was your age, it was already too late for me to go to MIT or Stanford and receive the kind of education someone needs to compete in the world today. The men I work for—and women, by the way, women too—they're geniuses. I don't dispute that. But they have also been the recipients of untold advantages. Oh, well, we do what we can. Isn't that right? And now it's your turn. It should make you feel good, Toby. Because up until now, let's face it, your life has been meaningless. I know how you live. I know where you live. I know what you do to stay alive."

"You don't know shit," Toby says, but without much conviction.

"You sell your blood. That's very foolish, you know. You can get in trouble."

"We's already in a lot of trouble. Rodolfo says you can't drown a fish." Toby dries the corners of his mouth with the back of his hand.

"Those two you were giving a ride to today, Toby. The twins. Alice and Adam."

Toby looks at him blankly.

"We'd like to work with them. They are of particular interest to us."

Toby shrugs, looks away.

"It's okay. We know where they are going. We'll see what we can do to convince them to help us out."

"What you's wanting?"

"Everything, Toby. Everything. Bloodwork. DNA. Psychological testing. Anything that will give us the means to duplicate what makes you all so special. Fountain of youth? Maybe. Fertility? Well, that's already been demonstrated. Whatever it is that you kids have in you—it makes testosterone look like a cup of weak tea." He runs his fingers over the back of Toby's hand.

"No."

"For a boy with such a rich beard, you're not very hairy elsewhere, are you," Keswick says. "Your hands are smooth. Your arms—not too bad. How about your legs?" He reaches down, yanks the cuff of Toby's pants, lifts it. Dark down covers the shin, not remarkably different from what you'd expect on a teenage boy. "Good! You may be very important to our research."

"Me's feel like crap," Toby manages to say. He reaches back, runs his hand over the top of a large bush behind the bench. His hand clenches, and he pulls several little leaves off the bush, each delicate one the size of a mouse ear. In an attempt to revive himself, he shakes his head vigorously and tries to stand up, but his legs refuse to cooperate. Everything within him—his blood, his breathing, his thoughts—seems to be going slower and slower and slower and slower. Except for his heart, which is pounding with fear, racing as if it wants to outrun and escape his failing body. "Hey, me's needing some help here." He takes hold of Keswick's wrist.

"Hang in there, son. Your ride's here." As Keswick says this, he gestures to a battered white van parked at the curb. By all appearances, it's a van belonging to a plumbing contractor. It says *Watertight Plumbing* on the side, and there is a drawing of a faucet with a single drop of water leaking from it.

Keswick hoists Toby up and half drags him to the back of the van. "We're going to fix you right up, son," he says. "You don't have a thing to worry about."

CHAPTER 5

Dinner. Cynthia was certain she could cook to the taste of any twelve-year-old, but cooking to the taste of a twelve-year-old who is certain that calories will trigger puberty, and puberty might be the beginning of some practically unimaginable beastliness—that's a whole other matter. She prepares what she hopes is an irresistible meal for the twins in her new, astonishing kitchen—so spacious, so well stocked with everything and anything a semi-ambitious amateur cook could desire. First of all, her signature popovers, simultaneously buttery and light. Burgers grilled. Her own variation of macaroni and cheese, with an herbed bread-crumb crust. Fresh-made lemonade. Cookies from a nearby bakery—at thirty-five dollars a pound, they had better be *legendary* cookies!

The twins sit uncertainly in front of their plates. Their napkins are on their laps. Their hair is brushed, their faces scrubbed, they look obedient, compliant, painfully well behaved. She wants to tell them, *Relax! You're home!* But—as they say in the Rooms—one day at a time.

"Dig in, kids," she says. She hears the excess of gaiety in her voice and reminds herself to keep things light. To a child, all adult emotions are outsize. Adjusting what you project so as to be tolerable to a young psyche means bringing the intensity down several notches, like an actor going from the stage to the screen—what worked on Broadway seems like pulling faces and shouting at the multiplex.

The twins put exceedingly modest amounts of food on their plates, leaving the platter of burgers untouched.

"This is really good," Adam says, taking a cautious nibble at one macaroni.

"This looks like a hat," Alice says, holding the popover.

"Careful," Cynthia says, "it might be hot."

Alice shrugs, as if nothing could be of less concern.

"Are those meat?" Adam asks.

"The ones on the left are regular hamburgers," Cynthia says. "The ones on the right are chopped-up veggies. I heard you guys talking about maybe becoming vegetarian."

"Yeah, we might," says Alice.

"Animal rights," calls out Adam, holding up his fist as if he were at a PETA demonstration.

"I guess I should do that too," Cynthia says. "How would that be? I have plenty of vegetarian recipes. San Francisco, where I used to live? A lot of people there don't eat meat. It's probably the wave of the future."

The twins look at each other uncertainly.

"I guess that would be okay," Adam says finally.

"Do you look like our mother?" Alice asks, breaking the popover into pieces, letting them fall onto her plate.

"She was a little younger," Cynthia says. She has been pre-paring for quite some time for questions about Leslie, but suddenly, faced with the reality of the children and the nearly palpable sense that in each frail chest beats a severely broken heart, she is at a loss for what to say. "She was very pretty. You both have her looks."

"You're pretty too," Adam says.

"Oh, everyone always said your mother was the one who got the looks. I was the studious one. But thank you, Adam. It's very nice of you."

"So, do you?" asks Alice.

"Look like Leslie? Oh, I suppose so. Similar height. Similar build. She had redder hair. And those eyes."

"What eyes?" There is a lightning strike of alarm in Alice's voice. And it reminds Cynthia: the children's most recent memories of Leslie's eyes are probably terrifying—eyes blazing with animal hunger.

"Emerald green, flecked with gold," Cynthia softly says. *How to change the subject?* "Oh, kids, I almost forgot. I made lemonade. Fresh lemonade."

In the kitchen, Cynthia takes the pitcher of lemonade out of the Sub-Zero fridge. She sets it on the counter and takes a deep, steadying breath. The smallness of those children, their startling skinniness, their helplessness, their aloneness. Her own love for them is suddenly so bright a flame that it burns away even the pity, leaving only love's purest ember.

She gathers herself. They don't need to see their new mother with weepy eyes and a red nose. Once upon a time, she would have suppressed this rush of emotion with a stiff drink, and now, as has been her habit for years, she thanks God for her sobriety. She is here. She is present and accounted for. She has embarked on the greatest journey of her life.

When she walks back into the dining room, the twins' chairs are empty. They must have left just a few seconds ago. She can hear their little footsteps scurrying up the stairs.

*   *   *

Cynthia is in her bedroom, which used to be her sister and brother-in-law's bedroom and which Cynthia initially had not wanted to make her own. But in this sixteen-room house of four levels, with a library, three parlors, a game room, and enough sleeping quarters to accommodate fourteen people, it is still the best bedroom, with plenty of sunlight in the daytime yet angled in such a way as to protect it from street noises at night—New York is not only the city that never sleeps but also, she has come to realize, the city that doesn't want you to sleep either. It's a city that would like you to keep it company during its endless insomnia. The master bedroom is an airy, spacious room, majestic, really, with a white marble fireplace, parqueted floor in a starburst pattern, and, the one modern touch, a huge, hedonistic bathroom with a steam shower, a Jacuzzi, heated towel racks, and full-length mirrors that must have broken Leslie's heart to look in after those fertility treatments wrecked her once-beautiful body.

Like all old houses, the town house on East Sixty-Ninth Street speaks its language of thumps and twitters and creaks and squeaks, especially at night. It takes getting used to. If you let yourself get frightened by all the odd noises, you'd never have a moment of peace. It's a little after eleven at night, and they've lived here for a week.

A full moon sails over the spires of Manhattan, almost unreal in its brightness and perfection, and it seems to pause for a while to send its cold silver light through the slats of the shutters on Cynthia's bedroom windows. Cynthia, wearing an old T-shirt and underpants, sits yogi-style in the middle of her bed, sipping from the tumbler of Saratoga water. She sips, swallows, and listens, wondering if the twins are sleeping. They had both been in foster homes where bedtimes were early and inflexible, and Cynthia had expected them to celebrate their homecoming and their new freedoms by staying up late and keeping to a helter-skelter schedule.

But they seem creatures of habit, and as the grandfather clock in the second-floor parlor strikes ten each evening, they are already making their way up the stairs to the third floor. And how deeply they sleep! Every day, they sleep later. It seems the more comfortable they become, the more tired they are. They are like travelers who have been waiting to come home, yearning like sailors on a distant sea.

And now they are home. To Cynthia's surprise, they both insisted on sleeping in their old rooms—Cynthia would have guessed they would rather have slept on the porch or the roof than spend a night in rooms into which they'd once been locked (night after night after night) and from which they had once been forced to escape. But no, they wanted their old rooms back, and that's where they are sleeping right now.

She places her water glass on the bedside table and picks up her journal and her old Montblanc ballpoint.

Three times in her life, Cynthia has kept a journal. The first was when she was ten years old and her father disappeared, never to return. She wrote in her diary for a few weeks, but she was so consumed by the worry that either her mother or her sister would find it and read it that she wrote the entire thing in code, and the code itself was so complicated that even she couldn't really understand what she had written.

The second time she kept a journal was many years later when Gary Ziltron, her boyfriend at the time and her partner in Gilty Pleasures, also disappeared. But whereas her father disappeared like a lost sock, Gary's leaving was explosive. He left a crazy, mean-spirited letter that undermined her sobriety, said rude things about her body, and all but announced he had never loved her. On top of all that, he took about three-quarters of their cash on hand. The post-Gary journal lasted for nearly two years, and she credited her eventual recovery from the pain and the shame of Gary's leaving her to all that stream-of-consciousness writing.

Now, in New York, she has purchased a beautiful notebook at nearby Dempsey and Carroll, the navy-blue cover fashioned from heavy linen paper, each page faintly watermarked with the company's logo. Her life right now is strange and thrilling to her, and lacking people with whom to discuss it, she has quickly come to find solace and even a weird form of friendship in her journal. *Maybe I always wanted to be a mother,* she writes, and then stops, smiles, remembering that in the seven days she has been writing her thoughts into this notebook, she has already written that sentence seven times. *I always felt sorry for the mothers I knew. Always so preoccupied, so drained. Kids are like vampires; they suck the blood out of you. Or so I thought. But now in the silence of this beautiful house, savoring the late hours when my thoughts are my own, I can hardly wait to hear their footsteps, their voices. Tonight's dinner was not a total success, but still, it was something, a first step. I know I can do this. I know we can get this right. I can hardly wait for morning to come when I can meet them in the hallway as they pad down the steps from their bedrooms on the third floor. I can hardly wait to ask, Anybody hungry? Who wants breakfast? I love them. I love them so much. It's like a fever that you pray will never break.*

She turns the page.

It's amazing how well they've adjusted. All those days and nights apart, living in foster homes. However it affected them, they have buried it—at least for now. Mainly, they are delighted to be with each other. Sometimes I feel almost jealous—no one in all my life has loved me the way those two love each other. Need to read up on twins!

I know they are thin—frightfully thin. But that's going to change. And they look sort of great, to be honest. Like little models.

I also need to take it slow. They are not going to bond with me overnight—no matter how much I would like that to happen.

The project of getting them out of the house is still on the old to-do list. They will sit on the porch and watch the passing parade of people—which never stops, by the way. New Yorkers walk everywhere, and they are out and about day and night. But in terms of exercise for the kids and real fresh air (if there is any to be had in this city!)—forget it. I have tried to tempt them, offering to take them shopping or out to eat (yeah, right), but so far all they want is to hang out with each other in the house. Arthur Glassman mentioned a couple of times that I might want to keep them out of Central Park, but so far, it's not an issue. My issue is how to keep their cute little behinds off the sofa and their lovely brown eyes from staring for hours at the TV, which I should never have bought in the first place. And would not ever have brought into our lives if I'd known what video junkies those two little angels were going to be. The only good thing about the TV is that they sometimes snack while they watch—if you can call cucumber slices in seltzer a snack. But who knows? Maybe it will lead to something with a lot of high-fructose corn syrup in it.

At least they don't watch violent shows. Mostly Cartoon Network and family sitcoms. They go for the real super-gentle high-sugar-content fare, the shows where the studio audience is always going Awwww *when one of the kid characters says something adorable or a puppy pokes his little head out of a basket or someone learns a lesson and a hug-a-thon ensues.*

She hears a noise. It is something not in the house's usual nightly vocabulary. This actually sounds as if someone is on the porch, trying the door. She lifts the pen off the page, holds it midair, listens with all her might.

Silence.

A distant rumble. Someone speeding down Lexington with a faulty muffler.

She waits another moment, shakes her head.

Tomorrow morning, Adam has therapy. Wednesday, Alice. They've been seeing therapists since Child Protective Services took over. And of course, of course. They should have that, they need it. Both their parents dead and everything else they've been through. Some of which I doubt I will ever know. But I worry about these shrinks and their theories and I most of all worry about how quick some of them are to put them on meds. I don't want that. All those medications have side effects. Suicide, especially. Both their parents killed themselves, right? So why would any responsible doctor want to risk the twins' safety like that? I don't even know if most of those so-called wonder drugs work anyhow. I'm not sure they're not mainly cash machines for huge pharmaceutical firms.

This is where I put my foot down. I have that right. I get to decide. I am their mother.

God, it feels so strange to write it.

But it's true.

I am their mother.

Dear God, please guide me. Please help me do the right thing.
Again: that sound.

It's more disturbing the second time. Cynthia holds her

breath, cranes her neck, tilts her head. It's the door, the down-stairs door.

But why would it be?

She goes to the window, unconcerned that she wears only a T-shirt. She lifts one of the slats of the interior shutters and peers through. But what makes the master bedroom the best room for sleeping also makes it the worst room for surveying the outside world. Her only view is the back of a few town houses on Seventieth Street—pastel blue and gray by day, black by night—and her own garden, lush now with wild grasses.

She tells herself that she is just nervous. She tells herself that the city's million sounds are freaking her out. She tells herself that right now, the best thing to do is climb into bed, switch off the light, and have a long, delicious sleep.

Except that her heart is pounding like a regiment of monkeys running in place.

She makes her way across the bedroom and opens the heavy, twelve-foot-high oak door. The hallway is dark except for a star-shaped night-light plugged into an outlet halfway between her bedroom and the staircase. A breeze from somewhere touches her bare legs; the down on her thighs stiffens and rises.

She wishes she had a weapon—not that she would know how to use it. As she reaches the top of the stairs—she waves her left arm in front of her, searching for obstacles, like a blind woman in unfamiliar surroundings—she remembers there are two heavy brass candlesticks on a delicate pine table flush with the wall under one of the few ancestral paintings that survived Alex and Leslie's descent into penury. It's of the paper-mill magnate Thomas Twisden, painted in 1887, when he was obvi-ously in physical decline, a thin old man with wispy hair and a crooked smile who seems to be realizing in the foreverness of the portrait that all the money in the world would not save him from death.

Cynthia fumbles in the dark for the candlestick. Nothing. Nothing. Then—she grasps it! She wraps her fingers around the dull coolness of its long neck, feeling the deadly weight of its heavy base.

She walks slowly down the stairs toward the darkness of the first floor, which waits for her like a pool of black water. Houses are meant to shelter us from all the dangers of life—yet they can be so terrifying. What if what you hoped so ardently to lock out is exactly what you locked in? For a moment, the headlights of a passing car illuminate the end of a sofa, a lamp, and then all is darkness again.

She reaches the bottom of the staircase, feels along the wall for the light switch. But no…she does not want to announce herself, and she does not want to be seen. There is a lovely Queen Anne single-drawer desk in the foyer where Cynthia stacks mail and upon which are two cups, one for pocket change, the other for her keys. In the drawer, along with a jumble of little objects for which she has yet to find a place, is a flashlight—she has lived most of her life in earthquake territory and knows that a house must have several flashlights. By feeling her way along the walls, she makes it to the foyer. She opens the drawer as quietly as she can and removes the flashlight. She carries the candlestick in one hand and the flashlight in the other, moving it up and down as she walks, like a priest with a fragrant, smoking censer.

She is close to the front door now and she points the flashlight beam at the locks. The main lock, which is engaged by twisting from left to right, appears to have been moved—not by much, maybe ten degrees, but moved all the same. Her heart is beating furiously, destabilizing her, making her worry that she might lose consciousness. She takes the lock's turner in her thumb and forefinger and twists it until the bolt is more firmly in place.

On either side of the door is a long narrow window made of thick, shatterproof glass and covered for privacy by thick white curtains. She moves one of the curtains gently to the side, bends, and peers out at the street.

And that is when she sees him, though she has no idea who she is looking at or if he had anything whatsoever to do with the noises she heard in bed. But there is something about him. He is standing across the street, leaning against the wrought-iron fencing of the salmon-colored Federal with the black-and-gold banisters beside the steep outdoor steps. To further accentu-ate their house's pedigree, the owners keep their faux gaslights flickering throughout the night. The lamps create more atmo-sphere than actual light, but there is enough illumination on the man as he lurks there for Cynthia to note his pale, somehow moist complexion, his short spiky hair glistening with gel. He wears black pants belted high, and a Yankees T-shirt. Every-thing about him says loner, creep, weirdo, especially the black Bible he holds in his hand—at least, she thinks it's a Bible. He holds it in his right hand and rhythmically hits his open left palm with it, as if this book were something with which to bludgeon sinners.

Just then, Cynthia hears a scream—high-pitched, feminine, and crackling with terror. It takes her a moment to realize the scream is coming from inside the house. Alice!

Cynthia drops the candlestick. It thuds noisily to the floor and rolls back and forth. Taking the stairs two at a time, waving the beam of the flashlight left and right, Cynthia races to the top floor of house. It feels as if the staircase is growing extra steps as she runs toward the twins' rooms. Her breaths feel as if they are outlined by fire. The screams stop, and when she finally reaches the third floor, she sees the doors to the twins' rooms are open and the light is on in Alice's room.

Adam is there, sitting on the edge of her bed.

"It's nothing," he says to Cynthia. "She was having a bad dream."

There is something surprising in his voice, a commanding quality, a depth of timbre. It brings her up short. And what a little man he looks, sitting there in nothing but his boxers. His shoulders are broad, his muscles prominent, his legs sturdy as tree trunks, with a moss of dark hair clinging to them from the knees down.

When Alice sees Cynthia entering her room, she flings her arms wide.

"Oh, baby, sweetheart, baby, shh, shhhh," Cynthia says, enfolding Alice in an embrace. "It's okay, it was just a dream." She pats the back of Alice's head—her daughter's head! Her daughter! She feels the thick smoothness of her hair, smells the slightly spicy pungency of the girl's nighttime breath.

"Oh, oh, oh" is all Alice can say, all that can get through the torrent of tears. For she is crying now, for the first time in who knows how long. Weeping, sobbing, like a poor creature consumed by sheer animal fear and the most terrible human loneliness.

On the other side of the city, it's as if Rodolfo can hear her crying. When Toby failed to deliver her to the apartment on Riverside Drive, Rodolfo's disappointment was so profound and his unhappiness so enervating that he barely reacted to Toby's disappearance.

As far as he can tell, he is the only one awake in the apartment. If the others are running wild in the park or after something on the streets of New York, or if they are dancing or eating, their energies are boundless, but if they are inside and well fed, then it's lights-out—they all tend to fall asleep rather early, rarely making it past ten o'clock. A few of them have sacked out in the front room, having fallen asleep on the floor while watching TV. The others have managed to make it to their beds.

Rodolfo, however, is unable to sleep, or even relax. He is like a shipwreck survivor on a flimsy rubber raft who cannot cease scanning the horizon, checking the skies, who must at all moments remain alert for signs of rescue.

"Rodolfo?"

Rodolfo turns toward the voice. It's Polly. She is wearing a pair of maroon gym shorts bearing the crest of her old school, and a baggy white T-shirt. Her legs are long, thin, though not very shapely, and her skin is smooth. Some of the other girls, if they want to wear shorts, have to shave or wax every few days, but Polly, already fifteen, seems not to have that problem. Yet.

With the crew, it's always *yet*. What happened to the parents because of the fertility treatments varied greatly from one family to the next. (There are some who went to Slovenia for the shots who are still perfectly normal. There are others—Mayor Morris, for one—who are able to maintain normal and productive lives, confining their rages and their more outré appetites to carefully controlled zones of privacy.)

What happened to the children varied too. For the most part, the crew consisted of kids in the midrange: fast, furious, and furry, but able to cooperate with one another, kids whose blood is so full of the zizz and vigor of their animal natures that everyday people injecting just the tiniest amounts of it can experience great rainbow rushes of lust and joy.

But there are also the products of those treatments who, once they reached puberty, began a rapid transformation into wild creatures ruled by appetites and instincts, unteachable by any school, ungovernable by any authority, fierce, powerful, not terribly bright; rampant, unruly little beasts who represent the most extreme behavioral elements in Rodolfo's New York crew.

There are even a few kids who exhibited extreme behaviors well before puberty, kids who bit and kicked and clawed as babies, who tyrannized their playgroups as toddlers, exhausted and even frightened their teachers; kids who were (ridiculously, as it turned out) treated for everything from celiac disease to ADHD until they either were "lost" by their parents or ran away of their own accord—usually after accidental meetings with one of the crew, followed by the relieving realization that they were not alone in the world, that there were others out there just like them.

They were the kids whose blood was without commercial value. If one of the crew's ever-growing customer base were to consume the merest droplet of blood from the most extreme members, it would result in an overdose, and the whole business might end up in ruins.

On the other extreme, there were a few in the crew who were, like Polly, seemingly (and as yet) like any other kids, except faster and stronger—and mortally afraid of their parents, who had not fared so well after fertility treatments administered by Dr. Kis. Polly is wiping her mouth with the back of her hand. Rodolfo can guess. She has emptied the contents of her stomach. She is not the only one to follow the regime— exercise, nibble, purge. The idea is to keep firing in the nonstop war against puberty. Word is that the body given just enough nutrients to survive will not mature. Secondary hairs will stay locked deep within their follicles. For the girls, breasts will not appear. Hips will remain slender, deprived of the hormonal knowledge that room must be made for a child to pass through. Menstruation will not occur. Even a couple of the boys are playing hide-and-seek with their own puberty. Little Man survives on four hundred calories per day. He is fifteen and looks ten; his genitals are like a cashew nut and two grapes surrounded by down. His breath has a vomity tinge to it; his teeth have lost half their enamel to the constant stream of stomach acids cascading over them.

Rodolfo decides to throw Polly a bone and not ignore her—he understands that leadership means being a bit of a hard-ass and then, when it is least expected, showing the troops something soft and magnanimous.

"You're awake," he says to her. "You okay?"

She knows he knows she has been purging, and she lowers her eyes, grateful and shy.

"I was looking in the refrigerator," she says. "We're carrying a lot of hits." The crew call the vials of blood they sell under the brand name Zoom various things: hits, bumps, picadors, bobbies, bubbies, bubbles, and picks. Polly calls them hits because Rodolfo calls them hits.

"Yeah, we's multitudinous."

"It's almost twenty-five thousand dollars' worth, right here."

"That's good," Rodolfo says. He furrows his brow as she moves a bit closer to him. His nostrils expand as he involuntarily tries to decode her scent. She smells of fresh laundry and mouthwash.

"Are you waiting for her?" Polly asks.

"No," he says, and he is quick to say it.

She smiles. She can see through his lie and it makes her feel close to him to do so.

"You want to see what I can do?" she asks.

"What can you do?"

"This." She springs backward, a perfect flip, and again and again, barely moving from her original spot. The abandoned glasses and bowls rattle where they have been left, on the tables and mantelpieces. Her face is slightly flushed. She raises her arms like a circus acrobat at the end of her performance.

"Neighbors," Rodolfo says, pointing down.

"And this," says Polly. She sticks her tongue out. It's dark pink and it glistens in the overhead light.

"So?" Rodolfo says.

"Wait, okay? Just wait." She swallows, relaxes her shoulders, and sticks her tongue out again, only farther this time. Her eyes widen. And so do Rodolfo's—it's a little startling to see the tip of Polly's tongue reaches to her chin. But it gets more unsettling. Polly continues to unfurl her tongue and now the tip of it...reaches down to the hollow of her throat.

"Whoa," Rodolfo manages to say.

But she's not finished. The tip of her tongue sinks lower and lower and now it hangs as a fleshy pink pendant at the middle of her chest. Her mouth strains open to its fullest as she releases more and more tongue, until she can—if she wants to—stick it into her own belly button.

"Put that shit away," Rodolfo says.

She retracts it—the tongue zisses back into her mouth like a metal measuring tape returning to its casing. She dries the corners of her mouth, takes a deep breath.

"What are we, Rodolfo?" she says. "I mean, really, what the fuck are we?"

It is past midnight, nearly one in the morning. Cynthia lies in her bed, miles from sleep. She is thinking of that man lurking across the street with his Bible. She is wondering if he had anything to do with those noises she heard. She tells herself she is being foolish. Nonetheless, she keeps wondering.

The old house's ruminative noises continue. The later it gets, the more the house has to say. The water pipes have their opinions. The joists have their complaints. The wooden floors are inconsolable. From somewhere comes a buzzing— a dying lightbulb? A chewed electrical wire ready to bloom into hot flame? A stiff summer breeze pushes the branches of the dogwood tree closer to the house, and its twigs and leaves and withered blossoms scratch madly against the windows.

But there is one sweet sound too. The sound of Alice's deep easy breaths as the child sleeps beside her. She wears pale cotton pajamas, childish, with a teddy-bear pattern. Her fingers clasp the cuffs of her sleeves, even in sleep. Every button is fastened. She sleeps on her back, her arms crossed over her chest, like a child in a tomb. Her hair fans over the pillow. The reflection of a passing car's headlights briefly touches her face, her rosy lips, her long eyelashes.

Cynthia was amazed—and relieved—that Alice was so easily convinced to come down and spend the night with her. With such utter guilelessness, with such perfect trust, the girl had let Cynthia take her hand and lead her to the master bedroom. Silently, Alice slipped into bed and fell almost immediately into a profound sleep.

"Little Alley-Oop," Cynthia whispered to her, and the little girl smiled her sleepy little smile.

But now…something seems out of place. Something is not right, not yet.

There is someone else in the room.

Or so Cynthia fears.

No. This is more than fear. This is not some vexing trick of the mind. This is not worrying that the banging of the pipes is really the *clump-clump-clump* of an intruder. This is not trying to figure out if what she hears outside might be someone trying to get into the house. This is not fear. This is real. This is as real as real can be.

Cynthia lifts herself up on her elbows, hoping not to awaken Alice. She peers into the darkness of the bedroom, but it is like trying to see to the bottom of a can of black paint.

She has no choice but to turn on her reading light.

There are two worlds, the same but different: the world of darkness and the world of light. They exist simultaneously, they live one inside of the other, yet their realities are profoundly divergent. With a click, the lamp is on, and darkness with all its mysteries and dangers disappears as if it had never existed, and taking its place are bedposts and carpeting, shutters, freshly plastered walls, an upholstered chair upon which the day's clothing has been deposited, her navy-blue journal that slipped off the bed hours ago. Yet, just as darkness can tease and torture the mind, it also offers hope—a degree of deniability. But now, in the stark light of the room, Cynthia sees something that terrifies her so much, she quickly covers her ears, as if to dull the sound of her own screams. But she is so deeply startled that she cannot even scream—someone is in the room, curled up on the floor, covered by a pale blue blanket.

She reaches for her phone, wishing it were a gun. She would fire it, no questions asked.

Yet in that moment right before rising fear turns into uncontrollable panic, she sees something else. Something familiar. His hair. His hand.

She puts the phone down.

It's Adam. Half an hour ago, he was standing in Alice's bedroom with his arms angrily folded over his chest, watching with great disapproval as Alice allowed herself to be led down the staircase to the second floor. But now it seems as if he's had a change of heart. It might be more than he can manage to stay up there on his own. Or it might be contrary to his nature to be away from his sister if he can help it. Or maybe the solace that Cynthia has offered Alice is something that Adam wants and needs too.

Whatever motivated him, he is here. He sleeps on the floor, using his forearm as a pillow.

It's quite possible that this is the happiest Cynthia has ever felt in her life—and what a strange kind of happiness it is too. Not a jumping-up-and-down, fist-pumping, throwing-your-hat-up-in-the-air kind of happiness, but the kind that swells your heart and moves you to the brink of tears, a happiness that fills you like the sound of an orchestra, a happiness that reminds you that life is fragile and fleeting...

Cynthia switches off her lamp and slips quietly out of bed. The house is still basically a strange environment, but she has at least memorized the path between her side of the bed and the bathroom, and she can confidently make the thirteen-step journey without benefit of light—with her eyes closed, in fact.

She has also memorized the contours of the bathroom, and

she lowers herself sightlessly onto the chilly toilet seat and, with a long sigh, empties her bladder.

There is something strange about it, however, and as she pees, she furrows her brow, trying to puzzle what is different.

The sound! Not the bright lively sound of her urine stream splashing into the water, but a dull quiet thud, like rain hitting broad, fleshy leaves. She half stands and peers into the darkness of the bowl. She gropes for the light switch, flicks it, floods the room with lumens.

It's a bat, a bat in the toilet, her bare bottom was inches from it, and she has peed on it. Like most people, Cynthia has uttered the three-word phrase *Oh my God* countless times, but now she whispers it and she has never meant it more. Pulling her underwear back up, she leans against the wall for balance, so frightened and repelled that her legs seem practically useless.

Is it dead? Now and then, a bat used to find its way into her place back in San Francisco. The first time it happened, she called the police. It didn't do her any good, of course, but it at least gave the guys in the precinct a laugh. The second time, she threw a coat over her head and fled the house. She had made a point of learning a few things about bats. She learned they were essentially harmless—the greatest danger they posed was bacterial, but they did not suck your blood or like to fly into your hair and scream and claw, and they did not turn into Bela Lugosi or Christopher Lee or Gary Oldman or Frank Langella or any of the other gloriously creepy men who'd played Dracula. They were mice with wings. She tried to find comfort in that— but could not. This bat in her toilet had obviously been trapped there while searching for water. Bats could not lift off to fly; they needed to perch on something with a bit of height, let go, glide, and then start flapping. And so the bat (she tries to think

58

of it as *the poor thing* but she is too disgusted by it to show the proper pity), unable to rise from the water, must have slowly drowned.

There's nothing to do but flush it away. But to her dismay, the thing is too big—with its leathery serrated wings spread, it's about the size of a Frisbee—and it spins and bobs up and down but doesn't come close to making its way into the plumbing. Hoping for better luck the second time, Cynthia waits for the tank to fill and then flushes again, and this time the water rises. Some of it sloshes over the toilet's rim and onto the floor. Frantically, she drags a little ecofriendly bamboo mat over with her bare foot, hoping to quickly absorb the tainted water.

The water level in the toilet subsides. But the bat is still there, floating on its back, its wings spread, its black eyes wide open looking like repulsive, shiny licorice-flavored candies, perfectly round, disturbingly bulging, utterly sightless.

She has to get it out of there. Somehow get it into the little ceramic trash basket and then into the heavy-duty plastic garbage pail outside. She opens the narrow utility closet and takes out the plunger. Holding on to the rubber end, she pushes the wooden handle into the toilet and navigates it under the bat. But every time she tries to lift the flying rodent out of the water, she manages to elevate it only an inch or two before it slides off the stick and back into the water.

After five unsuccessful attempts to get the thing out of the toilet, she resorts to basically catapulting it out. She puts the handle of the plunger beneath the bat and flips it up, hoping against hope that she will get lucky and the bat will land in the wastebasket, at which point she can drop a towel over the basket, rush the thing out to the back of the house—and dispose of it.

But she flips the bat out of the water with far more vigor than she had intended. The thing hits the ceiling with a dull, wet *thwack*. She looks up, horrified, expecting the worst.

And she gets it.

The water and the velocity of the bat's upward trajectory combine to make the bat adhere to the ceiling, but just for a few moments. The bat, the dead bat—it is dead, isn't it?—all at once becomes unstuck from the ceiling, and with its wings outspread and its awful mouth wide open, the thing falls directly onto Cynthia. It hits her on top of her head and from there it touches the side of her neck—each nanosecond of contact with it is unspeakable. It slides down her T-shirt. She is screaming now, with no thought of waking the children. She claws at her shirt, pulls it away from her body, and the bat—it is dead, it must be—lands on its back on the black and cobalt tiles of the bathroom floor.

Its blind eyes are open. Why are they even born with eyes? Was there ever a better argument against intelligent design? It seems to be staring up at Cynthia.

And its little bony chest, container of its virulent little heart, is rising and falling.

"Oh no!" shouts Cynthia as she realizes that the bat is breathing.

The bat emits a sound, some nerve-shredding blend of a click and a squeak.

Its little rodenty curled foot twitches. It looks like withered grape stems.

And then, worst of all, the bat attempts to flap its wings. In this position, and in this state of near collapse, it can only move them a quarter-inch off the floor, once, twice, a third time, before giving up.

But not giving up, not really. It survived going into the toilet for a drink and getting stuck there, it survived being urinated on, and it survived being flung against the ceiling—the creature might well be indestructible.

She is still holding the plunger. There is only one thing she can do. She raises it over her head to beat the bat to death before it manages to rise from the floor. Except for insects, she has never killed anything, but she prepares to do so now without hesitation. She holds the plunger a couple of inches above the concave rubber head, rears back to maximize the force with which she will bring it down upon the bat, and starts her downward swing, making a sound between a grunt and a screech, like one of those Russian women tennis players striking a backhand.

But the swing is stopped midarc. The sudden stop wrenches Cynthia's shoulder and wrist. Startled, confused, she turns around.

"Do not," Adam says, holding on to the end of the handle. "Please." Still holding on to the plunger, he guides her to one side.

He crouches down next to the bat. Adam is so beautiful, Cynthia must avert her eyes. He is murmuring something to the creature, but she cannot make out what he is saying.

"Don't touch it, Adam," she says.

"Adam?" It's Alice, who's standing in the doorway of the bathroom, rubbing her right eye. She has sweated through her little-girl pajamas. The teddy bears, born blue, are now black.

"It's okay, Alice," he says, looking up at her. Crouched there, his eyes on his sister, he would not be out of place in a Museum of Natural History diorama illustrating the earliest cave dwellers. He covers the bat with a towel, carefully scoops it up—clearly more mindful of the bat's safety than his own—and gently shakes the towel until the bat slides into the wastebasket.

"I'll be right back," he says.

When he is gone, Cynthia and Alice stand in silence until Alice says, "He loves them and they love him."

"Bats?" Cynthia says. "Really? Bats?"

"Everything," Alice says. "Everything that's alive."

CHAPTER 6

They are coming from all directions—uptown, downtown, Queens, Brooklyn, the Bronx, Westchester, even Staten Island—and they are coming on foot, on skateboards, on bicycles, by subway. A few of them, though young and with no legal right to do so, even drive cars, and now, like any other New Yorker hoping to avoid astronomical garage fees, they are circling the blocks around Central Park, trying to find places to park. They are traveling in ones, twos, and threes, though, like teenagers everywhere, they like to be with a crew, a pack mentality that applies to these teens in particular. But they do not wish to draw attention to themselves, and a convoy of youngsters converging on Central Park in the middle of the night— it's actually morning, three o'clock, and hot and humid, the full moon appearing and disappearing and appearing again in a clotted black sky—would most assuredly attract unwelcome attention.

Later in the day, in another part of the park, Mayor Morris is going to appear at an event that has been weeks in the planning. David Chilowich, one of the few New York hedge-fund managers whose difficulties with the Securities and Exchange Commission and the attorney general of New York have never resulted in legal action and who has been compiling a spectacular public record of civic engagement, has donated three hundred million dollars to the Central Park Conservation Guild, and he will be handing the mayor the check in a ceremony that, if all goes well, ought to boost Morris's sagging poll numbers (he's been fading for months) and increase Chilowich's odds of walking out of court a free man should his ability to evade prosecution ever falter. A stage has been set up overlooking one of the park's many lagoons, and seating for five hundred so-called dignitaries has also been set up. Microphones, speakers, closed-circuit TV, all are at the ready, and several cops from the Central Park Precinct, as well as Central Park Conservation Guild employees and volunteers, are on hand, even now, in the middle of the night, to make certain none of the careful preparations are disturbed.

The upcoming ceremony means that park security has been increased, but the security is concentrated near the north end of the park, around the Jacqueline Kennedy Onassis Reservoir, and tonight's pack meeting is twenty blocks away and on the park's west side, at the Diana Ross Playground. And now in the little play area, named to commemorate the singer's concert in the nearby Sheep Meadow decades ago, the band of runaways and castaways congregate beneath the full moon, which has at last emerged from the congestion of clouds.

Rodolfo is their undisputed leader and he has gathered them all tonight because, counting the disappearance of Toby, four of their kind have vanished in the past month. Dressed in artfully torn jeans and a flowing muslin shirt, Rodolfo stands at the top of the silver corkscrew slide in the pocket park's center while the others arrange themselves on the wooden climbing structures or the tire swings, or simply stand there and listen with the rapt attention that Rodolfo always manages to command.

Though he must address some seventy people, Rodolfo delivers his speech in a voice barely louder than a whisper. They have gathered in darkness and they must be as quiet as possible. The luxurious towers of Central Park West loom nearby, and the teenagers in the park, whose lives are ones of flight and stealth, do not wish to be heard.

Some of these teenagers, raised not far from where they now stand, used to play in this little park within the park when they were small children, under the eye of an overworked nanny or the anxious gaze of parents—parents who hoped against hope that somehow the project of creating a family would turn out all right. A couple of them sit on the very tire swings that used to carry them aloft when their legs were pink and smooth and they would close their eyes and imagine they were magically endowed with the power of flight.

"Ye's and me's, brothers and sisters," Rodolfo passionately whispers, striking himself vigorously on the chest and then spreading his arms wide to embrace all who have congregated.

"Ye's and me's, brothers and sisters," whispers the row of teenagers closest to Rodolfo.

"Ye's and me's, brothers and sisters," the row behind them whispers to the next row back.

Five times it is repeated, until everyone has heard.

"Tonight is not about business; tonight we's here to talk survival," Rodolfo whispers, and he waits for his words to be conveyed row by row.

"They are taking us's brothers and sisters. Who is doing this to us's? This we's must know."

He waits for the message to be rewhispered. His chest is

heaving. He feels so alive, it would not surprise him if he were to burst open and become nothing but pure light. He would not admit this to anyone, but power excites him, this kind of power, to have those faces turned toward him, to have them listen…

For the most part, the whispered speech is transmitted without difficulty, though, as always, there are a few of the gathered — lads, usually — who are restless and distracted. If they were in school — and most of them have not stepped inside a schoolroom in years — they would surely be diagnosed as hyperactive, or suffering from (and making others suffer from) attention deficit disorder, diagnosed either officially by the school psychologist, or unofficially by a teacher or a parent who had simply run out of patience. These manic few do their best to follow Rodolfo's speech — and, indeed, they do hear it and have a basic understanding of what Rodolfo says; surely, they hear enough to decide they don't really need to hang on every word. But these kids cannot stand or sit still, so their listening is done along with hacky-sack kicks, games of you-push-me-and-I-push-you, hands drumming their knees, or, for one poor soul, a compulsive and slightly repulsive puckering and unpuckering of the lips.

"Listen now," Rodolfo whispers. "We's not talking no more to people we's not familiar with. Don't matter for nothing how money they look or if they's handing over to you a big juicy Chewtown hamburger with all fixin's jus' the way ye always liked it. Keep away. We's havin us no idea who doing this mischief. Maybe a man, maybe a mommy. Could be cops, CIA, FBI, DEA, NSA."

"Could be PETA!" a voice from the back calls out. And the laughter that it causes is even louder.

Rodolfo laughs too while gesturing for everyone to keep it down, keep it down.

"If you in the bidness, know this, brothers and sisters, the danger be ten times more," he says with his hand over his heart, a look of the gravest concern on his face. "They want us's blood, they want to feel what we's feel, so big, so money, so fast and alive. But we's got to be a million carefuls. Of the pigs, go without saying. But we's got to remember how this runs. If we's sell the wrong blood, the bidness is fucked. Not all of us's carrying blood we's wanting to sell. We's been through this many times, brothers and sisters. Me's thought we's all clear on this."

Rodolfo drops to a squat, dangles his folded hands between his knees.

"If ye smooth gots no desire to be doing terrible tings, if ye like your meat cooked, if ye know how to read, then come see me's and we's look you over and you can be a supplier. Suppliers get a bigger share, they do, but everywe gets something, and in the end we's all gonna be rich and life is going to be sweet. Okay? But if we's start selling hot blood and we's customers start getting heart attacks or hairy asses…"

A ripple of nervous laughter, like a sudden smudge of phosphorescent light in dark water.

"Then we's all going to lose. The bidness will be over. These rich people, they not fools. They be talking to each other. One gets in trouble and they alls run away."

Rodolfo stands again and holds up three fingers.

" 'Nother ting," he whispers. "Sex." He puts his finger over his lips, shakes his head. He doesn't want to risk any excitement, any noise. "We's all like what our bodies do. No problem there, brothers and sisters. But we's must be careful. Use a condom; use two if you be fucking one of we's. We's not going to reproduce."

"Why not?" whispers someone in the crowd, and the question is delivered to Rodolfo row by row.

"Why not? I'll show you. Shulamith and Kevin. Now, we's all know Shulamith and Kevin, they be together forever, since the days we's eating squirrels and living in the Brambles. They love each other. And we's loving them." He gestures and two figures rise from a bench outside the playground.

Shulamith is a lean, dark-haired girl with a narrow face and full lips. Kevin is broad-shouldered with a low center of gravity; his facial expression at rest is both merry and secretive. Shulamith carries a swaddled infant in her arms, and those who have gathered in the Diana Ross Playground move to the side to make a path for them as they walk toward Rodolfo. With no more effort than a normal person would expend to move on a flat surface, they quickly walk up the corkscrew slide and stand next to Rodolfo.

Rodolfo says something private to them and then commands, "Tell everyone how old this baby be."

"Gort is seventeen weeks old," Shulamith says, forgetting to whisper.

"And?" Rodolfo asks.

"He's a very good baby," Shulamith says.

"And?"

"And we's love him."

"Anything else, Shulamith?"

The teenage girl hesitates for a moment—but the decision to do this was made hours ago. She slowly unwraps the blanket from her child and lets the blue cotton square fall to the ground. The child has been sleeping, and the sudden touch of the night air, even on this steaming summer night, awakens him. He lets out a peevish peep.

68

Shulamith turns him around and touches her nose against her baby's little nose. And at the same time, she exposes the infant's back for all to see. Those farthest away don't know what to make of it, but those who are standing in the first couple of rows see it very clearly: where the child's shoulder blades would have been, Gort has sprouted two pale gray wings.

CHAPTER 7

Sometimes the twins call her Cynthia, and sometimes Aunt Cynthia. The Aunt Cynthia is a bit disheartening to her—it seems permanent, a dead-end job with no promotion possible. It surprises her to be continually colliding with that small, tender, and undefended part of her that would love it if one day Adam and Alice called her Mom.

But no matter. One way or another, they are becoming a family.

The children cleave to her. They don't help but they closely observe her every move when she makes her bed. They sit and talk to each other right outside the bathroom door while she takes her shower. They eat quickly and they watch quietly while she finishes her breakfast. It's heartbreaking and slightly annoying, and it's also sort of amusing, and on top of all that, it is touching and even a tiny bit gratifying. This is what she is learning: In family life, no one thing is just one thing. Everything holds a multitude of meanings.

There is no downtime. Especially not with these two. Their needs, as yet unspoken, overwhelm her. The fear they lived with, the gruesome things they saw, their months and months and months tumbling through the social-service system. What do they dream of? What do they say to their therapists?

A week that feels like a month goes by. She wishes she were younger, in better shape. Yet older now—she is forty-five—she is perhaps able to tolerate their using up every minute of her day, every ounce of her energy, without feeling impatient or trapped. If the worst thing you feel in your life is exhaustion—not pain, not loneliness, not hopelessness, not rage, not hunger, not terror—then you might as well consider yourself among the fortunate.

Another week passes. The New York summer is the kind Al Gore predicted: the sun a dirty yellow scream, the sky a crazy jumble of clouds, the nights thick as oil spills.

She knows she ought to have found a meeting by now, but it's been years since she's had a drink, or even thought about using, and there is something about being in New York that says fresh start to her. Drinking and its attendant dependence on AA feels like something she left back in California.

Cynthia has many contacts in the New York antiques world, and though it doesn't seem realistic to think that she will soon have her own shop—when she closed Gilty Pleasures back in San Francisco, she did so with the knowledge that she might never run an antiques store again—she has to begin earning some money, and a job has been all but promised her, working for Fay and Jiwani a few doors down from the Pierre, and there is a good chance at another position at a place called American Pastoral. But right now, who has time?

The twins must be fed. Every day. Three or four times a day. Though they are still determined to limit their caloric intake, they are also—despite all their talk about becoming vegetarian—ravenous for meat, which they seem to grab with one hand and push away with the other. She is happy—delighted, really—to feed them all the meat they could ever want, and often the huge kitchen smells like a barbecue pit. And they must be clothed. Cynthia doesn't want to be snobby or grand about it, but they don't look right in those Target and Kmart outfits they came out of foster care with. She takes them to City Outfitters, drawn in by the funky mannequins wearing casual clothes, but feels faint when she sees that a pair of pre-torn blue jeans costs $250. Luckily, the twins do not object when she steers them out of the place. Eventually, she gets them clothes she hopes will take them through the rest of the scorching summer and into the (she hopes) more temperate autumn. She must get them at least one outfit each that they could wear to church or a nice restaurant, and she must get them clothes to run around and be kids in, and she must get them school clothes.

She must also enroll them in school. Sending them back to the Gothic structures of Berryman Prep, their old private school, is out of the question, psychologically and economically. Without a doubt, they will be attending public school. But even in their neighborhood, where real estate prices seem to have been calculated in post–World War I German currency (when it took a wheelbarrow full of paper money to buy a pound of Black Forest ham); even here, where a medical doctor's salary puts him in the middle class and a professor would be unable to live without the help of an inheritance; here, where the Yorkshire terriers wear diamond-studded collars, and nine-year-old girls get four-hundred-dollar haircuts; even here, the nearest public school building is a monument to government neglect: a dingy, one-story afterthought with wire mesh over its windows and brickwork from which graffiti has so often been removed that the stones themselves seem wan and unstable. Here, the student body consists of the children of live-in nannies; rich little boys with behavior problems who have been bounced out of their private schools and who have gladly traded in their blue blazers for basketball jerseys; and a surprising number of children from actual and bona fide nonwealthy parents, children who the strollers and shoppers along Lexington and Madison Avenues thought lived miles and miles away and whom they might have expected to see only in a heartrending documentary about Want in the Midst of Plenty but who reside a few blocks east in tenements that have not yet yielded to the wrecker's ball.

The twins must also see their therapist—since Jenny Carlat, who had been assigned to Alice, moved to Cleveland, both children see Adam's therapist, a lanky young man named Peter White, an MSW who after two years working for the City of New York is already a burned-out caseworker.

White's office is on East Thirty-Second Street. Unfortunately, despite Cynthia's efforts to move the appointments around, Adam is scheduled to see White on Mondays at ten, and Alice sees him on Wednesdays at two, and so Cynthia must accompany them twice a week. They go as a threesome. They do virtually everything as a threesome.

Peter White's office is in what real estate agents call the garden level (but which is in fact the basement) of a shabby old brownstone, once a private home for a family of six and now divided into fourteen rental units, two of them windowless in violation of the law. To reach the entrance of White's office, Cynthia and the twins must take the steps that lead below street level, squeeze around the trash bins, and ignore the sour juniper scent of alley-cat congress. The office itself is scarcely two hundred square feet, devoid of so much as a ray of natural light.

The space is divided in two by a wall, with the waiting room on one side and the consulting room on the other. When a client opens the door to the waiting room, the first bars of "Some Enchanted Evening" play in the consulting room, informing White that someone has entered. The first time Cynthia took the children there, she was surprised she could simply let herself in—even in relatively slipshod and easygoing San Francisco, people locked their doors, and here in New York, even the antiques stores had a system by which customers were visually inspected before being buzzed in. She mentioned her uneasiness with White's open-door policy, saying, "Anyone could just walk in here," and Adam said, "I guess," and Alice added, "But who'd want to."

Adam seems indifferent to his appointments with Peter White, but Alice hates them, and today is her hour. She is not one to complain, but as they descend the concrete steps leading to White's door, her eyes are cast down, her shoulders are slumped, and her lower lip is extended in a classic pout of dejection.

"I don't see why we don't have the right to just forget about bad stuff if we want to," she murmurs, as much to the cosmos as to Cynthia and Adam.

"It's the law," Adam reminds her, which is his interpretation of Child Protective Services' making their continuing therapy one of the requirements for their adoption to be finalized.

Cynthia opens the door and hears the recording of "Some Enchanted Evening" played by carillon bells coming through the closed door of White's consulting space.

Alice glances at her watch. Today, she is wearing the American Girl, and Adam has the Swiss Army.

"Expecting someone?" Cynthia says, really as no more than a joke.

But Alice frowns. The girl has a talent for suddenly placing her foot in your path and forcing you to step on her toes.

"Kidding," Cynthia says, hoping to reassure.

"I don't like it here," Alice says.

"You know where I've always wanted to go?" Cynthia says. "And maybe before school starts we can go there. Just the three of us."

"Where?" asks Adam.

"Mount Washington," says Cynthia.

"Where's that?" asks Adam.

"New Hampshire. Right in the middle. It's totally wild. And high. And windy. They say sometimes the wind gets up to three hundred miles an hour."

"Wouldn't that kill you?" asks Alice. "Why would you want to take us to someplace like that?"

"Because it's beautiful and it's wild. And it's only windy like that sometimes, in the winter."

A moment later, the door opens and White appears, rubbing his hand on his cheek and chin, perhaps wondering if he can go another day without shaving. He is six and a half feet tall, with long dry hair the color of a parched field of wheat. He holds his long pale hands in front of him and glances at them continually, as if they might do something awful. He treats his hands as if they were on parole. White looks at the three of them expressionlessly.

"Are we early?" Cynthia asks, annoyed by the shrink's lack of affect. Today is the day she might tell him that if you break the word *therapist* into two pieces, you get *the rapist*.

Yet why does she resent him? Why does she not acknowledge the fact that she *needs* him? It could be as simple as this: She wants the twins all to herself. She is giving them intravenous infusions of pure unadulterated love, and she does not want that to be interrupted.

"You're right on time," White says.

"We'll wait right here," Cynthia says to Alice reassuringly.

"Actually, Ms. Kramer," White says, "I wonder if you and I could spend a few minutes alone before Alice and I begin."

Cynthia is surprised to hear this. A nervous flutter in the lower digestive region. Despite Peter White's wracked, two-packs-a-day, ten-cups-of-bitter-coffee appearance and the fact that he is at least ten years her junior, she feels as if she is being called into the principal's office. Has he some sort of heightened emotional radar, has he guessed she has had dark thoughts about him? That *the rapist* thing was meant to be funny…She reaches into her handbag and gives Adam the sudoku puzzle book she'd brought along to pass the time.

"Sit tight, kids," she says, her voice unaccountably merry. It is a failing of hers, she knows, this desire to keep every moment upbeat, engaging, and interesting, as if she were a TV host afraid they would switch the channel. "Okay? Little Alley-Oop?"

"Okay," Alice says.

"How come she gets a nickname?" Adam asks. He is embarrassed by his own question. He can barely look at Cynthia.

"You want one? I wasn't sure. You're such a serious kid."

Adam shrugs. "I don't care. Whatever."

"Oh, so that's how it's going to be. All right…Braveheart, have it your own way."

White switches on the white-noise machine on top of the table strewn with magazines and escorts Cynthia into his office, closing the door behind them. When they are seated, he wastes no time getting to the point.

"They are both very upset youngsters, Ms. Kramer. They are bright, engaging, and, when they choose to be, quite articulate. But Alice spends half her hour here crying."

"Alice?"

"Yes, Alice. Adam doesn't cry. At least not here. But he brought me this drawing." White unlocks the top drawer of his wooden, well-scarred government-issue desk and pulls out the drawing, slides it toward Cynthia. It is an astonishing piece of work, a pen-and-ink drawing so filled with images that the paper feels drenched. Trees, planets, houses, and statues bearing swords and bayonets all swirl around in a kind of airborne madness that looks partly like ecstasy and partly like the end of the world. In the center of this vortex stands a half-man half-beast creature who is holding a dog that he is preparing to devour; sticking out of his mouth are a dog's head, a rat's tail, a child's foot—the remains of what he has already consumed.

"This is an amazing piece of work," Cynthia finally says, putting the drawing down. She places her hands in her lap, not wishing White to notice they are trembling. "I mean, a real artist did this. In fact, I doubt it was Adam." She shrugs. "He's too young, for one thing. This isn't the work of a twelve-year-old." She slides the drawing back to him.

"It is the work of a twelve-year-old, Cynthia. And Alice does cry in this office. We need to see what really *is,* not what we wish there to be."

"Of course," Cynthia says.

"I want to put them both on medication, Cynthia," White says. In fact, he feels regretful about this, since his slice of the psychological pie is talk therapy, but he camouflages his regret with a certain aggressiveness in his tone. "They both need selective serotonin reuptake inhibitors."

"Antidepressants? Why? I don't see them as depressed."

"Weeping in my office? This?" He taps the horrific drawing with his index finger.

"But you can't even prescribe them anything, Mr. White. You're not a medical doctor. You're a…what? You have a master's degree in social work? And now you want to pump those kids full of chemicals?"

"You sound rather angry, Cynthia."

"The fact is, you can't prescribe medications."

"I work very closely with the best child psychiatrists and psychopharmacologists in New York. Those children need treatment. I do believe that with time they could find their way through the thicket and come out as fine and productive members of society. But talk therapy is slow—and they need help right away. They are gaunt.

"Alice appears to be starving herself, Cynthia."

"I know, I know. We're working on it. I'm giving her grass-fed organic meats with no hormones. I think she's worried about…about getting her period. Puberty. All the additives and chemicals in the commercial food supply push kids into puberty way too early. It's a crisis, worldwide. All those children's choirs? Like in Europe? They can't find kids who can sing the soprano parts. Even the ten-year-olds have these deep voices."

"Why do you think they fear puberty, Cynthia?"

"What do you think? They've been told that for some of the kids whose parents went through those horrible fertility treatments—they've been told that things start getting crazy for those kids once they hit puberty. They're afraid. We all know that. Why shouldn't they be? It's not inappropriate; it's not crazy behavior. They feared their own parents were going to kill them—and fucking *eat* them. Of course they have fears. It would be psychotic if they *didn't* have fears."

"They're going to end up back in the hospital if we don't intervene quickly," the therapist says.

Cynthia shakes her head. She wills herself to calm down.

"It's a big step, Mr. White."

"I appreciate that, Cynthia. And I commend you for your conservative approach. Too many of the parents I see are all too eager to give their kids whatever new pill comes down the chute. They're desperate, I suppose."

"I'd like some time to think it over. Which antidepressant do you have in mind?"

"Oh, there's a host of them out there. And new ones coming out all the time. And maybe they'd benefit from something else on top of that. Something to stabilize them. Help them put on some weight. Help them get past some of their fears. It's just astonishing the things that can be done biochemically. Amazing stuff is being done."

"That's what they told my sister and her husband about fertility drugs."

White lowers his eyes, like some nineteenth-century gentleman showing his respect when a funeral carriage rolls by.

"No," Cynthia says, suddenly adamant. "I don't think we're at that stage, not yet. I want to give them what they've never had."

"Which is?"

"Love. Just pure unconditional love. A good stable home. The basic things that every child has a right to—things they have never had."

"You can't love away the damage that's been done, Cynthia. It's not possible."

Just then, the recording of those carillon bells playing "Some Enchanted Evening" fills the little room.

"Could they have left?" White asks, frowning, rising from his seat.

"I seriously doubt that," Cynthia says. She turns in her chair. "Kids?"

Looking as if he's trying not to panic, White walks across his office and opens the door to the waiting room.

The sudoku puzzle book is on the floor, and other than that, there is no sign of either Alice or Adam.

"Kids?" cries Cynthia, with more urgency and less hope.

"They're gone!" White exclaims.

"They wouldn't do this," Cynthia says. "I know them. They just wouldn't."

The door leading to the outside is open. Garbage-y summer air wafts in. The white-noise machine on the table continues to make its breathy sound, like a stadium crowd cheering a mile away.

CHAPTER 8

Boy-Boy leaves Ezra and Annabelle's apartment and rides the elevator down to the lobby. Today was lucrative; the old man bought twice his usual amount and put an extra Benjamin in the envelope for a tip. No question about it: being dangled from a balcony brings out the best in some people. Ezra has been ultra-polite since that first time. Annabelle, however, hardly even glances in Boy-Boy's direction. All the sexual satisfaction Boy-Boy's product has made possible for her has had the opposite effect of dangling her from a balcony. It's made her a bit rude. *She act like me's not there,* Boy-Boy muses as the elevator makes its squeaky descent.

Speaking of not there, Boy-Boy wishes the elevator operator weren't there. Everyone in the crew, from Rodolfo on down, is on high alert.

Us's and thems like us's, we's going down one by one, Rodolfo reminds them all every time they go out to work.

Could the elevator operator be the one doing all this extermination? Boy-Boy wonders. Could this dark old man in a toy-soldier suit be working with whoever is picking off the crew? Or maybe the old man is the exterminator himself! No, no, makes no sense. The exterminator ain't working no fucking elevator, Boy-Boy reminds himself, calming down. But what if the real elevator operator is tied to a chair someplace, conked on the head, handkerchief stuffed in his mouth?

Nervously, Boy-Boy chews on a cuticle. The skin around each and every one of his fingernails is red and raw. He finds his own skin comforting and sort of delicious. Forget *sort of.* It's just plain delicious. He knows he has to be careful, though; it's a dangerous appetite. A couple guys in the crew took it too far, and the result was something even Boy-Boy cannot bear to think about, even though he prides himself on being a street-savvy warrior with nerves of steel.

The elevator moves so slowly. *Fuck me, the peeps in this place must be made out of time.* But at last they reach the lobby and the operator opens the grate, turning all those triangles into exclamation marks, and after that the outer door.

"Thank you," Boy-Boy says, exiting as far from the elevator operator as possible to guard against some poisonous last-minute lunge. Across the tiled lobby, with its columns and potted plants, freedom waits, just beyond the heavy doors with their polished brass handles and all that money sunshine shining through.

"Son?" the elevator operator says as Boy-Boy leaves. "Sometimes a shower is in order."

Up many flights, in Ezra and Annabelle's apartment, the shades are drawn, the ringers on the phones are off, and the music plays fairly loud, because although the walls in this stately old apartment building are thick, practically soundproof, Ezra and Annabelle plan to kick up a bit of a ruckus, and they want to make certain no busybody with time on his hands and an ear to the wall picks up on any of it.

They are undressed now, soaking delightedly in the enormous tub in the master bath with its bright blue border of Turkish tiles and solid gold faucets in the shape of swans. Out of some residual sense of modesty, as well as a lingering reluctance to put his aging, sagging, scarred body on prolonged display in front of his young wife, Ezra has poured several capfuls of Ethiopian bubble bath he recently purchased at Henri Bendel. His old exhausted penis lies curled beneath the scented froth of a trillion bubbles while Annabelle, perhaps mocking his modesty or perhaps having a bit of fun, has taken two scoops of bubbles and placed them over her nipples—it's how people in Ezra's business used to have to show girls in the bathtub, several decades ago, when a hint of pink could get you shitcanned.

The tub is fourteen feet long and eight feet wide, and so deep that it took a full hour to fill it. Clunky square tuberose-scented candles purchased from a store near the Piazza Navona burn along the edge of the tub. They also have two bottles of Icelandic springwater. The four vials of blood bought from Boy-Boy lie on their sides next to the water bottles, and, after drying his hands on Annabelle's hair, Ezra uncaps two of the vials and they both drink quickly, after which they both take swigs of the Icelandic water to wash the taste of salted copper from their mouths.

"If pennies could drool, this is what it would taste like," Ezra says.

"It's like tomato soup that's been in the can so long it's gone weird on you," says Annabelle. She dabs the corners of her mouth with the back of her hand; the little trace of blood pinks the soapy bubbles. She looks at it for a moment, aghast, but finds a way to laugh. She plunges her hand in the water to wash it clean. Baptism by Ethiopian bath gel!

"Shall we?" Ezra says, picking up vials three and four.

"It's a lot," says Annabelle, suddenly cautious.

"You can never tell if you've had enough until you find out what it feels like to have too much," Ezra says. It is one of the great pluses of being with a younger woman—you get to be the sage! You are an ever-burbling fountain of goddamned wisdom, is you what you are.

Ezra downs vial number two, and Annabelle does too.

"Feel it yet?" Ezra asks.

"Feel nauseous. Drinking some kid's blood? Fuck me."

"I intend to."

"I'm serious, Ez. This is crazy."

"People do all kinds of things, my dear, to get to another level. Change things around, make things better. Crush up leaves and smoke them. Ferment grain and drink it. Swallow worms, right? Mescal? Eat mushrooms that grow out of cow shit?"

"I really prefer a nice California chardonnay," Annabelle says. "Now and again, maybe an ice-cold Pontchartrain Porter, if I'm having a crayfish boil." She closes her eyes for a moment as a memory of home washes through her—how could she have hated the place so much and yet miss it even more?

"When I met you," Ezra says, "what were you? Nineteen?"

"I was twenty-seven, Ezra."

He shrugs, as if she were splitting hairs. "You were wearing cutoffs so short your pussy was practically hanging out."

"Don't be gross, Ezra. Please."

"I didn't take the scissors to those old blue jeans, darling. That was your doing."

"I had beautiful legs. I was proud of them."

"You still do!"

"No, no. Not like back then. I'm thickening. I'm congealing."

"You starting to feel something?"

"It always takes a while."

"I don't know, I figured we double the dose, we get there quicker."

"It's sort of scary, don't you think, Ez? It's like you're not quite human after you drink that stuff."

"I've been human long enough. I think I've earned a little holiday from human."

"I hope we're not drinking Boy-Boy, that's all I hope," Annabelle says. She feels a stirring within, a little shift in the blood, like the body of a sound sleeper adjusting itself without waking. And then it is gone.

"You just felt something, didn't you. I saw it in your eyes."

"I don't know. Maybe." She looks at the empty vials on the side of the tub, with the residue of blood clinging to the sides. "The first time we took this stuff was the best. The first time was lovely."

"Lovely? It was fantastic. My *shvanz* was like a leg of lamb, and you, my pet, were a vat of mint jelly."

"Ezra. Please. You say things that actually make me sick."

"I know, baby. I know." He is grinning, as if by telling him he has a powerful effect on her, she has just paid him a compliment.

Annabelle leans back in the tub, bends her legs so that her knees emerge from the water like pink islands. She stretches her arms; suds drip from her elbows. Strange. The hair on her forearm looks darker than usual. Very strange indeed.

Ezra playfully scoots over on his rear, pries her legs apart so he can be right next to her.

"I don't feel right," Annabelle says softly.

"Oh, come on. Take off your Bible belt. We're not doing anything wrong. We're enjoying ourselves."

"I know."

"The things that happen in this town. There's about fifty S-and-M bars. I had a guy who used to work with me—well, *for* me, actually, I was his boss—who paid hookers to crap on him. I'm serious."

"I don't want to hear about it, Ezra. Anyhow, I think you already told me this."

"He used to lie naked under a glass-topped coffee table while they—I'll say this delicately because I honor your feminine sensibilities, my princess—while the whores moved their bowels. But whose business was it but his own?"

"I feel sorry for the women."

"Really? Do you? Or is that just something people say? Some idiot gets five hundred dollars for hopping onto a coffee table and taking a crap? I think there's a lot worse things happening in the world."

"I don't," Annabelle says. She glances again at the hair on her arm—how could that silvery fuzz have darkened so? Is it a trick of the light? "I think that is exactly what's wrong with this world."

"Hey, guess what," Ezra says, touching the tip of her nose with his finger. "I'm totally fucking feeling it." He grabs her breast. His so-called moves haven't changed very much over time; he is as greedy and desperate as he was at his first sexual encounter, when he was a student at Syracuse, trying to get the deed done with his marketing professor's doughy, slow-witted daughter before anyone attending the party upstairs became curious as to what the two of them were doing in the paneled basement, with its jettisoned barbells and medicine balls. The urgency he is feeling now is not far removed from the urgency he felt then. No drowning man groped for a lifeline with more desperation than he felt in moments of peak sexual arousal, and what Ezra is feeling now is the peak of the peak, the kind of crazed need for connection and release you feel when you are just starting out and lust does not so much cloud the mind as devour it in a few quick bites.

"Put your heels on my shoulders," Ezra says in a slur. He imagines his penis has just gotten impossibly hard, rock hard, blue-steel hard, consult-your-physician hard. Could it just be in his mind? He reaches under the bubbles and feels himself. Holy syndication! It doesn't even feel like his. It's a unicorn's horn!

"I guess I'm starting to feel it too," Annabelle says without much enthusiasm. She places her heels on Ezra's shoulders. For an old man, he has nice shoulders, smooth and rounded, with a smallpox vaccination scar high up on his right arm, a little starburst of shiny smooth skin about the size of the old-fashioned seal his lawyer put on the last page of their prenup.

"Sex in tub," Ezra says.

"Uh...yes," Annabelle says uncertainly, not because she doubts that is what is about to happen, and not because she isn't ready for a little old-fashioned slap-me-Henry, but because suddenly Ezra sounds as if someone has dropped a brick on his head.

His mouth is open. His fingers, webbed by soap bubbles, wave in the air, as if he were making certain he could move them. His eyelids are at half-mast—perhaps out of respect for his recently deceased brain. He lifts her up—his strength always takes her by surprise, but now it is more surprising than ever—and places her strategically on his lap. Bing: He's inside of her. He is pulsating. She feels his member like a weird alien heart in her.

"Be sweet, Ezra," she says.

"Moooooove."

"I am moving, baby. I am." He tries to kiss her. "Oh, don't," she says. "Your breath." She recoils. It's like being kissed by a scab, but she doesn't say this, she doesn't want to hurt his feelings or make him angry. But it is. It's as if someone had taken a cupful of blood, let it dry, and then molded it into two greasy, smelly lips.

But her moving away incites and excites Ezra—just as a dog can be stock-still staring at a squirrel for a long minute and lunge the moment its prey moves an inch. His thrusts grow fiercer. He knocks her off balance and she starts to slide. She tastes the sour fizz of the soap bubbles, spits.

"Wait," she says, commandingly enough for him to actually listen to her.

"You okay?" he manages to say.

"I think we took too much, Ez."

"I want to pop," he says.

Annabelle closes her eyes. *Pop* is what he calls reaching orgasm; every time he says it, it makes her just a little bit sadder. She wants to go home. Home! Home! Oh, please, God: home.

She places her hands on his hips and moves him out of her. It's not as if she does not want to have sex; she just doesn't want to have to look at him and smell his bloody breath.

She turns around, grips the edge of the tub, cranes her neck to keep her face as far from the suds as possible, and lifts her rump out of the water, inviting. She even waggles it back and forth. Hell, if they are going to do this, it might as well be fun...

"Niiiiiiiiiice," he says, hot little pebbles of beastliness rattling in his throat.

This is good, Ezra thinks, or sort of thinks, when he sees her be-my-Valentine behind. He buries his face in her, hears her distant gasp. Flesh, soap, water, heat. Taste. What is he tasting? Something. The little wrinkled ring of her final resistance. So good.

It hurts his knees to kneel. Instead, to enter her, he squats.

"Careful," she says, but the body says differently: she backs into him with a mighty thrust. Almost knocks him over.

It delights him. As she thrusts backward, he thrusts forward, instinctively waiting a beat before his move so they can establish a rhythm. Boy. Girl. Boy, girl. Ba-boom, ba-boom. Rather close to *baboon,* but no: this is music. This is rock and roll, this is swing—hell this is even John Philip Sousa. This is all that matters. This is the point of everything. Every other thing is just extra, what you do before and after you do this.

And, oh, by the way: Ezra wants to pop.

He moves inside her with more urgency. He is lodged so securely in her. Feels as if he had been born here. He has one hand on her hip, the other on the small of her back. She is starting to sink. She is starting to thrash. He hesitates for a moment. Oh, well, these things happen.

There is no way for him to stop. It is as if the fate of the universe hinges upon his reaching completion. Her legs are fluttering. Her muscles are contracting. Oh my, that feels so good. Water is sloshing out of the tub. The back of her head has completely disappeared. She is invisible to him now, but he surely can feel her.

His face is burning. His ears ring. His blood, mixed ever so slightly with the blood he has consumed, courses through him like lava. His hamstrings tighten. His heart rages like a madman locked in a room.

Only Annabelle's fingertips touch the edge of the tub. And one by one, they lose their purchase on the marble border. Her legs make a last, furious flutter. A trail of bubbles flows out of her open mouth, and the bubbles are consumed by the larger, denser, perfumed bubbles into which they flow.

At last, Ezra reaches his goal. His semen twists and jolts out of him, slightly painful, massively pleasurable, startling, exhausting, renewing. He thrusts again and again and again, not wanting the pleasure to end, and he is only now realizing that any resistance from Annabelle has ceased, and not only that, but there is no response at all. He slowly pulls out of her and sits back on his haunches, waiting for her to sit up again as well.

He has been rendered so stupid by the blood and the sex that he waits for nearly a minute before common sense kicks in and he frantically pulls her out of the water, but by then it is too late.

CHAPTER 9

Peter White and Cynthia race up the block, going east to west, and once that desperate act is completed, they don't really know what to do next, and so they quickly traverse the same block again, this time going west to east. White looks annoyed, but Cynthia is frantic. She grabs the therapist's arm.

"They could be anywhere," she says.

"I told you," White says, making no attempt to disguise his displeasure. "They need medication."

"Oh, for God's sake," she says, turning away from him. "Not now."

Because right now in the world, there are more than seven billion people who are neither Adam nor Alice Kramer, and it seems to Cynthia, standing here on the sun-struck street in Manhattan, that a goodly number of that nameless multitude are streaming right past her. Tall and short, stocky and lanky, stumbling and nimble, old and young, stooped and straight, fragrant and rank, sane and insane, dressed to the nines and clad in castoffs, black, white, yellow, and brown, hirsute and smooth, hopeful and crushed, chatting on cell phones, gorging on street food—all these souls: none of them Alice, none of them Adam.

*　　*　　*

They have made their way to Bethesda Fountain, to the spot where Alice, running for her life from her parents, first met Rodolfo. Back then it was night, and she was alone. Rodolfo was one of several wild boys practicing their clattering stunts on their skateboards. He had been friendly to her in his own slightly terrifying way. And as their friendship went on, he was friendlier and friendlier.

"We're going to get in trouble," Adam says now.

"Help me look," says Alice.

The fountain, presided over by a dark stone angel, gushes water that turns bright silver in the sunlight. The pool beneath it trembles. A low stone wall surrounds the pool, and people sit on the wall, some reading, others eating or meditating or talking on the phone. The brickwork around the fountain is pigeon pink, the same color as the feet of the busy birds who patrol the area hunting for scraps. Beyond the fountain and its trembling pool, one of the park's lakes stretches, filled today with rowboats, plus the occasional toy under remote control.

"You see anyone?" Adam asks.

Alice shakes her head. There are plenty of skaters around, all ages, races, and genders, but no familiar faces. A hundred or so feet in front of them, the crowd suddenly parts. A boy is running, and behind him are two police officers, both young and fit.

The boy is small, with long dark hair that fans out as he races. His build is slight; his eyes pools of bright blue madness. He wears jeans and a T-shirt and looks dirty, uncared-for. Yet he is uncommonly swift, and the distance between him and his pursuers gradually increases.

A man with a graying crew cut wearing shorts and a tank top decides to come to the aid of the police and steps in front of the fleeing urchin. The boy throws the man to the ground in an easy motion, as if discarding a broken umbrella. The man's head thuds on the pavement. Blood pours out of the man's mouth. But it looks worse than it is—it's only that he hit the pavement with such force that he bit off a chunk of his tongue.

When the boy races past Alice and Adam, they don't give it a moment's thought; they start running alongside him.

CHAPTER 10

In the silence and solitude of the house on Sixty-Ninth Street, Cynthia can still smell the sweetness of the freshly painted walls—she had instructed the contractors to pour a little bottle of vanilla extract into every can of paint, so when she and the children moved in, the place smelled like a bakery. What a good idea it had seemed, but now the cheerful, friendly aroma mocks her senses.

Her eyes ache from crying. She wonders if it's possible to weep yourself blind.

She had no alternative but to go to the police. In her fevered imagination, every cop in the precinct would know that the twins were her adopted children, and their disappearance would be used to prove her unfitness as a mother. But the reality was something quite different. The officer who took down her information—a young, somehow Turkish-looking fellow with dramatic eyebrows and an aggressive smile—showed no inclination to question her competency as a mother, nor did he show much interest in the report that two young children were missing. Apparently, not enough time had passed for the police to make looking for the twins a high priority. In fact, as Cynthia left the precinct, she doubted that searching for Adam and Alice was a priority for them at all.

She continued to look for them, but now she is home, waiting for someone—the kids, the police—to call her. Or for the greater miracle of the children coming home.

An hour passes. She sits in the parlor with her legs crossed and her folded hands in her lap. She must remind herself to breathe.

Every so often, the waiting becomes intolerable and she springs from the sofa and races to one window or another, parts the curtain, and peers out at the street. She is coming to believe that at a certain level, hope and insanity cross paths. And she is at that level.

Who can she call? There is no one in this city she knows except for Arthur, and she has already tried his numbers and her calls have gone unanswered. Who else? The people in the antiques world? You might as well call a Siamese cat to save you from drowning. Why, oh why, has she not bothered to establish herself with any AA meetings in New York? Did she really believe that she would somehow do better on her own?

She drinks ready-made iced tea. Suddenly famished, she tears open a box of crackers and devours half of it. She turns on the TV in time for the local news. The anchors appear to be a former football player and a recently retired runway model.

"The hottest summer in New York history continues to rack up record numbers, and another bonds trader comes forward in the Banco del Mondo scandal that continues to rock the financial world," the runway model says with an expression that suggests a wry appreciation for a world careening out of control.

"And police," intones the retired athlete, "find the bodies of two young people in Central Park, apparently killed in broad daylight." He glances at his co-anchor and shakes his head, as if to say, *Why must it be up to me to report these most terrible things?* "And also Earl with the weather, Lilani with sports, and a special treat later in our broadcast—celebrity chef Tangerine Dream will demonstrate five easy dishes that actually promote weight loss."

"Sounds intriguing," the model says, patting her virtually nonexistent tummy.

"Back right after these short announcements," the athlete says.

Cynthia is standing, her hands on top of her head, her mouth open. She must now wait through three long minutes of advertising for gold, denture cleaners, life insurance, and, most wicked of all, a pitch for a new drug for children who are judged not to be living up to their full potential in school—Excello, prescribed for a large scattering of childhood behavioral patterns, from forgetfulness to foot jiggling, and sold in this ad through a grandmother character, who looks as if she wandered off the set of *Little House on the Prairie,* reassuring her daughter, who looks hip (tattooed) but responsible and concerned (eyeglasses, a worried expression), that it is perfectly safe to give Sean (failing in school, alienated from his friends) Excello. "I wish it was around when you were a little girl driving everyone crazy," the old woman says, to which the daughter says, "Mom!" and gives her a playful but totally respectful little shove.

At last, the newscasters' faces fill the screen. Cynthia has an impulse to turn off the TV, but she forces herself to watch. Film of two bodies, both on the small side, covered with Mylar sheets. The whirling red and blue lights of several emergency vehicles flicker in the leaves of the abundant trees. Yards of yellow tape isolate the crime scene; hundreds of people who look as if there is no place else in the whole world they'd rather be stand off to the side, watching the bodies being taken away.

Who are these people? she wonders. *Who are these people standing and watching?*

And yet, she is one of them. She is staring at the TV screen, waiting for the unlikely moment when one of the blankets will fall to the side and reveal who is beneath it—or show a hand, a shoe, anything…

The on-site reporter, a young, cooperative-looking man in his late twenties wearing a striped seersucker jacket over a white T-shirt, is speaking into the camera in a rather droll, laconic voice. "Right now, Tina and Doug, police are not releasing any details about the two victims, awaiting positive identification."

"Is there anything we know so far about them, Rafael?" Doug asks in some vague approximation of actual conversation.

"Well, my sources tell me the victims appear to be somewhere between fourteen and sixteen years old. They were carrying no identification. Interestingly, they had quite a bit of money on them."

Money? thinks Cynthia. She latches on to the oddity of this—it gives her hope.

"Both young men were well-dressed, and right now no cause of death has been given," Rafael continues.

Young men? Without realizing she was doing so, Cynthia had lowered herself into a kind of crouch in front of the TV, and with this last bit of news—both victims male—she falls forward onto her hands and knees, drops her head, and simply stares at her hands and the pattern on the Persian carpet.

The reporter is still talking, but Cynthia is no longer taking it in. All she knows is this: both victims were male. Which rules out Adam and Alice. And besides that: Who could see them and mistake them for sixteen-year-olds? More likely to mistake them for ten-year-olds. And they had no money on them, at least none to speak of. She feels crazy and horribly tainted—to be so elated that the dead children are not her own. A sin, certainly. And as a longtime citizen of San Francisco, she believes that the laws of karma will one day have their way with her.

"Thanks, Raf. Try and stay cool out there," Tina says.

Cynthia switches off the set and paces the room. She is momentarily overjoyed. She wants to tell someone the wonderful news: the corpses found in Central Park are not the twins! Yes, it's come to that: Slain children not her own qualify as good news.

She goes to the window and looks out, expecting to see them. But they are not there. She returns to the sofa, sits, rubs her eyes with the heels of her hands. Is there really nothing she can do to bring these children home? No call to make, no favorite place to look, no one to help her? Hillary Clinton used to say it took a village to raise a child, but right now, Cynthia would settle for a barbershop quartet or a couple of cousins or, really, just one extra person: someone who could be here in the house in case they return while Cynthia goes up and down the streets of New York, hoping to get lucky.

She needs a drink. Why, oh why, did she have the thousands of other drinks, none of which she needed as much as she needs one right now? If only she had not already once—well, actually, twice—wrecked her life with alcohol, she could do what any normal person would do in a situation like this. She could pour herself a modest little drink. She could put two ice cubes in a glass and pour a bit of vodka over them. A splash. Nothing crazy. Just a splash, a goddamned splash. The warmth of the vodka would startle the ice, and the cubes would creak and crack and secrete a little bit of moisture, mixing in with the vodka, and she'd move the glass in a tight little circle to stir the ice water and the vodka, and then she'd take a sip. The vodka would be cold and astringent on her lips, on the tip of her tongue, in the back of her throat, and then, as it went down, it would miraculously mutate from cold to warm to very, very warm indeed. And by the time it was in her stomach, it would be like a lovely hydrangea made out of pure shimmering heat. Would it be the solution to all her problems? Of course not! All it could do was settle her nerves, which, she reasoned, would probably make her a more useful person than she was right now. Now she was approaching the edge of her endurance, and her thoughts were repetitious and maddening. This is what every person in recovery dreads: the voice inside one's head, reasonable, persuasive, and utterly evil, repeating over and over that a shot, a snort, or a drink is the only thing that will help.

And yet...it could be argued, the case could definitely be made that if she did not have something to calm her nerves, she would soon go mad. And what better thing to soothe her than a modest little sip of alcohol? This was tried-and-true. This was ancient—older even than prayer. She had read somewhere that the consumption of alcoholic beverages dated back to the very dawn of human society. In fact, as she recalls, pacing now from one room to the next, the article seemed to have suggested that without fermented drinks and the good vibes they engendered, human society might have been delayed by another couple of thousand years.

So how was it that people—beginning with the ones who lived so long ago that they could barely walk upright all the way to the several million folks just beyond the glass of her house's many windows—could all of them enjoy an innocent little snort of something lovely and relaxing while she, the accursed Cynthia, had to white-knuckle it? Where was the justice in that? Why was she being punished?

And then it occurs to her: If all this viciously enforced sobriety is a prison, she is, in fact, her own jailer. She has the keys right in her own pocket! She can walk out to freedom—the freedom to choose, the freedom to exhale—any time she wants to.

There is not a drop to drink in this house. There is not even cooking sherry or aftershave. She wonders how close the nearest liquor store is, pretending for the moment that she doesn't know full well—she knows, in fact, the location of every liquor store within a ten-block radius of the house, carries the invisible map of their locations. She even knows which ones deliver.

She is holding the phone. Much to her own surprise. She wonders when she picked it up, how long she has been pacing around with it in her hand. She pushes the Talk button, listens to the dial tone. Testing. Testing. In a kind of panic, she throws the phone onto a sofa. Get thee behind me, Satan!

Okay, one thing for sure. She is not going to have a bottle of vodka delivered to the house. First of all: What a waste of money! Second, the last thing in the world she needs is to start forming relationships with liquor stores, to be opening accounts, talking to clerks, tipping delivery people. No way. No fucking way! If she wants a bottle of Grey Goose, she can walk to the corner of Seventieth and Lex and get it herself. And by the way, Grey Goose is out of the question. If she's going to take a little vacation from sobriety, she's not going to indulge her love for certain brands; she will make do with the cheapest vodka they carry. Once, back in SF, she recalls, smiling weirdly, she bought a gallon of a vodka called St. Pitersberg for $4.99. The dumbbells who bottled it couldn't even spell Petersburg! It left an aftertaste that reminded her of a fly she had accidentally swallowed when she was seven years old.

The afternoon turns to evening. The evening light, a dark dusty blue, hangs on like someone clinging to the edge of a cliff, and then, suddenly, it lets go and the darkness rushes in. Completely lost now in faulty thinking, Cynthia tells herself, *Well, it's now or never,* and she hurries toward Lexington Avenue, scarcely able to breathe—each breath is like swallowing a rag soaked in gasoline. Passersby seem to be glancing at her, shooting her looks that say *Don't do it.* Of course, nothing could be further from the truth. She knows this. And yet, she also does not know it.

The clerk at Lexington Quality Spirits has a head shaped like a lightbulb. He decides to torture Cynthia by asking her if she'd like him to gift wrap her bottle of cheap vodka. "Just put it in a bag," she manages to say. As she trudges home, she holds the sack away from her, like those people on dog walks carrying bags of their pet's shit.

Home! She left the door unlocked in case they returned in the five minutes she was absent. "Kids!" she calls, walking in. "Kids? Kids?"

The door slams behind her. She whirls around. Why did it do that? Oh, well…

She unscrews the bottle. Great word: *unscrew.* Like removing your sexual experiences, sip by sip, until you are just a slab of meat programmed for metabolizing alcohol. Anyhow, it's good to get the suspense over and done with—this bottle has not been brought home for storing away. This quart will be drunk. Only one question remains: Just a few restorative snorts, or drain the thing down to the glass stalagmite on the bottom of the bottle?

She sits with the vodka, delaying that first drink. She sniffs the fumes rising from the bottle's neck. Wow! Horribly wonderful, wonderfully horrible.

And then she realizes: She is not alone.

Her heart is racing, completely out of rhythm. "Alice? Adam? Kids?"

She lifts the bottle as if it were a club, forgetting she uncapped it. The vodka cascades over the heel of her hand, her wrist, up her arm to her elbow. She curses, puts the bottle down on the table. She licks the trail of wetness—and this is it, after all, this is how her unbroken string of sober days is suddenly ended, not with a toast, not with any pleasure, not with a slap or a tickle: just a hurried, half-conscious series of little cleanup licks.

Darkness rolls through the house like black water that has breached a levee. Room by room, she keeps ahead of the darkness, switching on lamps.

Each lamp illuminates the piece of furniture next to which it stands. The Queen Anne sofa with the lilac damask covering, one of the few lovely pieces that somehow survived the chaos of Alex and Leslie's final days. An engraving by John La Farge of a ragged boy with a lyre mesmerizing a pack of wolves. The deep dark leather chair Cynthia bought in a home-decor shop near Union Square, part of her weeklong shopping spree as she tried to fill a huge house that had been all but denuded of usable furniture by her sister and Alex as they descended into animalistic madness.

Each time she turns on a light, Cynthia hesitates, listens. All she can hear is the life outside, the traffic noises that get in despite the soundproof windows. The house is silent, but within that silence, she feels there is a presence, something lurking.

Something crouched.

Something waiting.

She pulls a brass poker out of its stand next to the fireplace in the dining room. She doubles back into the living room and stares for a moment at the open bottle of vodka. *What an unbelievably lucky break,* she thinks, *having it here.* Her old friend and protector.

Yet something stops her. Some surviving thread of resolve. A promise remembered that rises from the ashes and is suddenly alive, shouting to her. *Pour it down the drain,* a voice commands her.

The voice is persuasive enough to prevent her from guzzling the whole bottle in one long, nihilistic swallow, but not quite so convincing as to get her to do its bidding.

It's a standoff. She glares at the bottle, points at it in a warning sort of way, and then turns her back to it—but leaves it full. And she continues to sniff her arm, sickeningly thrilled by the scent of the booze on her skin, the way she aroused herself as a young girl by paging through at the girlie magazines her idiot father thought he had securely hidden—how those Hindenburgian boobies transfixed her, whipsawed her senses between admiration and revulsion.

Oh, the body, the human body: what a source of humiliation and horror. Suddenly, Cynthia is desperate to relieve herself. Her bladder is full and it has blotted out every other sense, just as the dopey little moon can eclipse the enormous burning sun. Her hands clenched into fists, she hurries to the nearest bathroom. She hikes up her skirt, lowers her knickers, glances into the bowl—she will never again sit on a toilet without checking to see if some hideous creature is floating in the water. Her urine comes out of her in a long scalding twist; it goes on and on and on, for she has been holding it in since the morning.

She leans forward, resting her elbows on her knees. She allows herself to close her eyes—but a moment later, she gasps with terror. Something cold and horrid has touched the back of her neck. In her fright, her feet get tangled in her underwear and she falls to her hands and knees. She rolls onto her back, scuttling away, using her heels to propel her. She looks up and sees on the ceiling a dark spot, roughly the size of a human heart, and from its center comes the *drip-drip* of water.

Moments later she is pounding up the stairs, calling out for the twins. In the back of her mind she is trying to remember which room on the second floor is above the bathroom she was just using. As far as she can recall, it is not a room with water— it's a room with floor-to-ceiling glassed-in shelves, dark wainscoting, once the home of framed antique maps, precious old globes, and various artifacts culled from scientific and touristic expeditions Twisden ancestors took part in.

The room now is empty—freshly painted, but as yet unfurnished. There is an accumulation of water on the wide plank cherrywood floors. Cynthia looks up and sees the huge water stain on the ceiling—and here the water is coming down much more quickly. Each drop is the size of a thumbnail. As the plaster falls away, insects that have been living behind it start oozing out. Are they ladybugs? She's not sure. A clump of them, the color of ear wax, bubbles up, the collectivity of their little wings fluttering into a whine.

She races up to the third floor. She can already hear the water lapping out of the tub in the twins' shared bathroom. The door is closed and she stands there with her hand on the knob, afraid to open it. "Adam? Alice?" She waits for a moment and then twists the knob, pushes the door open, and walks into a world of thick soapy steam, choking in its sweetness. The steam touches her skin like a million tendrils. Fear like a finger opens her mouth, and the steam fills her lungs.

Coughing, she waves the steam away from her as it rushes toward the cool air of the open door.

"Kids?"

She switches on the overhead light. It's dim behind the layers of steam, like a lozenge moon in a cloudy sky. She stands over the tub, peers in. There's no one in it—but she doesn't trust her senses; someone could be lurking beneath the surface.

She is standing in two inches of water. The overhead light is starting to sputter and spit sparks. She has a vision of herself stiff and charred from electric shock, an image so sharp and convincing it seems more like a memory than a premonition.

She twists the porcelain hot- and cold-water faucets closed, but water continues to flow over the lip of the tub and onto the floor. She must pull the black rubber plug that covers the drain. She reaches into the murky water, gropes for the plug. And something wet and rough wraps itself around her wrist. In fright, she yanks her hand out of the water—but it's only a washcloth, a dark brown washcloth purchased a couple of weeks ago from Bed, Bath & Beyond.

She stands there watching the water drain out of the tub. She doesn't know for the life of her why she is transfixed here. It could be as simple as this: Her mind is overloaded and she can't think of what to do next. As the water glugs down the drain, she throws some more of the Bed, Bath & Beyond bounty onto the floor, trying to soak up the water and prevent further damage—though soaked floors and falling plaster seem the least of her worries.

The tub is nearly empty now. Clinging to the sides is a layer of dirt so thick it seems almost like fur. In fact, it looks so thick that she must touch her forefinger to it, just to make certain. Whoever has bathed in this water was unspeakably filthy.

Now she does not think there is someone else in this house; she knows it. She wonders if she ought to dial 911…But how would it look if she called the police to find her own children in her own house? And who trusted the police, anyhow? With their guns drawn, their trigger fingers hyperreactive. If only this house were smaller.

She goes from room to room, each one as inanimate as a painting. Yet the more evidence she acquires that no one is here, the more certain she feels that she is not alone. She can feel the invisible presence like cold air against her. Unseen fingers almost touch her, just graze the ends of the down on her arms, the wisps of hair on the back of her neck.

Finally, every light in the house is on. And every room in the house has been inspected. Closets opened, clothes parted, hangers sent clattering. Beds looked under. They're not here. And yet, she is sure they are.

And if they are not, who is?

On her third pass through the front sitting room, she once again confronts the open bottle of vodka. No, not today, not today. She grabs it roughly by the neck, as if to master it, and pours the contents into the nearest sink, which happens to be in a tight little half-bath wedged beneath the staircase to the second floor. On the way out of the bathroom, she sees the heavy oak door that leads to the cellar.

Once that cellar was a crime scene. It was the place Alex and Leslie kept the pets they devoured more and more regularly as their appetites became more feverish and uncontrolled. And it was the place where they first ventured into cannibalism, eating a young Cuban immigrant piece by piece. It was into the cellar that Cynthia herself ventured after heeding her sister's call to come to New York, and it was here that she saw that poor caged young man, his arm devoured.

In readying the house, Cynthia instructed the contractors to take everything out of the cellar—not only the cages, and the sinks, and the darkly stained concrete slabs, but also the boiler and the hot-water heater, which were relocated to a small shed specifically built for that purpose behind the house. And once the cellar was but a shell, Cynthia padlocked the door, and she has not opened it since. The lock is huge and heavy, with a thick steel shank the weight of a log. And the lock, she sees now, is missing.

Whoever is in this house is right down those stairs.

She places her hand on the doorknob but then quickly moves it away, as if burned.

No. She must do this. She must.

She opens the door. It's so heavy. The cold dampness of the cellar rises up as if resurrected by the light. She gropes blindly for a light switch until she remembers that there is no electricity in the cellar—disconnecting the power was part of the room's eternal banishment.

She must get a flashlight. Kitchen. Drawer. Batteries? God, please let there be batteries.

She is about to close the door when she hears a high-pitched twittering noise, like a tree full of peepers, and then a light drumming sound, like a hundred small fingers nervously tapping on a table. Before she can ask herself what is making those noises, the answer becomes sickeningly clear: rats.

Rats.

Dozens of rats. Maybe a hundred. Locked down in that cellar, maybe born there for all she knows, and now raging up the stairs like a marauding army, drawn to the light and perhaps the promise of food, water. She sees whiskers, snouts, the pale pink of hairless feet. Screaming, she slams the door shut. The lead rat is already halfway through, and the thick door cuts it in half. Its furious little eyes go from wet paint to dry paint; its horrid little tongue protrudes halfway out its toothy, efficient little mouth.

With the poor blameless rat wedged so, she cannot fully close the door. She has a choice. She can open it up a little and clear the rat away with her shoe—unfortunately, open-toed sandals—or she can exert all her force and push the door until it cuts the creature in half. Plan A risks God knows how many other rats racing in—she can hear them squealing and scratching right now—and plan B (which already seems the more likely course of action) will probably mean a little geyser of gore spewing out of the dead rodent.

The other rats have already climbed on the dead rat's back. Tiny little claws show through the crack in the door. They seem to be throwing themselves against it, as if they had enough strength to force it open.

But then she hears a voice—a little weakened call of distress coming from the cellar.

"Help us!"

It's Alice. Alive! Here!

Confusion and relief fill Cynthia like a howling wind. For a moment, she is incapable of thought or movement. Then, with a surge of strength, she shoulders the door shut. It closes with a wet whoosh. The front half of the rat drops to the floor, immobile. One glance. No more. Look away.

"I'm coming!" Cynthia screams, hoping her voice can penetrate the heavy door.

She goes to the kitchen and finds the fresh, barely used broom standing in the closet, a bright copper dustpan attached to its handle. She also finds a brand-new red plastic flashlight. She clicks it on, checking the batteries. The flashlight's broad face yellows brightly.

She returns to the cellar door, sweeps the half-rat to one side. An inch of spine is showing, and a livid fringe of veins. She inhales deeply, as if to put the breath of life into her courage. Breathe in, breathe out. Her courage at first gives no sign of living, but finally, after the fifth deep breath, it stirs.

She waits. Her hope is that the rats that ascended the staircase became discouraged and retreated downstairs. She doesn't know what she will do about them downstairs, but anything will be better than having to cope with them on the staircase. She must move quickly, before her little bit of courage returns to its stillborn state.

She yanks the door open, screaming wildly—to frighten whatever rats might be lurking there and to let the kids know she is on her way. It hurts to scream. It hurts her throat, and it hurts her soul. It's like having her humanity taken away.

And the rats are indeed lurking there. She sweeps the beam of her flashlight frantically from left to right, and with her other hand, she attacks the swarm of rodents with her broom. Some of them tumble down the stairs—she can hear the thump and thwack of them as they disappear into the darkness. Some of them run away on their own. There are no rat heroes in this bunch; just hungry, frightened rodents. One of the rats, however, in trying to escape the sharp hard bristles, climbed onto the head of the broom, and now Cynthia lifts the broom and hits it against the wall with all her might—either killing or stunning the one brave rat. Either way, it surrenders its frantic purchase and is gone.

She directs the beam of the flashlight down the steps—the bar of golden light must raise hope in the twins; they rise to it like flowers to the sun.

"We're here!"

"Hurry! Please hurry!"

Who is more terrified, her or the rats? She is banking on the rats being more scared…

Swatting wildly at the steps, she descends as quickly as she can, mindful that if she falls, all is lost. The beam from the flashlight sweeps over the dun-colored backs of the retreating rats—they flee like villagers from a dragon. Cynthia stands now on the floor.

But there is one that is fearless. Perhaps it's a female; perhaps she has just had a litter of helpless, practically translucent little pinkies whom she is coded to protect. Whatever motivates this solitary rat, it rises on its hind legs, juts its narrow, despised face forward, and gives every indication of standing its ground.

"Kids?"

"They're getting closer to us," one of them says. Adam, she guesses. He sounds resigned.

"Just kick at them," Cynthia says. "Fight back."

The rat facing her drops to all fours and takes a couple of steps forward. Cynthia swings the broom at it, hoping only to scare it off. She scores a direct hit.

But rather than run away from her, the militant rat some-how ends up with its claws dug into the straw of the broom head. It takes a moment for it to get its bearings, but then it moves slowly toward the collar that joins the handle to the head, and now it has one paw on the handle, and now it has two paws on the handle, and now . . .

In a panic, Cynthia throws the broom and its passenger across the cellar. It clatters against the wall or a post—and now all she has is her flashlight.

The rats that fled her seem to know this. In clumps, they emerge from crevices along the walls until they have all coalesced into a kind of rodent army five feet wide and five feet long. In unison, they run along the wall—bewilderingly fast, like a bolt of lightning.

Afraid to move, Cynthia keeps them in the flashlight's beam. The rats seem to be in mad conversation with one another.

"Kids? Let me hear you. Where are you?"

Are they too afraid to speak? Has something happened to them?

"We're over here!" Alice calls out in a frantic whisper.

Her voice is coming from the far corner of the cellar where the old coal chute used to be—this whole house had been heated by coal until shortly after World War II. The chute is gone and the door to the outside where the deliverymen used to shovel the coal into a vast bin that stood at the bottom has long been bricked over. However, there remains a ledge, and it is here that the twins have perched, their legs dangling ten feet above the concrete floor. It passes through Cynthia's mind: *How in the world did they ever get up there?*

But it doesn't matter. Not now. She has found them. They are alive. Nothing else really matters.

She stands below them and they reach out to her beseechingly. She reaches for them but she can't get very close—they are at least four feet from the tips of her fingers.

And they are not alone. Some smaller creature—oh, it's a

child; at first she wasn't sure—is crouched between them. A poor filthy thing. He shields his pale eyes as the flashlight's beam brightly interrogates his little face. When the light touches his hands, his fingertips emit a bright red glow.

"We have to hurry," Cynthia says. She points the beam back at the rats. They are starting to approach her again, but the light stops them—at least for the moment.

She places the flashlight on the ground with the light pointing at the rats.

"You first, Alice," she says. "Jump. I'll catch you."

Cynthia expects to have to convince the frightened child to jump, but Alice surprises her—she leaps from her perch without a moment's hesitation. Cynthia is barely prepared to make the catch, but she does. The girl—her daughter!—is in her arms. They stand there for a moment in the near darkness.

"Alice," Cynthia says, her voice trembling with relief.

"Mom," Alice murmurs.

It takes Cynthia's breath away. Mom! She feels the rush of tears, the surge of hot blood to her own face.

Now for the others.

But when she looks around, they are already standing on either side of her.

"Adam! You scared the shit out of me."

"Your mom swears," the little boy in their company says.

"Who's this?" Cynthia asks.

"Dylan," Alice says. "He's our friend."

"Dylan Morris," the boy says, thrusting out his narrow chest. "My father is the mayor of New York City!" He is holding a box of Carr's Table Water Crackers. He pulls one out, bites it in half, and chews it vigorously.

"Give me that," Cynthia says, taking the box away from the

boy—who is too stunned to say anything; his eyes widen with amazement. The gang of rodents is slowly approaching them, and Cynthia throws one of the crackers in their direction.

The cracker is so light, however, and her toss is so nervous and incomplete that the cracker falls no more than two feet away from them—so rather than occupying the rats, the cracker instead draws the rats closer to them.

She claws out the cellophane sleeve containing the rest of the crackers and tosses them quickly and with as much force as she can muster. The pale pile of them is irresistible to the rats; they pounce on it and begin devouring the crackers with such ferocious energy that the twins and Dylan cover their ears.

"Come on," she says, picking up the flashlight. "Let's get out of here before they start in on us."

She picks up Dylan and carries him, and she and the twins make their way toward the stairs.

The light of the flashlight again passes over the little boy's hand, and in response to the light, his fingers turn deeply and brightly red. He sees that she notices this and scowls angrily at her.

When they are halfway up, she hears a scream that sounds almost human. She turns, points the flashlight toward the noise: some of the rats, in their frenzy and delight, have started eating one another.

CHAPTER 11

Dennis Keswick stands in front of the nameless, nondescript building a block off Kissena Boulevard in the great borough of Queens. The moon is bright and he knows there are hidden closed-circuit cameras everywhere guarding the periphery of the building, but he sees no reason to disguise himself or to hide and peek or to in any other way prevent his employers from knowing he has come to look things over. This building—squat, colorless, with iron grillwork over its few windows—is where the wild children he harvests are taken; these are secure Borman and Davis laboratories, and try as he might, Keswick cannot fully imagine what procedures take place there.

Borman and Davis is a well-respected international pharmaceutical firm, and though Dennis understands that its executives, like those in every other corporation, are motivated by a desire to maximize their profits (a drive lightly disguised in the quaint costume of Responsibility to Our Shareholders), he also believes they are beholden by the firm's very size to act more or less responsibly. Those boys and girls he has delivered to them and who are somewhere behind the bland façade of that pale gray building are being treated at least as humanely as the chimpanzees once were in the halcyon days of the past, before a bunch of angry spinsters and Big Government made experimentation on primates illegal.

How many wild boys and girls are in there at this very moment? Are they kept in one large room? Or individual cells? No, not cells. Rooms. Are the scientists drawing blood? Spinal fluid? Bone marrow?

Oh, the scientists, the scientists, the miserable, stuck-up, arrogant, superior, ugly-assed scientists. The smocks, is what he calls them. The smocks. Do they treat Dennis as an equal, a colleague? No, they certainly do not. They treat him like a delivery service. Thank you for the body, Dennis, see you next time. Do they invite him in to see the facility? Oh, absolutely not. Do they invite him in for a drink of water, a quick trip to the can? No. The loading dock at the back of the building is all he knows. Sometimes a guy whom Dennis calls Igor meets him out back and carries the catch of the day inside. Igor wears a purple sweater and black pants no matter what the weather. Sometimes three of the scientists come out, youngish fellows, probably going a little stir-crazy and wanting to take advantage of Dennis's delivery to grab a few moments of fresh air. The young chemists are polite, vaguely friendly. One of them calls Dennis "man," and another says "dude." All that MIT/Stanford/Harvard training, and he says "dude"!

Dennis could have been one of them, if he'd been given a decent chance. With the right mother and a father who wanted to be a father—Dennis put few limitations on what he might have been able to achieve had he been given a proper start in life.

A warm wind wafts by, carrying the scent of burned sugar. An Asian couple appears, carrying bags of groceries. Maybe they are Chinese; maybe Korean. Dennis cannot tell the difference and does not care to. The Asians are ascendant and a few of them are probably high up on the Borman and Davis food chain. Screw them. Screw them all.

The thing is this: If the smocks succeed in isolating whatever it was that made the kids practically superhuman, fortunes will be made. Of course, the biggest, fattest, tastiest slice of the cake will go to the five or six suits on top, but those chemists and endocrinologists and molecular biologists inside that building— they are definitely in line for a major payday.

Maybe Dennis himself will get a raise. Maybe they'll throw a few grand his way as a celebratory gesture. Maybe.

In the meantime, he peers at the building, wondering what the H-E-double-hockey-sticks they are doing with the human bounty he so faithfully delivers to them.

Oh, joy! Joy! Joy! The sweet breathless feeling of absolute joy!

First Rodolfo, then the others—boys, girls, and the undeclared—darting up rocky hills, over moon-bright lawns, through the thickets, into the trees, thundering through unlit tunnels, bounding over dark dewy benches, grabbing each other, evading each other, calling out in their wordless secret language of hoots and hollers, whoops and whistles. The laughter. The danger. The sex. The sense of absolute freedom— freedom from families, freedom from hunger, freedom from the word *no,* from a shaken head, a pointed finger, a frown. Freedom! Freedom from judgment; freedom from fear. It is theirs.

And so is Central Park. It is three in the morning. Long past the time when the last horse and buggy has clip-clopped the last drunken tourists along the twisting drives, long past the time when the last lonely soul glumly staring at his phone got up from the bench and trudged home. Halos of white light hover around the lampposts. The glamorous scent of the city is in the air—

perfume and the exhaust from limousines. The temperature has barely dropped a degree since sundown; the humid air holds on to the heat like a miser grasping a handful of wet dollar bills.

Here and there the homeless—many of them mad—sleep under a bush or on the steps to the fountain. Rodolfo and his crew will not disturb them; they have come to an unspoken truce. Most of the homeless people do not even open their eyes when the wild things race by, and those who do lift themselves up on one elbow, watch for a moment, blink, and lie down again on their impossible cardboard beds. They will never report what they see. Why would they? And who would believe them? Not the Central Park police, housed in their picturesque barracks along the Seventy-Ninth Street drive, patrolling the park on horseback, on bicycles, in cruisers—and more likely to run one of the homeless in than take his testimony.

Tonight the wild children are running free, burning their energy. Living indoors can take its toll—even with the money, the food, the videos, the games, the beds. They are not meant to live indoors. They are not meant to live outdoors either. They are meant to have both. And now they do.

The pack of untamable boys and girls numbers close to a hundred, but only nineteen of them have blood that Rodolfo dares put on the market. He likes to pretend it's scientific, but really it's only by guesswork that he makes his choices. If they sell blood that is too wild, there could be trouble—the idea is to give the customers a buzz, not to fucking electrocute them! And if they sell blood from one of the pack who is essentially no different from any other teenager—maybe faster, maybe quicker to anger, maybe a little more loyal, but basically nothing more than that—then they will end up selling beat shit, and the thrill ride the customers so greedily seek will definitely not be forthcoming. All they will get for their money is a little tube of blood, and maybe, just maybe, a placebo erection. And eventually word will get out. Those boomers hunting boners— they network. They are all in one another's business; they talk all the time—what else do they have to do? So the important thing is to protect the integrity of the product. In a word-of-mouth business, the integrity of the product is key. Protecting product integrity is Rodolfo's major activity. There are a million things to keep track of: were they running out of needles; was the stuff being properly refrigerated; who was owed a complimentary dose for bringing it to new customers. The doses themselves had to be kept track of; you did not want to sell Boy-Boy's blood to someone with a weak heart who just wanted enough extra energy to keep his slightly younger wife amused on their anniversary, because if you did, they could both end up in icy drawers at the morgue.

Rodolfo's dream: One day they will use the blood money to buy a place in the country. It shouldn't be too far away. They will always need the city; business, after all, is business. Maybe a hundred miles up the river. A big house, large enough for dozens of them. Up a long driveway, with a locked gate at the mouth of it. Porches. Balconies. A big old lawn, a million trees. A pond, a lake, a pool. He can close his eyes and see the moon riding the ripples of the water.

Though normally when they romp through the park they are kind of a formless pack, tonight, Polly is always at Rodolfo's side. Bounding up a hill, playing on the swings—wherever he goes, she is right next to him, matching him step for step, with her moon face and long braid, her babyish nose, and her bright green eyes behind thick glasses.

Unlike most of the crew, Polly was never in danger in her

old home. Her parents were two of the few who managed to kill themselves—most of the other parents were too beastly to take their own lives; animals do not commit suicide. Yet Polly's folks found a way. She woke up one morning and her parents were in their bedroom, orderly for once, clothes put away, chairs upright, bed made, both of them looking oddly peaceful and demure and, of course, dead. They were old, in their late fifties, professors, and in a different world, Polly would have one day become a professor too. All she did was read. She never let anyone touch her. If you found her standing next to you, it was because she wanted to talk.

And the way she talked! Her great subject at the moment was that they were all post-human. "We are the beginnings of a new race. We're new. There are extinct species buried in the Burgess Shale we can't even imagine. Creatures with fifty legs and two heads," she says now.

"That's barking," Rodolfo says.

"Not everything makes it up the evolutionary ladder," Polly continues. "And even if it does, no one knows even half of what's here. Science knows only about ten percent of all the species on earth. The world is full of living things, animals and plants and everything, and no one has studied them, they don't even have names for them. And they don't have names for us either. Just look at us! We're faster, stronger, and I wouldn't say we're stupid, that's for sure. That's why they hate us. We have to be careful until there are more of us."

And she says it all in the old-fashioned English her parents taught her. Some of the pack mistrust her, with her school-teacher way of talking. It was the voice of the enemy; they heard it like an Allied soldier in World War II would hear *achtung*.

"How many of us have they gotten so far?" Polly asks. She

and Rodolfo are on the swings in the Diana Ross Playground. The chains squeak. She holds her feet with the toes pointing straight out to make herself go higher and higher.

"We's fine. Me's finding who be the doing of it, put him down good." He lifts his chin, purses his lips. He can hear his boys, and the girls too, somewhere in the darkness. Dueling with sticks. Wrestling.

"Owww!" someone cries. "Don't throw me's so hard."

That must be Little Man. Always losing, always complaining. If he were in a litter of pups, he'd be the one getting shoved off the teat…he'd be the one some little girl would be feeding through an eyedropper.

"But how many, Rodolfo?" Polly persists. "How many are missing?"

"Six?" He shrugs, as if it were a matter of indifference to him, but his heart surges and twists at the very thought of it.

"They want to wipe us off the face of the earth," Polly says. "I was reading—"

Rodolfo laughs as if she has just confessed something slightly embarrassing.

"About this factory in China. You know what they make?"

"Chopsticks."

"Mice. All different kinds. They sell them to labs. Bald mice. Schizo mice. Mice that can only walk backward. Mice that get old in one day."

"Peoples is mean like monster movie," says Rodolfo.

"They can do it by changing just one chromosome," Polly says. "That mouse factory has a thousand different kinds of mice, like flavors of ice cream, and they sell them to whoever wants to experiment. The only thing is, they can't control what happens in the next generation. That one missing chromosome changes the DNA, but it's not predictable. So even if you get two bald ones to mate, their babies might be biters or maybe glow in the dark, like those fish they sell in pet stores."

"Me's love to glow in the dark!"

"Maybe your children will. We've got a baby with wings."

"He cute."

"The point is, Rodolfo, what are we? I don't know what we are. And neither do you."

Rodolfo launches himself from the swing seat. He hovers for a long moment midair and then lands with a soft crunch on the pebbles.

Polly is standing there, right beside him. She takes his hand. *So she touches,* Rodolfo thinks.

"There's not enough of us. We can't protect ourselves. There's no hope for us."

"We's fine. We's getting rich."

He gets back on the swing, and so does she.

She bends and extends her long slender legs; they are in perfect rhythm. He has an impulse to touch her legs, but he grips the chains harder.

"Selling our blood so a bunch of old perverts can feel young? How long is that going to last? And how do you even know whose blood to put out there? Use the wrong batch and someone goes crazy and then the police and everyone else comes looking for us like we blew up the Empire State Building."

"So many worries, Polly. You's needing to relax." He laughs, reaches over, and tugs at her long braid—it's like a rope that rings a church bell.

"You want my blood, you can have it," she says. "I know I am mostly not wild. I think maybe I am twenty percent animal. So my blood is safe. Some of us—wow! Too wild."

"Me's wild too," Rodolfo says.

"Not really. I mean, yes, sure, you are. But not like some of the others." She grabs his wrist, and his swing reacts, twisting and turning. She holds tight and pushes up the sleeve of his white shirt. She runs her hand up and down his arm. "You're smooth. And you're smart. And you're gentle."

"Me's not gentle," he says, pulling his arm away.

"You should take me someplace," Polly says.

"Where? Everything's here."

"I just would like to be alone with you."

Rodolfo feels the heat of embarrassment rush into his face, and he turns away, not wanting her to see. Polly is a pretty girl, in her own way. And smart. And, really, he does not mind how she talks, like a princess on TV.

"Me's down with that," he says. "Back home?"

"I love the apartment, Rodolfo. But it's too crazy there."

"Me's got a room, solitary."

"I know. But it would be weird. Going in with you? Everyone on the other side of the door. Philip, Little Man, Suzie, Captain Blood." She moves her fingers as she counts them, her long, slender fingers. She still does her hand exercises so she will be able to easily reach an octave if she ever gets the chance to sit at a piano again. "Boy-Boy, Bump, Lola. They all worship you."

It makes him smile. Warmth oozes through him, like honey through a crack in the jar. He closes his eyes and pumps his legs, propelling the swing higher. It wouldn't take much more elevation for him to go up and over. Or maybe he will jump—the energy generated by the swing plus his own energy, he might stay airborne for five seconds. He feels a cooling breeze on his face. The night air fills his shirt.

He glances up at the tops of the trees; the flashing lights of a patrol car illuminate the leaves, and they tremble blue and white. Moments later, the cop car appears, and to show how seriously put out he is, the officer driving steers it over the curb, over the paved walkway, and onto the grass, stopping as close to the playground as he possibly can.

Normally, the crew can almost instantly disappear when they see the police—if a cop ever sees them, the boys and girls move so quickly that the officers on patrol don't even register their presence, or they rub their eyes and look at each other quizzically, as if they had perhaps just glimpsed a coyote. But tonight is different.

Tonight the children do not run, nor do they steal into the shadows.

Rodolfo looks at Polly. She has dug the tips of her shoes into the gravel to stop her swing. She holds on to the chains and looks back at Rodolfo, waiting for him to indicate what they should do next.

From the tops of the boulders, from the bushes and the Great Lawn, from the four points of the compass, the brood appears, in twos, threes, and fours, until there are twenty of them encircling the playground. Tonight they are unafraid. Tonight they have reached the end of hiding, and they have reached the end of wishing that people would leave them alone. Tonight they are no longer wishing they were just normal children living in apartments with normal parents. Tonight they are tired of being hated and they are tired of being hunted. Tonight they are curious what will happen if they simply hold their ground.

The two police officers are both out of the Central Park Precinct—their headquarters are just two minutes from here, the building bucolic and barn brown with raised white letters proudly displaying the precinct's name. One of the officers is

Olivia Martinez, and this is her first month on the job. Her black hair is cropped short as a choirboy's, and she is slight— so slight that she struggles with the gear she must carry: the club, the cuffs, the flashlight, the radio, the revolver, all ponderously hanging from her belt. Her partner is John Kluggel, a tall, fleshy officer in his sixteenth year on the force. This assignment is a demotion for him; he was pushed down the pay ladder from sergeant to patrolman after ordering his ex-wife's husband's car towed not once, not twice, but three times. Kluggel has watery blue eyes that say *Don't bother me* and a large red birthmark on his cheek the size of a slap.

Kluggel unsnaps his holster, and though Martinez thinks this is absolutely not the way to proceed with what appears to be, after all, just a bunch of teenagers hanging around a playground, she does the same, aware that by not doing so, she would be tacitly criticizing Kluggel.

"Watch and learn," Kluggel mutters to her as he approaches Rodolfo and Polly. (He says, "Watch and learn," no matter what he does in her presence, from filling out an arrest report to ordering hazelnut coffee.)

Martinez, glancing upward, left, right, then left again, is not sure if John has failed to see the dozen or so others who now basically encircle them or if he has seen them but chosen to ignore them and go for the two on the swings.

There are two ways to approach someone: You can walk fast or slow. John used to favor the slow approach, liking the cowboy swagger of it and the implication that he had all the time in the world and was not in the slightest bit tense or concerned. The slow approach gave whoever you were going to stop and frisk time to get real worried. But fairly recently, he switched to the rapid approach, coming up to people with startling speed, moving as if powered by an engine at full throttle. He covers the distance between the cruiser and the bed of white stones around the swings in four or five vigorous strides.

"Get up," he says to the two on the swings, resting his hand on the butt of his revolver. He waits a moment and then repeats his order, this time his voice at a thick boil. He is a loyal subscriber to the shock-and-awe theory of police work.

But the two teenagers appear serene. The boy seems to be smiling, and the girl adjusts her long braid so that it hangs down the very middle of her back.

"We's not bothering," Rodolfo says. He almost sings it.

"You heard me," Kluggel says.

"You truthin' on that, Mr. Bang-Bang," Rodolfo says.

The girl grins, and Officer Martinez recognizes the quality of the smile, sees the expression of a girl who is just the slightest bit frightened but who has had the misfortune to lose her heart to a troublemaker. Some girls like to ride the emotional rodeo until they are bucked off and go flying, until they get gored, until they get good and used up. Poor saps...

John, like every cop in the Central Park Precinct, knows that there is a bunch of weird kids roaming the park at weird hours, leaving weird things in their wake—bones of small animals, discreet little piles of human scat—and being weirdly elusive too, so elusive that spotting one of them (and these two on the swings surely fall into the category of Weird Kids in the Park, as do the other knuckleheads slowly encircling them above) is tantamount to a hiker spotting Bigfoot. And every cop in the precinct also knows that the mayor has a special interest in these little fuckers, an interest that is as weird as the bones and scat that the cops and everyday citizens find in the park from Columbus Circle all the way up to Harlem. Weird because each time the mayor, that rich little snob strutting around Gracie Mansion, applies a little heat on the matter of the park kids, he also makes a point of adding that if any cops see someone young running with the pack, they'd better not harm a hair on his (or her) head. Now, why would Mayor Morris say that? Speculation is that the mayor's own missing kid is now one of them, but of course, whenever anything big happens (and Dylan Morris's disappearance is huge), there are always conspiracy nuts who manage to "see" a pattern of secrecy and cover-up. John's explanation for the mayor's directive is a lot simpler, having to do with the mayor's wanting to avoid the public-relations disaster that would inevitably come if they were to harm some ten-year-old. But these two on the swings? Old enough to know better, and old enough to kick the shit out of, if need be.

"We're not doing anything wrong, Officer," Polly says. She doesn't say it pleadingly, just states it as a matter of fact.

"Show me some ID," Kluggel says.

"I don't have anything on me," Polly says.

Kluggel smiles like someone who enjoys the smell of rotted meat.

"What are you doing out here?" he asks.

"Just hanging out," Polly says.

"Just hanging out?"

"Yes."

"What about you?" he says to Rodolfo.

"Lick me's ass," Rodolfo says, pronouncing the word *ass* as if it had an infinite number of *s*'s at its end.

Kluggel looks over his shoulder, checking to make sure Martinez is doing her job. She is. She's just a few steps behind him. She looks scared, though. That does not help.

"Stand up," he says to Rodolfo.

"Me's swinging here, Officer."

"Stand the fuck up or I'll..." But he doesn't have to make his threat explicit. Rodolfo rises from the sling seat. Holding on to the swing's chains, he lifts himself off the ground, somersaults backward, and, after landing, throws his hands straight up in the air, a move he learned watching the 2004 Olympics on his parents' TV when he was a little kid.

Polly starts to get up too, but Kluggel yanks out his billy club as if it were a sword and points it at her. "I'm asking you to stay where you are, miss," he says with an awful approximation of good manners. She sinks down again and Kluggel's spirits lift. He will never get tired of people doing what he tells them to do.

"Pat her down, Officer Martinez," he says.

"You's not to do," Rodolfo says; his long finger goes back and forth like a windshield wiper.

"You be careful here, son," Kluggel says. "You don't want to go opening your mouth when you're in deep shit."

"Oh, me's so scared," Rodolfo says.

"Please stand up for me," Martinez says to Polly in what is meant to be an apologetic tone.

With inexplicable speed, Rodolfo intercepts Martinez and tackles her, ramming his shoulder right above her knees. She is sprawled on the ground, blinking up at the thick night sky.

It gives Kluggel every reason in the book to unholster his weapon. But no sooner has he withdrawn it than Rodolfo wraps his legs around Kluggel's legs, and with a quick violent twist, as remorseless as the crack of a whip, he brings Kluggel to the ground.

A moment later, Rodolfo sinks his teeth into the fleshy pad of Kluggel's right hand. Kluggel had been pretty badly bounced around by his own father, had a tooth knocked out in a fight at

Far Rockaway the morning of his senior prom, had been bitten by his mother's Chihuahua, had once had a cinder block dropped on his foot, was in a five-car pileup on the Hutchinson River Parkway five Thanksgivings ago, and had shot off the lobe of his own right ear while cleaning his revolver. But nothing he ever experienced prepared him for the pain of Rodolfo's teeth sinking into his hand. If the pain were a color, it would be the brightest red, and if it were a temperature, it would be 213 degrees.

It's not just the bite. It's the tearing, the grinding. The gun slides out of Kluggel's hand. A voice within him sounds a warning, though he can barely understand the words—it's like someone trying to speak over the howls of a hurricane. But it tells him that under no circumstances can he allow this boy to take control of the firearm.

"Sorry," Polly says to Martinez, pinning her down. She doesn't appear to be using much force, but Martinez is unable to move. It's as if she were in a coffin; consciousness races and lurches, but the body is finished.

Rodolfo springs up and kicks the gun away, and it spins under some bushes. He spits what he has bitten off, a little jagged chunk of flesh, a salty spray of blood.

"You's sick in body and soul, Officer Bang-Bang," Rodolfo says. He wipes his mouth with the back of his hand. He hopes he has not just contracted some crazy disease from the officer on the ground.

John may have had departmental difficulties—his career on the force has been far from exemplary—but he retains a kind of dedication, even a vague sort of idealism. And he has always been a real competitor. He is dizzy with pain, but he is also determined to bring these kids in—and now he has something real to charge them with, something that will 100 percent stick. Cradling his wounded hand, he struggles to his knees. He glances back at Martinez. Useless. And then at his car. Too far away. He hopes against hope that another patrol car will come gliding by. Or anyone, really. Anyone.

He resists the temptation to look at the wound on his hand—it will only make everything worse. It's taking him longer than usual to get on his feet. One foot is planted, but his weight is primarily on his knee. Okay, on three. One—

That's as far as he gets. The wild boys and girls of the park come swarming from every direction. They plow into him as if he were a tackling dummy and it's the night before the big game. He ends up on his stomach, his face pressed into the pebbles. The little white stones jam into his nose, enter his mouth, press into the lids of his tightly shut eyes. He is helpless.

He hears the boy on the swing yelling at the others, telling them to cut it out, slow down. "We's okay, we's okay," he shouts. "No more! Take it easy."

But it doesn't feel as if any of the others are in a state of mind conducive to taking it easy.

What follows is an evisceration beyond anything anyone ever imagined, a vicious, savage devouring of his flesh and his bones, and the extinction of his life. Perhaps the horror of it can be inferred by two and only two moments at the end of John's life. The first is the moment of hope he experienced as the brood piled on him, the hope that there was something playful in their intent. Their heads, their knees, their bony chests, all knocking into him—monkey pile on Johnny!

The second moment is later, maybe three minutes into the attack, after they have rolled him onto his back or perhaps after he managed to roll onto his back himself. By then he is almost completely overwhelmed by the physical pain that is being inflicted on him—the tearing of his flesh, the twisting of his limbs. In an instinctive move to defend himself, he takes a wild swing at the blur of bodies, a real roundhouse, delivered, he thinks, with enough force to dislodge and perhaps knock unconscious at least two or three of them. But nothing happens. He doesn't feel the impact of his fist against...anything. No one says *ow;* no one reels back. The punch has not been thrown. But why not? And then he sees why not...the arm he thought was going to deliver the blow is not attached to him. It has been yanked clear out, and now one of those fiends who lives inside the darkness has it in his dirty little hands and he raises it above his head to show it to the others.

Rodolfo has given up on trying to get them to stop attacking the officers. He stands to one side with Polly, noting which ones are most out of control, which ones are going at it because they are being led by the hungriest and angriest of the crew, and which ones are simply watching. It's information he needs to determine whose blood gets drawn and sold and whose behavior is so extreme that their blood would simply be too dangerous on the open market.

CHAPTER 12

CENTRAL PARK CLOSED
Aftermath of Wild-Dog Attack of Two Police Officers

Don't know where to begin. The kids disappeared. Still can't get a straight story about where they went, or why. They came back with another kid who claims to be the goddamn mayor's son! And I almost drank. (Well, technically, I did drink. I bought the bottle of vitamin V, opened it, and a little of it touched my lips. But my lips did not blister, I did not go on a bender, and the vodka was drained—by an actual drain!)

All right. I'll start again. The kids disappeared. Oh! Hearing that horrible little song in the therapist's office that tells you the outer door has opened and then going out to see that empty waiting room and looking all over town for them—needle, haystack, etc.—and not having (and still not having) any idea where they went, or what drove them, not knowing if they were taken or if they were running after something or maybe just running away from me...Oh my God, the things I do not know. I am a fountain of no information.

I was unable to find them. They came back on their own with little Dylan Morris, if that's his name, in tow. Dylan has to be the most disquieting child I have ever met. He looks at you, not to know you and not to communicate with you, but simply to see what you are going to do. Are you going to try to touch him? Are you going to move left or right; do you have food or something else he might want; do you intend to do him harm? It's like walking on a path in the woods and accidentally coming upon an animal and both of you are completely surprised. But Dylan's strangeness is more than a creepy lack of human affect—if he's a runaway, I can understand why he might be hard to reach. Who knows what he's been through, what he's running away from, and what he's had to do to stay alive? The thing about him is—Jesus, I don't even want to write this down. It will be like proof that I've started to go mad…and if I do go mad, those kids will really and truly disappear into the grinding machinery of the child-care system that processes kids like sausage meat. But here it is anyhow: Dylan's hands glow in the dark.

Okay. I've been sitting here staring at the last sentence I wrote. What if I really am losing my mind?

Yes, maybe I am. And here's further proof. I have let Adam and Alice convince me to let Dylan stay here. Just for the night, they say. I have never seen them so adamant, so fierce and unyielding, and in all honesty, I gave in out of fear—the last thing I could tolerate at this point is their disappearing again. As I saw it, my job, my mission was pretty straightforward: Keep them in the house at all costs. Keep them safe. And sometimes you get the job done by easing up on the rules. What would I rather do, defend the principle that whatever Mama says goes—or Aunt Cynthia, or whoever the hell I am to them—or defend their lives?

We were at the dining room table. I sat there and watched them shoveling in food. What a relief! Despite a day straight from the pits of hell, seeing them eat made me happy. (They haven't gained an ounce on my watch!) When Dylan reached for something—he has the manners of a ferret—and the light from the chandelier touched his grabby little hands, his skin glowed fresh strawberry red. I know I already said this but I am saying it again. I've got a kid asleep upstairs who glows in the dark. And what made it even crazier is that when I gave Alice a look, she just cocked her head, like she was trying to figure out what I was looking at her for, and the same thing went for Adam. Either they didn't see it, or they didn't care, or it was all some terrible trick of my mind. Anyhow, the deal we finally made was this: Dylan can stay the night, and in the morning we figure out what to do with him. I'll shake him loose from his nutty story about being the mayor's son and find out where he actually lives and that will be that.

And this house. This house is full of rats. How many? A thousand? Try getting an exterminator in this town! It's like getting an appointment with a neurologist— "We're booking into September, miss." I need someone here yesterday! Anyhow, I finally found one who at least was willing to blow some blue sky up my ass and tell me he'd be out here in the next day or two…

As for Alice and Adam: They have got to tell me why they disappeared like that. Maybe they don't even understand that when you are a part of a family, that is simply not the way you behave. Maybe they don't understand how I worry about them, what it puts me through. Maybe they don't even understand that they have value, and the idea that something might happen to them simply does not frighten them, or even register. I have to keep reminding myself that these two beautiful children have been living in the worst kind of poverty—emotional poverty. When have they ever felt secure in the love of a mother (or a father or, really, any adult)? And that is why I call you dear, *Dear Diary, because I can say to you what I trust no one else to hear, and that is this: I adore those children and I believe—with all my soul—that the love I feel for them is stronger than any medicine, any fucked-up drugs their silly, desperate parents took, and strong—*

She hears a sound and lifts the pen from the page, turns toward it, waits. The house is silent—or as silent as a house can be in New York. Thunder rattles around the dark sagging sky. She goes to the window, looks out. It is nearly midnight and it is beginning to rain—perhaps some relief from the heat is on the way. Though it is a weeknight, and late, there is more traffic than you would see in a dozen Saturday nights anywhere else. Cabs, limos, minivans in from Long Island, Jeeps in from Jersey, Teslas in from who knows where... A slow, gauzy ripple of lightning. On the sidewalk, pedestrians stroll, oblivious to the rain. Some even welcome it—spreading their arms, opening their mouths to drink it in. She scans the street for any sign of that creep. She doesn't see him, but there is scant comfort in that. He could be anywhere. He could be in a coffee shop a block away. He could be standing so close to the house she cannot see him. He could be in the house at this very moment...

Too much is happening; too much is going wrong. She can feel the pressure of events surging within her, ready to burst through the ultimately fragile seawall that is her self-confidence. That *was* her self-confidence.

Cynthia opens her computer and goes to her search engine and types in *Mayor Morris missing son,* just to make absolutely certain that this Dylan character the kids have brought home is completely full of shit. The query elicits more than a million responses and she clicks open the fourth—someone once told her the ones on top paid the search engine to put them there. It is a *New York Times* story, with a banner headline: MAYOR'S SON VANISHES. A subhead says: "Dylan Morris Missing Three Days, Police and Mayor's Office Finally Releasing Information."

She reads quickly. The article says the boy was taken from Gracie Mansion at some point on Sunday night. It explains the mayor's decision, made with the full cooperation of the police department, to keep the news away from the public so that nothing would interfere with negotiations with Dylan's kidnappers, though the reporter points out that sources have revealed there has been no ransom asked for Dylan, and apparently no contact whatsoever with anyone who might be responsible for his disappearance.

She quickly scrolls down and there it is: a picture of Dylan. Though dressed in the blazer, white shirt, and striped tie required by his school, and though his hair is shiny and well-combed, and his smile is broad and confident, there is no question that this is the boy she found huddled in the cellar.

A wave of fear breaks within her.

This cannot be! She cannot harbor this child. His parents are in agony—the city is in agony—wondering what has happened. How could she not have known? She feels insane, completely isolated. This is not her city. She is holding her phone now, uncertain whom to call. The police, 911? Yes, 911. Of course. She dials. An operator answers on the second ring.

"I have Mayor Morris's son in my house," Cynthia says, her voice frantic, though not much louder than a whisper.

"Where are you, ma'am?" The operator must see that the call is coming from a cell phone with a San Francisco area code.

Breathlessly, Cynthia gives her address. But then she hears

what sounds like an explosion. Paralyzed by the shock of it, she sits at the end of her bed, hunched over the phone.

"Ma'am?" The voice is courteous but insistent.

"I heard something," Cynthia whispers.

"You say you have Dylan Morris with you, ma'am? Is that right?"

"Shhh. Someone's here."

"We have a squad car on the way, ma'am. Is the boy unhurt, ma'am? The boy. Is he unhurt?"

Holding the phone in front of her as if it might protect her, Cynthia inches out of her bedroom and goes to the top of the stairs, looks down at the entrance hall. The front door is wide open. A clap of thunder, a splintering bolt of lightning. The rain is coming down in sheets, and some of it blows across the tiles in the foyer.

Oh no, she thinks. *Please. No more.*

She pushes the door closed. The floor is slick. The walls are spattered with rain. Her beautiful house!

But her real concern is the children upstairs. She races to the third floor. As she pounds up the steps, she can hear the 911 operator's voice calling out to her with less and less patience.

And when she gets to Alice and Adam's floor, she sees the thing she was most dreading: two empty rooms.

"They're gone!" she cries into the phone. "They're gone, they're gone, they're gone."

"You need to stay calm, ma'am. We have officers on the way."

And indeed, by the time Cynthia makes it down to the ground floor, a police car is pulling up in front of the house, its whirling lights coloring the driving rain.

*　　*　　*

Free! Free! Adam, Alice, and Dylan (who is slower than the twins and so rides on Adam's back) race across rain-swept Central Park. The driving rain releases the deep heat embedded in the ground after all these days of scorching temperatures, and the park is wreathed in mist, an ancient, haunted moor surrounded on every side by steel-and-glass towers.

They don't know if they are being followed, but they do know there is no time to waste. They don't know where they are going, but they do know they must get there as soon as possible.

They don't know who—or what—they are, but they know this: They must survive.

They stop beneath a giant sycamore for a moment to catch their breath.

"Maybe we should go back," Adam says, panting, as he puts Dylan down.

"Back?" Dylan exclaims, as if the idea were not only crazy but dangerous. He opens his mouth to catch a raindrop that has dripped from the leaves.

"Why should we?" Alice says. "Anyhow, I want to see where those other guys are living. Okay?"

"She took us, Al," Adam says. "We'd still be in foster if it wasn't for her."

"Yeah, I know. Bu—"

"And we wouldn't even be together," Adam adds. "And…"

"And what?" Alice asks.

"In foster I was always…" He looks away. Huge billows of mist roll across the Great Lawn, thick as smoke. "I was always sort of scared, is all," he says in a quiet voice.

"We'll go back to the house pretty soon," Alice says.

"Mom's okay, pretty much," Adam says. "Don't you think?"

"Mom?"

"What are we supposed to call her?"

"She's not our real mom," Alice says.

"She is now," Adam says. "And she's super-nice to us."

"Come on, you two," Dylan says. Great blasts of energy are always coursing through him. He contorts his body to accommodate the constant flow of adrenaline.

Dylan starts to run, and they follow him. They are running north. Now west. Faster and faster. And faster still.

Every time they pass beneath the gauzy globe of a street-lamp, Adam sees Dylan's little grasping fingers flash a deep red. *What is he?* Adam wonders.

He exchanges looks with Alice as they bound over a bench. They clear the topmost slat by five feet; the strength in their legs feels limitless. The sky seems to reach down, its gauzy arms lifting them higher and higher.

What are we? Alice wonders.

Rodolfo strides purposefully down the long corridor that runs front to back through the apartment on Riverside Drive. What he sees reminds him of an illustration he saw in his last year in school—seventh grade—when they were supposed to be studying the American Civil War but all Rodolfo could do was waggle his pencil and jiggle his legs and pray to God that the top of his head didn't explode. He remembers precious little of that year, but he does recall the illustration of a tent torn to shreds on one side, a makeshift hospital filled with wounded soldiers, even the most grievously wounded placid and resigned in their cots or on their bedrolls while a stony-faced doctor with a beard like an anvil, assisted by a nurse who was drawn to look like an angel, did what he could to patch them up. Here, in his lair high above the city, nine boys and girls sit on the floor with their backs against the wall extending their bared arms while Boy-Boy goes from one to the other, drawing their blood. He is the syringe master. Not only is he gentle and adept with an intravenous needle, but he is also the one who broke into a nearby Duane Reade and stole several boxes of needles, along with boxes of vacuum tubes. Little Man follows behind him, collecting the tubes, making sure the stoppers are tight, and ferrying them to the kitchen, where he places them in the refrigerator.

Rodolfo looks on with his arms folded over his chest, like General Sherman surveying the troops. It's Bump's turn now and Rodolfo smiles at Bump's obvious squeamishness. Bump, who is fierce and fearless, who can outrun any animal in the park and can climb a tree as if it were a porch stoop, is wincing, squinting, and turning his head as far to the left as possible while the needle draws his blood and the tube goes from clear to bright red to something close to black.

He hears a sound from the front hall, and he turns toward it with the instant, uncluttered concentration of a forest animal that has heard the snapping of a branch.

It's little Dylan Morris. Half the cops in the city are looking for Dylan, and he has orders never to come to this apartment. But here he is.

And he is not alone.

Behind him is Adam, and behind Adam stands Alice.

Alice!

Rodolfo runs to greet her. He runs, in fact, right into her, though it is just a glancing blow. He continues to run—his legs will not stop; they move like engine pistons when the accelerator has been pressed clear to the floor. He slaps at the wall, bounds over the furniture, and, with his eyes wide and his arms raised high, he zooms around and around the apartment in an ecstasy beyond his control. At last, he runs halfway up the living room wall, flips backward, and makes a perfect-ten landing.

"Me's know you come," he says, his chest heaving.

At five in the morning, Cynthia comes back to the house, released at last from police custody. The police have not shown much interest in the fact that Alice and Adam are somewhere on their own in the vast, perilous city; they are, however, vitally concerned that she saw the mayor's son, and for the first couple of hours she was in custody, they treated her as a suspect, with pleas for her to help them find Dylan Morris morphing into very pointed questions, which in turn morphed into out-and-out interrogation. She is in the company of Arthur Glassman, whom she called when they finally allowed her to use a phone. They step into the house, slightly hopeful that the twins have returned in her absence.

They are both exhausted. Cynthia has had no sleep; Arthur has had but two hours. Their stomachs are sour; their breath is foul. Cynthia feels humiliated at having been treated as a criminal, and Arthur is starting to wonder how many good deeds he must do out of respect for his two old friends Alex and Leslie. The sister is a piece of work. There is something fanatical in her loneliness. It may be time to start billing her.

There is a sawing sound everywhere. It is the rats—rats in the basement, rats in the attic, rats in the walls—gnawing on wood. They gnaw to file down their ceaselessly growing front teeth; otherwise, the teeth would grow right through their lips.

"Rats," Cynthia says in answer to Arthur's questioning look.

"You've got to get someone in here to get rid of them. It sounds as if they're going to come right through the walls."

"I think they're basically shy," Cynthia says.

"I'm sure," says Arthur.

Cynthia can sense the twins are not here, but it is a very large house and she must search through it, room by room. Arthur waits for her in the library. He comforts himself with a vision of breakfast to come. He checks his watch. Soon it will be six. He wonders if he is presentable enough to make the short walk over to the Regency and treat himself to the perverse but undeniable pleasure of spending on a cup of coffee roughly what a textile worker in Bangladesh is paid in a month. He is wearing a decent pair of shoes, though without socks. His slacks are wrinkled, his shirt has seen many hours of anxious duty, and there is a matter of personal hygiene, an innocent victim of his rude awakening. Yet the pols and the media types won't be there yet, and he can take an out-of-the-way table. The omelet *fines herbes!* The mixed berries! The seven-grain toast. He idly tries to remember the last time he ate white bread—once upon a time, grain processed enough to make white bread was a luxury for the rich, but when it became affordable for everyone, the rich suddenly discovered that white bread was sliced suicide, and now they all preferred the denser, peasanty grains. Arthur knows this, and he knows it is absurd too. But, nevertheless, he wants his seven-grain toast and cannot imagine eating a slice of Silvercup, or whatever the potbellied masses were calling their tasteless pale loaves.

"God damn it all to hell."

It is Cynthia's voice, coming from the front hall. She sounds furious, which makes Arthur roll his eyes. He is somewhat surprised by how little sympathy he has for her. It all began with her getting into the wrong car at the Surrogate Court, and his irritation has increased by seeing this immense house and suspecting that good old-fashioned real estate greed is part of the reason she has been so gung-ho about adopting those weird little twins. But the true engine of his annoyance is her calling him from the precinct and interrupting his sleep. Sleep has become sacrosanct to Arthur; those dreamy hours on his French linen sheets is what he looks forward to all day long. And not only that; he needs eight hours, preferably nine, the way he needs oxygen. Nonetheless, he lifts himself out of his chair, groaning mightily. But before he makes it halfway across the library, Cynthia comes in, wiping her hands on her hips and shaking her head.

"The door was wide open," she says. "The hall is soaked."

"Didn't you close it when we came in?" Arthur says.

"I thought so. I don't know...I guess not."

"Look here, Cynthia. I have to get going." Arthur checks his Patek Philippe watch—he hopes never to tire of gazing at the simple beauty of the watch's adorable little face. "I have a full day in front of me." His smile is really no more than a show of teeth—he might as well be brandishing a rake.

But she is frightened to have him leave, frightened to be alone in that house, and even more frightened by the possibility that she will not be alone.

"Please don't leave," she says. She can barely look at him, so ashamed is she to be acting like this.

The smile slowly disappears from his face—the rake is put away; the barn door slides shut. "I really must go. You're a mother now, dear. It's a difficult job, but you must do it. Carry on and keep your powder dry, as they say."

"Arthur—"

"It's okay, I'll show myself out. You might want to lock the door behind me—we don't want it…blowing open again."

He leaves quickly, and Cynthia bolts the door, wondering if she is locking trouble out or in.

"Kids?" she calls in a tremulous voice. "Kids?"

She is alone. And knows she is not. The knowledge brought to her by her eyes and her sense of logic is contradicted by that swirl of hunch and fear we call intuition. She knows she is not alone. She knows that in the next room, or upstairs, or up the next flight of stairs, or down in the cellar, someone (something?) lurks hungrily, motivated by only the basest evil.

The house is too large. There are too many rooms. How lovely it would be to live in a little apartment, a box, where everything was in view at all times. You could keep the bathroom door open, and the single closet too. There should never be more rooms than people. Unoccupied space is a breeding ground for…she cannot even put into words what she fears.

"Kids!" Her voice is full of urgency now. Even to her own ears, she sounds furious, slightly unhinged.

She walks through the sloshy foyer. Someone is here. She cannot prove it, but really, in the end, she thinks, aren't the most important things in life the things for which there is no rational explanation, the things we cannot prove?

She is standing in front of the heavy wooden cellar door. It is locked, from the outside.

That cellar has been nothing but the site of horror and catastrophe to Cynthia. The first time she walked down those steps, she discovered the hideous kennel/abattoir her sister and Alex maintained there, a place where dogs and cats, ferrets, squirrels, rabbits, and hamsters were fattened and devoured by the increasingly berserk masters of the house. And it was here that Cynthia stumbled upon the half-eaten, barely surviving Cuban man, who died—it was a mercy—in the hospital shortly after. She thought at the time she would never recover from the sight of him, but just as the memory of a slap recedes in the wake of a stab wound, and the stab wound seems less horrific, in fact almost tolerable, after you've been bombed, the memory of poor shredded Xavier Sardina, although it has not disappeared, has nevertheless been dimmed by the cloud bank of all that has happened since then—the *chug-chug* of those door locks in the Town Car, the bat in the toilet, the twins' disappearance, and the moving carpet of twittering rats.

And yet. The cellar must be checked—only this time, she will keep the door open and not venture down more than a step. Two at the most.

She walks to the kitchen and fetches a flashlight, turns it on to make certain the batteries are fresh. The torch's big moon face lights with a golden glow in the predawn shadows of this mansion. Oh! The mansion, the stately town house she once so envied and craved, this fortress, this crown jewel of the Upper East Side that Cynthia in her passion and her avarice was once so eager to call home—now she is trapped in this showcase, this emblem of a distant, terribly elegant age when masons fresh off the boat from Italy worked for next to nothing, when ruddy maids with lilting Irish brogues scurried and scoured for little more than room and board, and Twisdens of yore rested secure in their untaxed fortune.

She unlocks the door. Standing at the head of the steep staircase, holding on to the doorjamb with one hand, as if a sudden wind might sweep her down and down and down into the depths below, Cynthia feels along the cool dampish wall, trying to locate the light switch, forgetting for a moment that the electricity was cut months ago. Then, gingerly, Cynthia puts one foot and then the other on the topmost step—she is like a hydrophobe on a diving board.

"I know you're down there," she says in the most matter-of-fact tone she can muster.

Her voice echoes faintly. But beyond that, all is silence. Even the rats are silent—or they have moved elsewhere.

Fat chance.

Cynthia waits, and then decides to try it one more time. After that, she will get out of there. Lock the door. And hope to God she will never have to step foot in there again.

"All right, kids. Come on. I'm not mad. Okay?"

She is sure she is not alone—but what she is not sure of is who is in the house with her. She calls for the twins because that is her best-case scenario. It's the number one option, and number two is…is? Is what? A homeless person? Her sister's ghost? A killer?

"Kids?" She forces herself to take one more step down. She is still far from the bottom. She can still get out of there if she must.

Unless, of course, the door slams shut.

Which it does. With a deafening *boom*. No wind could have done that. No accident, nothing natural. It is a slam full of intention.

As quickly as her frozen senses will allow, Cynthia lunges for the door, but as soon as she touches it, she hears the heavy brass lock plunging into its receiving chamber with a low click, like a neck being snapped. She turns the handle. Nothing. She shakes it. She pushes on the door. A crazy person is screaming, *No, no, let me out,* a totally batshit, out-of-control, shrieking hopeless woman, and it takes her a few moments to realize that the poor tormented woman is her herself.

She pulls herself together with a few deep, steadying breaths. *Think! Think!* But she might as well be exhorting herself to fly or sing the role of Mimì in *La Bohème*. Where once there were thoughts, there is now bright light—a blinding white light. But wait! Through that white light a figure emerges, and when the figure is at the forefront of her consciousness she sees it wears a robe and has a long ghoulish face, not masculine, not feminine, not even entirely human, and it whispers, "You are going to die."

With renewed determination—strength born of panic, really—she tries to force her way through the closed door, as if her hands could break the lock.

"Don't do this," she begs. "Don't. Alley-Oop?" Just uttering the little pet name brings the girl into Cynthia's senses, like the smell of rain. She stifles a sob. "Braveheart? Are you there?"

She waits. And waits.

Her phone! She can feel it in her back pocket, a resistant parallelogram of hard plastic. Her smartphone, her fucking brilliant phone. The police will be here in minutes—they sure as hell know the way. She reaches into her pocket, but all she finds there is an expired subway pass, her MetroCard, blue and yellow, with a black magnetic strip at the bottom. It's no bulkier than the ace of hearts—how did she ever think it was her phone? Fear and the wild hope for rescue have deranged her senses. She throws the MetroCard down into the cellar, and it floats into the darkness. She closes her eyes, as if to quickly construct a levee against the rising flood of tears.

She sits on the step, hoping that her next move will somehow present itself to her. Oddly, it feels better to keep her eyes closed.

Her body aches. Exhaustion moves through her like a fever. She recalls reading something about hypothermia, how when the body's temperature drops to potentially fatal levels, people are often seized by an almost uncontrollable desire to curl up and fall asleep, and those who do rarely awaken. Breathe in, breathe out. Find reasons to be grateful. Find reasons to hope. In. Out. She tells herself: *Open your eyes.* She does.

But do not look at your watch. Don't count the minutes.

Time doesn't matter.

Remember that: It doesn't matter.

What doesn't matter?

Oh, right. Time.

Someone will eventually come and let her out. Whoever is on the other side of the door, whoever has locked her in here, obviously does not want to kill her, or touch her, or harm her in any way.

Who knows? He may be perfectly nice…whoever has done this.

Her eyes flutter shut again, but she forces them open.

Something is at the bottom of the stairs. It is not a corporeal body. It is just a texture, a kind of ripple in the darkness. It has no shape, no dimension. No smell. It makes no sound. It is just there.

The stirrings of terror are in Cynthia's heart. But mainly she is curious, intrigued. What is that?

But no sooner does she ask herself that question than the darkened, indistinct blob of atmosphere begins to rush up the stairs as if propelled by a fierce wind. Cynthia brings her arm up to shield her face, but she cannot stop staring at whatever it is that comes toward her.

It's Alice! Little Alley-Oop, racing toward her like a funnel of demonic smoke. Her teeth are bared; her eyes are dull and pitiless. When she is a couple of feet away, she stops, lands on her feet two steps below Cynthia, and assumes her normal form: a little under sixty inches of seemingly normal human flesh, bone, and hair, dressed strangely…she is wearing a shapeless blue dress; her feet are in wobbly old woman's shoes.

And then a voice within Cynthia says, in a squeaky, almost hysterical tone: *Idiot, if God had wanted you to have children, you woulda had 'em. So now look at you! Over your fool head, as usual.*

Whose voice is that?

Not Alice's, not little Alley-Oop's. The ghostly little girl just stands there, smiling faintly, little wisps of smoke still drifting around her. But then, with the suddenness of a leopard that must strike quickly for its prey, the little girl grabs Cynthia by the wrist.

"No!" Cynthia screams. In her terror and confusion, she momentarily loses her purchase on the stair, and she slides down three steps. Her vertebrae bang against the hard wood. And now that squeaking sound again. What is her mind telling her this time?

Except it is not coming from within her. Like a night sky dazzling with little red stars, the eyes of fifty or more rats are closing in on her. The sound of their little pink feet scuttling on the wooden steps. They are as organized as an army, and in no great rush. Cynthia scrambles up and races to the door. She turns the handle. She doesn't know why. The door is locked.

Except now it isn't. Thrown forward by her own momentum, she hurtles into the hall of the house, stumbling over her own feet. Quickly, she turns and slams the door behind her, locks it. She hears the rats scratching on the other side. Some are peeping peacefully, some are squeaking peevishly, and a few are actually screaming. The scream is like that of a terrified old woman.

Driven by motherly instinct, she races to the second floor, and then to the third, to Alice's and Adam's rooms. Their beds are empty, but the closets are open, and the dressers are open too, each and every drawer. Someone has been here and grabbed half the clothes the twins own.

CHAPTER 13

"Do you know why I've asked to see you?"

"No. Not really."

"That's funny. We've been sitting here for several minutes."

"I know."

"And yet you've shown no curiosity."

"I didn't think it was my place. You asked to see me. Isn't it up to you to say why?"

"You're a bit of a pain in the ass, aren't you"—Cal Rogers, with his ferocious iron-gray crew cut, bulging forehead, and mouth as tiny and tight as an asterisk, makes something of a show of glancing at the folder on his desk—"Mr. Keswick. Dennis."

Dennis feels a little release of tension. That Rogers is pretending to have forgotten his name is definitely reassuring. If Rogers is stooping to little mind games, it means that he is uncertain—uncertain if Dennis has done anything wrong, uncertain about what he wants Dennis to do next.

"I don't think of myself as a pain in the A-double-S, sir," Dennis says. He looks around Rogers's grim little office. Other parts of this unacknowledged Borman and Davis facility are spotless and hypermodern, germ-free and airtight, with something of the spacecraft in its design and eerie remoteness from earthly life. But Rogers's office is strictly middle management, windowless, with a faint odor of Fritos in the air and a desk that looks as if it had been acquired from some fly-by-night mortgage broker after the bursting of the latest real estate bubble.

"How long have you been working for us, Dennis?" Rogers asks, folding his hands on the desk and leaning forward, suddenly switching gears and perhaps hoping to appear friendly.

"Not very long."

"Three months, yes?"

"If you say so, Cal."

"And how long have you been with Borman?"

"Let me tell you something here, Cal. To you, I'm...what? Muscle? A goon? You've got my résumé right there in front of you. Why don't you look at the record of my education? If I had gotten a break here or there, maybe a little support on the old home front, I'd be back there running trials. Look at the transcripts, why don't you?" Dennis knew he was going on at length here, knew he was probably turning the gas higher under the pot of hot water he was already in, but this was his great subject, the wound his mind kept circling: He could have been a real scientist rather than a fucking errand boy! "Chemistry, biochemistry, it's all there. Do you think you and the rest of the smocks are doing something that only you, only the precious ones, the chosen ones, can do?"

Rogers remains calm. He's already been briefed—meaning warned—about Keswick, about his bitterness, the rage that rises out of him like methane. But Dennis is too valuable to let go; he delivers the live bodies that make the research possible.

Rogers smiles, but that only incites Dennis more. "Medical

school. There were a lot of med schools that would have accepted me. But it takes money, and I was broke. And it takes people who believe in you, and my parents did not give a you know what about me, and talking to them about education— you might just as well have told them you needed a hundred bucks to go out dancing with Tinker Bell."

"Well, you're still a young man," Rogers says. "Are you considering med school for your future?"

"Too old, and you know it."

"You're making a good salary now, Dennis. You must have some savings."

"I do all right."

"And Borman and Davis has a program for its employees. I'm not sure you're aware of it. Dare to Excel?"

"I'll bear it in mind, Cal."

"You'll want to talk to Dave Pritzer, over in HR."

Dennis decides to deploy his beloved blank stare.

"Dave will walk you through the application process," Rogers says. There is a little tremor of uncertainty in his voice. Knowing where the weakness is in a person is a source of great strength for Dennis. It's like splitting logs: You look for a crack, a fault line, and that's where you bring down the maul's blow— voilà! Firewood.

"I've got a lot going on, Cal. You want to tell me why you asked me to come in?"

"Three things, Dennis." Rogers linked the pointer finger of his right hand onto the crooked pointer of his left. It made him feel better—now, and always—to enumerate things. It suggested a grand design, and it projected authority. "You're aware of the directive regarding Mayor Morris's son."

"Ah. The elusive Dylan," Dennis says.

"Well, just make sure you keep in mind that His Honor would be furious with us if anything happened to that boy."

"We've been over this," Dennis says.

"Two." Now two fingers from the right hand are hooked onto the left pointer. "We've lost one of our subjects. The boy you brought in last week from the Upper West Side."

"He escaped?"

Rogers's eyes open wide for an instant, and his head snaps back, as if recoiling from the unspeakable horror of the thought of one of the subjects making his way out of the facility and back into the world. "Oh, no, not escaped. Expired."

"Really? What happened?"

"We're working on it. But we need to step up operations a bit. We want a substitute for him—it was frustrating because he was, right off the bat, yielding some very exciting results. But the thing is, we're expanding the whole project. The more we learn about these creatures, the more we are…I don't know what the word is here. I think I'm going to say *inspired*. Yes, we're inspired by what we are finding them capable of. We're bringing in new teams of researchers, we're expanding hours."

"Yes," Dennis says. Despite having his guard up, he is allowing himself to feel just a little bit collegial. In his heart, he is a team player, and it is his great misfortune, or so he believes, that his work has been mainly freelance, without coworkers and the camaraderie and intellectual stimulation that he imagines would be his if he were working inside this very building, if the powers that be would somehow find it within themselves to overlook his spotty credentials and recognize his intelligence and his dedication.

"I always thought there was a lot more we could be doing with this than coming up with another product to increase sexual health in older men." Dennis doesn't like even saying *sexual,* and he clears his throat, as if the word has left a weird taste behind. "I think people are having all the sex they should be having anyhow—they don't need to be taking pills or drinking something to be doing it to each other more." He cannot help adding that, although he knows full well that very few people agree with him, especially here in a laboratory where all the smocks are chasing after a formula that can turn a limp ding-dong into solid rock.

"Well, aren't you the quick study," Rogers says, unaware of the condescension in his tone. "You're absolutely right. There are many, many possible applications we are evaluating, every-thing from the cosmetic to the lifesaving. Needless to say, we are all completely excited. The only damper on the whole en-terprise is that we must do it with a degree of confidentiality. A high degree, actually."

"Like complete secrecy," Dennis says.

Rogers dismisses the candor with a wave. "Our path to fig-uring out just how to use the biochemistry we have here would have been a lot easier if a couple of conditions had been met." He looks at his hands, realizing he has already used both of them for the first countdown, and proceeds without visual backup. "First, if we'd gotten wind of this mutation a bit earlier and had had a chance to work with some of these little creatures before they matured, that would have been extremely helpful. But, alas, that was not the case."

"Some of them are still pretty young," Dennis says.

"Yes. And some have delayed maturation. Those twins who you were meant to collect for us."

Dennis nods.

"The ones you let get away."

"I'm working on it. I know where they live. I mean, you know, I have to be careful. I can't just grab them in broad daylight."

"Oh, I'm sure you have all kinds of little tricks up your sleeve, Dennis. Just make sure you do it." Rogers glances down at the folder again. "Twisden. Adam and Alice. We have reason to believe they are potential genetic gold mines. While they were in school, they exhibited virtually no antisocial behaviors. We have obtained records that track them through their various foster homes, and they were obedient, well mannered; one foster parent even described the boy as *meek*. Yet they have both done well athletically. And their parents were extreme cases. The mother, as you know, quite literally destroyed our Slovenian friend from whom they got their treatments. Of course, you can never be sure, but our hunch is that these twins may have the perfect balance. They have the hybrid vigor we are hoping to duplicate but are still human enough so we can get whatever we come up with approved. If we could reproduce what is running through their veins, it would save us a year, maybe more. And a lot of hassle with the FDA."

"I'm on it," Dennis says.

"We're already getting amazing results. We're turning our rats into damned geniuses. One shot of blood taken from those kids, and the rats are solving mazes thirty to forty times faster than the control group. Those idiots in Washington have made it tricky for us to get primates for our work, but we have our ways. And the results we've gotten in our chimp trials have been very exciting. Tumors shrunk. Thirty-five percent increase in connectivity between brain cells. Signs of aging reversed. Frankly, I can hardly wait to take it myself." He smiles. "And the way we've been working—round the clock!—we're all going to need it."

Dennis swallows. It's breaking his heart to hear all this. He should be in the lab, not in some fricking truck wrestling stinky teenagers.

But Rogers does not recognize the distress in Dennis's eyes—or if he does, he chooses to ignore it.

"You know, a lot of this would not have been necessary if we could have made use of the original research done by this Dr. Slobodan Kis, in Slovenia. But he was murdered, and shortly after his laboratory was dismantled; all traces of his work vanished. Government job, no doubt. We think his papers were burned, but perhaps they're somewhere on the bottom of Lake Bled. We sent people over and…" Rogers shakes his head sadly. "It's as if the man never existed. No one will say a word—no one ever worked with him or studied with him. It's like the Soviet Union in the 1940s. The man has simply been eradicated, purged, removed from the human alphabet. So we're on our own." He sighs, maybe self-moved by what he perceives as the trials and tribulations of his own life. "Onward and upward with R and D. Right? The good news is we've got a team of truly great and just altogether dedicated researchers working on this."

"Yes, that is good news," Dennis says, folding his arms across his chest.

"That's why we're going to need new subjects and plenty of them as soon as possible. Luckily, there are a lot of those little creatures in this city. Mainly they are homeless, living like animals in our parks, making messes, just being a nuisance—and, frankly, on their way to becoming more than a nuisance. You've seen it yourself, I'm sure. As they mature, they can go from mischief to violence, and we certainly don't want to be in a position where we have to hunt them down with high-powered rifles like a bunch of ranchers in Utah protecting their sheep from packs of coyote. I don't think that would look very good on the six o'clock news. You understand?"

"Yeah. Sure. That's point number two. You want me to step it up. But you said there were three things. What's the third?"

"The third is you, Mr. Keswick. You."

"Me?"

"You were seen coming here on your own at night. You were seen spending a lot of time here for some reason that had nothing to do with your job or with Borman business, lurking like a criminal just outside the perimeter of our property. We don't want that. Not from you. Not from anyone. It draws attention. We are going to have all the attention anyone could ever want once we roll out the drugs we are going to synthesize from our work here. But until then, we don't want any attention. None whatsoever."

Dennis opens his mouth, prepared to defend himself against the insinuations—hell, they were a lot more than insinuations; he was being accused, he was being threatened. But Rogers raises his left hand—relieved now from its counting duties— to silence him.

"This is more than a matter of your ability to follow the regulations, Mr. Keswick. This is an existential issue that goes straight to the heart of our ability to maintain security and fulfill our mission. If you are unable to comply with these very reasonable expectations, you will, without further warning, be terminated. You understand? Do you? Do you fully understand what I am saying to you?"

Dennis slowly nods. He fully understands. He understands that he was caught on CCC when he visited the site; he understands that despite his services, the smocks think of him as a goon who can easily be replaced, and he also understands that when Rogers (and the Borman brass that stand behind him) says *terminated,* he's not talking about a pink slip and two weeks' severance pay. He's talking about the real kind of severance, the kind in which, say, your head is severed from your body.

Adam stands in the tub adjusting the temperature of the shower. He frowns because the water pressure sucks here in this ramshackle apartment on Riverside Drive—it's worse than the worst of the foster homes Adam drifted through over the two years between his parents' deaths and his aunt Cynthia adopting him.

He winces. Thinking of Cynthia makes him feel bad for a moment. He knows she is worried. Oh, well, there's nothing to be done about it…

The water temperature is right, or at least as right as he is going to get it. He looks down and sees the water pooling over the drain, which, as Rodolfo warned him, is clogged with hair. There's an economy-sized bottle of Liquid-Plumr on the side of the tub, but when Adam picks it up, he can feel it's empty.

Adam steps into the spray of water broadcast by the shower's corroded head. He lifts his right arm and worriedly runs his finger along his armpit's moist skin. A single, nearly invisible hair is growing, and he pinches the top of it and yanks it out. He hunches his shoulder until it touches his cheek and sniffs. A very faint odor of something that reminds him of turkey soup. Uh-oh. He is on constant lookout for early signs that his body is transforming, and he knows that a change in your body's smell—a deepening, an intensifying—is an early volley puberty shoots across the bow of childhood. Next thing you know, the pirates of adolescence have boarded your ship…

Adam grabs the soap. Once this perfumed bar was animal fat, and now it seems to be reverting to its original state. Hairs, long and short, dark and yellowish, are embedded everywhere in that slippery pinkish parallelogram. Adam tries to pick the hairs out of the soap, but there are too many, and he is defeated by the hopelessness of the task. He decides the hot water alone will be enough to wash him clean. He steps farther into the spray, letting the water beat against the top of his head. He tilts back, opens his mouth, and lets the water fill it. He glances down at his lower half. Every time he visually visits this part of his body, his heart quivers with anxiety—one day his stuff is going to be bigger, encircled by a disgusting doughnut of hair; one day the silvery down on his shins is going to darken and curl. Who knows? Even the knuckles on his toes might sprout their own wiry vegetation.

He inspects himself through a squint. So far, so good.

His shower completed, Adam steps out of the tub. The racks are jammed with towels, and the black-and-white-tile floor is strewn with everything from washcloths to bath sheets, not one of them dry, all of them redolent. Adam chooses the least gross one he can find and quickly dries himself as best he can, keeping his eyes half closed so he won't see something on his own body he doesn't care to see.

Rodolfo—whom Adam has never trusted, and whom he now trusts less than ever—has come back from their house with two laundry bags full of their clothes. It's sort of annoying that the clothes that Cynthia folded so nicely have all been crammed together and wrinkled, but nevertheless, Adam is happy to see his Levi's with the perfectly frayed cuffs and his green Bruno Mars T-shirt that he has owned since he was nine and that still (sort of) fits him.

Adam emerges from the bathroom. The moisture from the shower is soaking through his clothes—but it's preferable to him than using any more of the towels. He shakes his hair to get some of the wetness off, and the shake moves down his entire body—his shoulders, his torso, his hips, his rear. *Don't do that,* he thinks. *You're acting like a dog.*

He walks to the front of the apartment, where he'd left Alice, Dylan, and Rodolfo before taking his shower. But they are gone. The visual clutter here is extreme—racing bikes, a broken Segway, video games, a foosball table, an attic's worth of furniture, crumpled potato-chip bags, crushed cans of energy drinks, candy wrappers—and at first, Adam doesn't see that someone is there.

It's Polly, kneeling in front of the sofa. On it is a yellow tin tray rescued from an old Thames and Kosmos chemistry set, but in place of the playthings that were originally held there are thirty vials of blood, each with a little piece of masking tape on it. Using a goofy ballpoint pen—the case is sparkling, and the back end supports a little rubber troll holding a chartreuse feather—Polly is numbering each of the vials.

"Hi," Adam says, not wanting to startle her.

"You looking for your sister?" Polly asks without glancing at him.

"I guess."

"She is in Rodolfo's room," Polly says in a tone that invites him to draw the most dire conclusions from that simple fact. She might as well have said they were taking their clothes off or were perched on the windowsill sky-grabbing at the pigeons.

"Where's that?"

"End of the hall. The big-door room." She finally does glance at Adam. "I wouldn't go there, though. Rule number two hundred forty-four: Come knocking when the door is closed, get ready for a punch in the nose."

"For real?"

"Totally."

Adam gives the hallway a long look. He hears music. He can't tell what the song is. Just the stiff bang of a drum, the deep slur of the bass, a voice that sounds as if it were coming from a tomb, a monster in a tomb, but in the fakiest way. Here's what Adam knows about monsters: Most of them look real regular. They like fish tacos and cry at stupid sad movies and some of them hold your hand when they walk you to school…

"So what's that?" Adam says, looking over at Polly and the neatly arranged, carefully labeled vials of blood. She is wearing a pair of black shorts and a white T-shirt that has a couple of bloody streaks on it. The sleeves are rolled up. Her arms are like sticks, like the arms of a little princess who'd never done a day's work, who didn't even have to carry her own toothbrush. Her legs are skinny too, and Adam guesses that under that T-shirt is a chest no different than a boy's. She is doing what Alice is doing, holding back the rising river of puberty with a dam built of low-calorie days.

"Didn't Rodolfo explain to you?" She has a kind of head-of-the-class voice, the tone of the kid who's always first with all the right answers.

"I guess."

"You guess?"

"Then no. I don't know. Explain what?"

"We pay for this place with these." She picks up a vial, shakes it back and forth.

"What is it?"

"It's us. Some of us, anyhow. Peeps out there pay to have a

little taste so they can be young and stuff. Me's—" She slaps herself on the forehead. "Ye gods, I'm starting to talk like the rest of them. I. I am in charge of organizing the product, keeping track of what goes out." She picks up a narrow ledger with a maroon cover. "It all goes in here."

"Where do you get the blood?"

"From arms. Where did you think? Needles. Stick it in, suck it out."

Adam makes a face.

"You're not very tough, are you?" Polly asks.

"Maybe I am and maybe I'm not."

"I think you're not."

"Wanna try me?"

Polly smiles. She slowly stands up. Her face is very, very serious. Her brows are hooded over her intense green eyes, and she holds her bony fists in front of her, moving them in a tight circle, like a slow-motion boxer. She moves ever closer to Adam, who reluctantly raises his hand, not to strike but to defend.

"I'm serious," he says.

"I am too," says Polly.

She moves ever closer. There are little flecks of darkness in her green eyes. The tear ducts are bright pink. Her nostrils dilate and constrict, dilate, constrict, dilate, constrict. And all of a sudden her head jerks forward like a snake striking its prey. Startled—hell, scared—Adam tries to get out of her way, afraid that she is going to head-butt him and knock him unconscious. But she has anticipated his move and her hand is on the back of his head. She holds him steady and…what? She kisses him full on the mouth.

It's a first. His mother used to kiss his cheek. His father used to tousle his hair. His new mother seems afraid of him, though she kissed his eyelids when she thought he was sleeping. Once, when he was in second grade at his old school, he fell in the hall running to class and Mrs. McBurney swooped him up— she was a giant of a woman, with a mole on her face as big and moist as a puppy's nose—gave him a gigantic, explosive raspberry on his bare stomach, and then put him down on his feet again and went on her merry way.

Polly's kiss is hard, inflexible—not like those tonguey, drooly ones on TV, where the two kissing seem to be having a contest to see who can get the most spit down the other one's throat. It is way more surprising than it is pleasurable.

She pulls away and pushes him back, shoving his shoulders as if he had kissed her.

From somewhere deep in the apartment, a door bangs open, followed by the sound of laughter and the pounding of feet. Moments later—with Adam standing there, still stunned, wiping the kiss off his lips with the back of his hand—Rodolfo comes galloping into the front of the apartment with Alice on his back, her knees pressing into his sides. She grips his long shiny hair as if she were holding on to the reins of a very spirited stallion.

"Put me down, put me down," Alice says, not very convincingly.

But like most boys his age, Rodolfo is drawn to do the opposite of what has been asked of him. He runs faster now. It looks as if he is going to go straight through the window and out into thin air, a last ecstatic giddyup before he and Alice are obliterated on the sidewalk two hundred feet below.

Alice screams with fright, but the giddyup game has made her giddy and there is a shimmer of delight in her scream, and though the mixture is nine parts terror and one part joyous excitement, Rodolfo chooses to heed only what he wants to heed.

He comes to a sudden stop, but then the pace of his equine rounds through the apartment picks up radically. Now it seems as if Alice is riding not a boy who is playing at being a horse, but an actual horse. An unbroken horse with its first human rider. He careens from one corner to the next, leaping over furniture, crushing Coke cans in his way.

Polly watches, her arms folded over her chest like an overwhelmed babysitter just about to blow her top. Her lips are pressed together, their color drained.

"Your sister," she mutters to Adam.

My sister what? he wonders. She's not doing anything wrong.

At last, Polly can't restrain herself any longer—as uncontrollable as the urge to cavort is in Rodolfo, the urge to stop him from touching Alice is just as strong in Polly. "All right, you two, stop!" she fairly screams. Her fingers curl; her teeth are showing. "You want to get us fucking kicked out of here, is that what you want?"

At first, it seems as if Rodolfo has not heard a word. He continues to charge around with Alice, but he makes his way back toward Polly, and just when it seems he is about to race past her, as if she were just a checkered flag in some weird Grand Prix, he comes to a full stop.

"You's say?" he asks, grinning.

"You're acting stupid," Polly says. "Really immature and stupid. Fucking stupid." *Stupid* seems to be the operative word. She must keep her anger torqued; if she were to relax even a little, she fears she might start to whimper. It is so unbelievably painful to see how he carries on with that little shrimp. She knows she is acting like a bitch, but better to let them all hear the full blood-soaked and bloodcurdling roar of bitchiness than the brokenhearted whimper that is underneath.

Alice slides off Rodolfo, rearranges her clothes, and tries to look as if she is relieved to be standing on her own feet again. She also tries to look a bit annoyed with Rodolfo's roughhousing—but her smile of delight, as inexorable as a sunrise, gives her away.

"Your hair's wet," she says to her brother.

"I'm sure he did not want to use one of the dirty, smelly towels in our bathroom," Polly says, showing she can sneer and explain at the same time.

"What's your problem?" asks Alice in as pleasant a tone as one can pose that question.

"The way we live?" Polly says. She gestures first to the vials of blood on the sofa—for all the wildness of his tour around and around the place, Rodolfo has managed to leave the product unmolested—and then, with a larger gesture, she takes in the entire apartment. "It's not for you. You don't belong here. Let me guess." She points at Alice. "You sleep in a little-girlie nightgown." Now she points at Adam. "And what about you? Gym shorts and a T-shirt?" Quite correctly, she takes their silence as confirmation. "Well, you know what we wear when we sleep around here? Nothing."

"So what?" Alice manages to say.

"We sleep nude."

"Since when you's stripping all the way down?" Rodolfo asks Polly. He stands close to her, and then closer. He bumps his forehead against hers.

"There's a lot about me you don't know."

"Is really stuff, or just the talking?" Rodolfo asks.

"Stupid," Polly says, but she is warming to him, and the warmth creates a little crack in her façade of anger and disapproval.

"Me's the stupidest boy in New York," he says gleefully. And with that, he swoops Polly off her feet and slings her over his shoulder as if he were a fireman rescuing a girl from a house in flames.

"Let me down, you stupid boy," Polly says, with only the faintest trace of complaint in her voice.

Alice and Adam stand there as Rodolfo charges down the long hall, off of which are three of the apartment's bedrooms.

"What's with him?" Adam asks.

"I don't know. He's okay."

"Where did he put our clothes and stuff?"

"Back there. We're getting our own room."

"Really? How long?" Nothing has ever been permanent in Adam's life, so why should this be?

"For as long as we want."

"Who says? Rodolfo?"

"Don't be against him. He's awesome." She sees the look of pained disapproval on her brother's face. "Well, he is. I mean, he's okay. He went all the way over to our house and got our stuff."

"Ever think about how he did it? You think he knocked on the door and said, 'Oh, Ms. Kramer, I came here...'"

"I know how he did it," Alice said. "He was brave."

"Who's even paying for this place?" Adam asks. "It's really big."

"It's not as big as our house. And anyhow, it's on the West Side."

"Were you back there doing it with him?"

"That's gross, Adam."

"Well, were you?"

"No." She shakes her head; her expression is pained. "Never."

"For real?"

"Look at me!" Alice exclaims. She steps back, moves her hand from her forehead to her waist. "I'm not like that."

Adam is silent for a moment. From the back of the apartment comes the bright silver burble of Polly's laughter. "I'm starting to smell," Adam says, his voice little more than a whisper.

"Maybe you're eating too much," Alice offers.

"I get so hungry."

"You can eat, just don't keep it."

Adam makes a face, shakes his head. "We better call Mom," he says.

"Mom's dead."

"You know who I mean. Cynthia."

"She's our aunt. Not our mother."

"We better call her. It's not even fair."

"So call her."

He pulls his phone from his pocket. It's almost out of power.

"What should I tell her?" he asks.

"I don't know. Say we're okay." She thinks for a moment. "Yeah. And tell her not to call the cops or anything. Just say we're fine."

"I think she's nice," Adam says.

"I do, too. But…"

"But what? Nice is nice."

"But she doesn't understand us," Alice says.

"What if she does?"

"She doesn't."

Their attentions are suddenly seized by a high-pitched, unstable noise. It sounds like a kitten in a tin garbage can mixed with the electronic bleat of an alarm clock. They turn toward the sound's source—it is coming from the long hallway.

"Gort!" a girl's voice calls. "Get back here!"

A moment later, a little pink face peeks around the wall at the end of the hallway. It's a child's face, a baby's. Yet it is airborne. Is someone carrying the child?

The twins hear a fluttering sound, as if a deck of cards were being shuffled. The infant's eyes are wide and full of bright green cunning. The baby turns toward Alice and Adam, and its mouth turns up in a delighted smile. The baby's tongue extends. Its eyes become brighter, more alive, yet at the same time less human somehow, less feeling.

With the suddenness of movement of a hummingbird, the child zooms toward the twins. They see now it is a boy, naked; his little penis is squat and flaccid, like the tied-off end of a party balloon. His belly is round and strangely textured, like the rind of a cantaloupe. His little fingers wave yearningly while the pale gray wings that spring from his shoulder blades beat furiously in the air as he hovers before them. The wings themselves look moist, larval. He takes another long look at Alice and Adam, who cower, terrified, before him. But he seems to mean them no harm. He hears his mother's voice calling again and he turns and darts quickly back to her.

"We have to go home," Adam says, his voice trembling.

Alice shakes her head. "We are home," she says.

CHAPTER 14

The Watertight Plumbing truck pulls into the loading dock on the north end of the vast, seemingly abandoned warehouse in Queens. A late-summer moon, dark orange, pocked and pitted like a rotted pumpkin, floats in the mottled sky, bright enough to draw the eye but not shedding any light whatsoever. It is never quiet in the city, even here in a so-called outer borough. There is always the noise of trains and trucks, the throb of music. The streets are never empty; there is always someone coming, someone turning a corner, walking a dog, jogging, looking for a parking space. In the constant back-and-forth, the unceasing activity, it is easy to go unnoticed. No one asks, *What is that building behind the high-voltage fencing?* No one wonders, *Why would a plumbing truck be pulling into a loading dock when it is almost midnight?* But the people running the project at this Borman and Davis lab have (successfully, so far) banked on the notion that the more witnesses there are to something out of the ordinary—an injured cat, a mugging—the less likely it is that any one of them will do something about it. If you feel you are the only person seeing something odd, dangerous, or illegal, you are likely to intervene, or at least report what you've witnessed. In a crowded situation, however, you have an out. You can assume (assumption being the sum of hope plus apathy) that someone else will take care of it, or that it has already been dealt with and so for you to register a complaint or call out a warning or enter into the fray in any other way not only is unnecessary but might actually muddy the waters and cause more trouble.

And so tonight, as on many other nights, Dennis Keswick drives his truck up to the locked gate of this mysterious building and rolls the window down so the CCC can see who it is. The smocks and suits have refused to issue him a proper ID card, prepared as they are to completely deny any and all knowledge of Dennis should something go wrong. He has stopped agonizing about this insult, this continuous underestimation of his worth, and now he waits nonchalantly while whoever is working security tonight presses the button that allows the gates to swing open so he can proceed with his human cargo. The gates are a little out of line; the metal scrapes along the cement as they open wide enough for Dennis to roll through. He is in what he calls major-production mode. He has taken Rogers at his word and stepped up his program of tracking, capturing, and tranquilizing the wild children. Normally, he would bring them in one at a time. On rare occasions, he has snagged two.

But tonight he's got three. A tall redheaded girl whose hair smells like burning leaves; a lithe Asian kid who had a fat roll of fifties in his jeans (*had* being the operative word, since Dennis relieved him of his financial burden moments after administering the see-ya juice); and, the most obstreperous of the three, a rather massive young man, six three if he's an inch, with a shaved head and a turquoise-and-red tattoo of feathers where his hair ought to have been. The big guy calls himself Salami; Dennis has him in the book as Gabriel Martin; his parents are or were Louise and John Martin. Gabriel has been on his own for six years, since he was eleven. Louise and John are unaccounted for, presumed dead. Most of the parents of the wild children arc dead now — heart attacks, strokes, aneurysms, inexplicable accidents; the mammalian, avian, and aquatic essences pumped into them were too much for their human, all too human, physiology to support. A few of them, though it is against animal nature to do so, even managed to commit suicide, evidently preferring death from a high terrace or beneath the steel wheels of the D train to a life under the constant control of their increasingly chaotic impulses and their decidedly outré appetites.

Keswick's haul is safely locked in the back of his van, each individually chained to the walls of the cargo space, not only for Dennis's safety but for their own. Not all of those wild things get along with one another — some, he has been told, have all the capacity for resentment and evil peculiar to humans combined with the mindless aggression of a cornered beast. (Dennis will never forget helping his aunt Joyce in Hillsborough, New Hampshire, get rid of some red squirrels that had invaded her little storybook cottage in the woods. She wanted to dispose of them humanely and insisted on Havahart traps that would lure them in with some irresistible treat such as organic crunchy peanut butter and capture them but leave them unharmed. What she did not know was that every red squirrel considers every other red squirrel its mortal enemy. And so, when the kinder, gentler trap happened to catch two squirrels, only one of them made it through the night. The bulging, burping survivor was found alive the next morning, round and sated, with a glassy look in his pinprick eyes, and the only evidence of what mayhem had transpired while Aunt Joyce slept in her four-poster bed was the tiny, apparently inedible feet of his vanquished cell mate left on the trap's metal floor.)

Now Dennis hears the rattle and clink of chains echoing in the van's metal back chamber. He is certain it is Salami who has regained consciousness. Not a real problem, more of a pain in the butt. Salami is such a large thing, with so much animal energy coursing through him, that one see-ya obviously did not suffice. Oh, well, more where that came from. He opens the glove compartment and takes out a screw-top jar that was formerly home to alcohol-soaked cleaning pads and now holds a baker's dozen of the mini-syringes—they look rather like pushpins—he uses to knock the kids out before donating them to science, ha-ha, wink-wink, nudge-nudge.

He drives slowly toward the loading dock. Earlier that evening, there was a quick, furious summer rain, and pools of rainwater have collected in the many potholes in the facility's old, neglected driveway. The bluish light that escapes from a few of the building's windows is reflected in the puddles, which shimmer and shake with the van's approach and break into bluish splashes when the tires roll through.

He pulls in. He is about to give the horn a little tap but stops himself just in time. He's already been reamed out for that. Come to think of it, maybe he *will* honk the horn. His hand hovers above the steering wheel. No, better not. Why reinforce every negative thought the smocks and their minions have about him? Instead, he flashes the brights on and off a couple of times.

A few moments later, a rectangle of bright light appears as a small side door opens. An elderly worker emerges, dressed in baggy dungarees and a T-shirt, pushing a handcart. *What,* Dennis wonders, *is this ding-dong thinking? Where in the Sam Hill did he get the idea that this is like unloading boxes of envelopes or bags of feed corn?*

He powers his window down and speaks to the old guy in an urgent whisper.

"Hey, chief, we need four strong men and a catchpole." He snaps his fingers, points at the old guy. "Pronto."

If the man minds Dennis lording it over him, he gives no indication. He simply shrugs, turns around, and heads back into the building. The bright light flares briefly as he opens and closes the door.

"Me's killing on you so hard, shithead," says Salami. Even through the closed door, his voice is harsh and heavy, with little striations of his boyish soprano still audible, threaded in like tinsel sewn into the fabric of a shirt.

Oh, this is going to be work, Dennis thinks with a sigh of resignation.

Moments later, four men equal to the task come out.

"Two are snoozing," Dennis says to the unloaders. "But the big one's awake, and he's upset."

"Open up," one of the unloaders says. He has the catchpole, with its heavy leather loop on the end.

"They're secure in there, right?" asks another worker.

"Unless they can break through steel," Dennis says.

"Well, can they?" asks the nervous one.

Dennis gives his most derisive laugh. "On three, gentlemen," he says. "One. Two. Three."

He flings the doors open. And there they are. Today's catch. Two are sleeping. The girl, at first glance, looks dead. Her face is the color of fillet of sole a day or two past its sale date; her eyes are closed; her mouth droops open. She wears a halter top, shorts. Her bare legs are scratched from thorns and stickers, and her bony ankles are scabbed. Next to her is another unconscious wild one, a boy, also in shorts. His legs are long and lean with very dark hair on the shins. He has a pointy face that looks defiant and mischievous, even with his eyes closed and his chin resting on his collarbone.

Salami, however, is fully awake, and he sits there glaring at Dennis and the other men. He has given up trying to break his shackles but has not surrendered in any other way. A sound like the grinding of gears emanates from his throat. He is gathering saliva and mucus, and a moment later he spits it out at his captors. The gob flies with the speed and accuracy of a stone launched by a slingshot. Dennis, used to the ways of these revolting creatures, moves quickly out of the path of the missile's trajectory. The Borman and Davis employee with the catchpole, however, is not as fortunate. He was, in all likelihood, Salami's target in the first place. The greenish gob finds its mark on Catchpole's chin, and it hangs there, trembling and semitransparent, like a piece of interstellar goo.

Catchpole may be a little short-tempered for this line of work. Shaking off the spittle, he goes after Salami, not with the catchpole's leather harness but with the pole itself. He brings it down with hard fury on Salami's shaved head, and the boy yelps and cries.

"Take it easy, take it easy," Dennis murmurs.

But Catchpole is having none of it. Over and over, he slams Salami with the steel pole, until blood oozes out of the boy's skull like juice out of an overripe orange. Salami makes a few futile swipes at Catchpole and, also futilely, tries to protect himself. But he is trapped, defenseless. His eyes go from furious to blank and finally roll slowly up into his head as the once-wild but now-vanquished boy loses consciousness.

Dennis unlocks the three kids, and in short order they are all dragged into receiving. Many times before, Dennis made an effort to follow his bounty in and see where they were brought, how they were processed, what happened next. But each time, he was prohibited from stepping foot in the building, and now he has stopped making any attempts. It's maddening enough to be bossed around by the smocks and the pencil pushers, but to be muscled by these stiffs in security and receiving—that is intolerable.

The metal doors slam. All is silence. Dennis stands there with his van, now empty.

Oh. Not quite.

Three vials of blood have gotten lodged between the corrugated floor and the side of the van. Dennis picks one up and inspects it. He shakes it. Sniffs it. And drops it into his breast pocket. It feels warm against his heart. Curious, his excitement growing, he pockets the other two as well. And then his eyes light up. There is a brown canvas backpack shoved into the corner. He reaches for it and hears the tinkle of countless vials. He's struck it rich!

"Nice place you got here," the prostitute says looking around Dennis's one-bedroom apartment on the ninth floor of a 1950s apartment house on Ocean Parkway in the middle of Brooklyn. She is a bit heavy but seems not to be self-conscious about it— she wears a short leather skirt and a tight, scoop-neck top. Her voice is derisive; her brightly painted, surgically enhanced lips curl into a sneer. She tosses her head, and her platinum pageboy, sprayed and lacquered into petrification, barely budges. Dennis, who may not be expert in improving his life situation but is more than adept at sensing anything remotely resembling a low opinion of his person, his intellect, or his lifestyle, can see the humid hovel he calls home through the prostitute's eyes. What did the escort service say her name was? Burgundy? Bree? It didn't matter.

And Dennis's name, as far as this woman and the escort service that sent her is concerned, is Carl Ravenswood. He totally loves using that name. His nom de screw. And it's the name on his lease too. The name on his buzzer downstairs. He would like one day to write his old friends and say, *Try living under an assumed name, you'll be surprised how relaxing it is.*

He sees his paid guest taking in the fourteen-year-old GE air conditioner, inherited from the previous tenant, who probably got it from the tenant before him; the sofa dragged out of a nearby Covenant House after a kitchen fire; the leaning tower of pizza boxes in the corner, which Dennis has been accumulating over the past three months, because he is playing a game with himself to see how high he can stack them before they collapse and another game to see how long he can stand having them here before he completely loses his mind—she's taking it all in and deciding Dennis is the kind of threadbare customer who has to dig deep in order to pay for his repulsive little nude romps and who will not be able to add a tip to her fee. And here's another thing that Dennis knows, or at least assumes: Bree, or whatever the hell name she is claiming, does not want to be here—none of the so-called girls want to travel to Brooklyn, and the fact that she has been sent means she is a second- or third-tier "provider."

Yet despite it all, Dennis is excited to have her here.

He reaches into his back pocket and hands her four fifty-dollar bills, fresh from Salami's pocket.

She steps back as if from a hot flame.

"Put it in an envelope and put the envelope over there," she says.

But he does not want to take instructions from a prostitute. He grabs her wrist and slaps the money into her open hand. She is not about to let it drop to the floor. She turns her back and puts the money into her purse.

"Ever see one of these?" Dennis asks her when she turns around again. He is holding one of the vials that Salami must have dropped.

"What is that? Zoom?" Everything she says sounds pissed off.

"Zoom?" Dennis asks. "Is that what people are calling it?"

"Zoom, Doom. All kinds of shit. That stuff is fucking evil. I heard it was blood."

"It is," Dennis says. He refuses to react to her cursing. It makes him sick but does not surprise him. It's not as if he were expecting someone with morals or manners.

"You should put it away," she says. "I don't even want to see that shit."

A feeling of pleasure is going through him as he senses her fear of the little vial standing on the tip of his thumb, held in place by his first finger. "It is definitely blood."

"That's ill shit. You on it?"

"What if I am?"

"Are you?" Her tone takes on a bit of uncertainty.

Dennis knows it's not exactly PC and feminist and everything, but sensing a woman's wariness and even her fear is kind of an aphrodisiac for him. "Well, my dear," he says in his debonair voice, picked up from long afternoons watching black-and-white movies while warehoused at his tipsy grandmother's house in Rock Island, "I propose we make a party of it and each partake of the fabled Zoom." He takes another vial out of his shirt pocket.

"If you touch one fucking drop of that shit, I'm leaving." She glares at him, and when she notices no particular change in his expression, she adds, "And I'm keeping a hundred for my travel and time."

"Ah, my fair damsel," Dennis says. "You cut me to the quick!" He has no idea where this kind of talk is coming from, but he is amused by this new identity and cannot imagine that it is anything less than irresistible.

"You got to be nuts using that stuff," she says.

"You've partaken of the mighty red, then, I presume?" Dennis says.

"No fucking way. Two of the other girls." She shakes her head. "The warning's out on that shit. Some freaks up from Mexico are bringing it into the city. Anyhow, that's what I hear."

"Really?" All her swears are like fingernails on a blackboard to Dennis. "That's what you believe in your infinite wisdom?" He grins at her—and if smiles were display cases, this one would be showing Phi Beta Kappa keys, degrees from Stanford, Harvard, and MIT, and a family tree of accomplished ancestors reaching back to the Magna Carta. "And what other valuable information do your confidants share with you, pray tell?"

"Oh, you're a funny guy. Well, there's nothing that funny about getting the shit fucked out of you and coming out with scratches all over. This old Canadian guy staying at the Hilton took a chunk out of Mirabella's earlobe. And swallowed the diamond stud her boyfriend gave her." Bree shakes her head.

"Well, then, we'll have none of this," Dennis says, dropping the vials back into his shirt pocket. His smile broadens. She said just what he predicted she would say. It's all going exactly according to plan…

Believing Dennis is cooperating with her, she relaxes a bit;

her voice softens. "You oughta be careful with that stuff, sweetie," she says. "You ain't a teenager." She pokes his soft stomach. "That shit'll mess you up, swear to God."

"Well, let's have a drink anyhow," Dennis says. He indicates with a wave two glasses on the cluttered coffee table. Though each of them contains a vial of Zoom—the former Zoom vials themselves had been refilled with V8 juice—they look like well-made Bloody Marys, each with a wedge of lime notched on the rim, and a celery stalk standing in the center. "I didn't add the vodka yet, in case you don't drink."

She looks at her watch. "Oh, I guess I can have a little vitamin V."

"Vitamin V, I like that," says Dennis. There is a bottle of off-brand vodka on the table—he can afford one of the fashionable brands, but he is sure they are for pretentious idiots. He unscrews the cap, pours a generous splash into each glass. He hands one to Bree and takes one for himself.

"To us," he says, clinking her glass.

"Cheers," she says.

She brings the glass up to her lips but then hesitates, seeing that Dennis has not lifted his glass. He seems balky and uncertain.

"What about you?" she says.

"Just taking in your beauty, my dear."

"You're not drinking?"

"Sure I am. Undoubtedly."

"How about we trade glasses," she says.

"Really? I...this is sort of my favorite glass."

"I say we trade. How about it? Be a good boy."

"If it will make you feel better, of course," says Dennis. He hands her his glass, takes hers in exchange. He gives her a look that says, *Now, are you happy?*

"It's a little early for me," she says.

"Oh, come on. It's later than it's ever ever ever been." He gives her glass another clink, this one with an edge of admonishment in it.

They drink. Dennis steels himself against the taste, which he assumes will be greasy and gross. But it's not half bad—the V8, the horseradish, and the hot sauce have done their job disguising the taste of those children's blood.

"Oooh, salty," Bree says. But she's drunk deeply; half the glass is empty. The ice cubes, coated pale red, are visible now.

"Sorry about that," says Dennis. "I'm actually a trained chemist. But apparently not much of a mixologist."

"I have to watch my sodium intake," Bree says.

"Oh, come on. Anyhow, didn't you hear me? Weren't you even listening to what I said? I'm a trained chemist. PhD, the best schools, you name it." He sees her eyes move; she is once again taking in the penny-pinched squalor of this shitbox apartment. "Trust me," he says, hurrying now. "There's very little salt in your drink. And we're also—you should keep this to yourself—we're in the process of disproving all this low-sodium, salt-free-diet stuff. According to the work we're doing in the lab, there's nothing to it."

"Whatever," Bree says, putting the drink down on the table.

"Ah, dear damsel, you cut me to the quick," Dennis says.

"You already said that," Bree says. She is frowning. She has a strange look on her face, as if she hears someone very, very far away calling her name.

"Well, I just don't see why you won't finish your drink. Watch how Professor Daddy does it." He drains his glass. *Professor Daddy! That's who I am, that's who I will be!*

"I'm good," she says.

Oh no, you're not, thinks Dennis. *You're actually bad. You are a whore. How can you say you're good?*

"Sure?" He is playing it cool.

He can.

He has outthought this woman three times over. He knew she might react badly to the sight of the vials and that's why he emptied them of Zoom and put the good stuff in the drinks. He knew she would see him hesitate to drink, and because she has a comic-book mind and is far more predictable than the weather, he knew that she would think there was something wrong with her drink. And that is why, of the three vials he portioned off for today's playtime, two and a half were poured into the drink she ended up with. And so even if she wants to be a pain in the behind and refuse to drain her glass like a good little whore, she has already consumed more than enough to make what comes next a most excellent adventure.

Bree now is licking her lips and swallowing her mouth's moisture in gulps, as if consuming dollops of cold mashed potatoes. She pats her breastbone, and her eyes go through a series of transformations: concern, followed by fear, followed by fascination, and ending up in a kind of animalistic blankness—the eyes go from being windows to the soul to being windows on pure appetite.

Dennis is feeling quite a bit of appetite himself—it's amazing how quickly that Zoom starts zooming. How long has it been? Ten seconds? It's difficult for him to stand still. He finds himself marching in place, but his demeanor is hardly soldierly. He is rotating his shoulders, flexing his fingers, sniffing and snuffling. All of his systems are in overdrive. His mind repeats the question: What do I do, what do I do? He wants to look out the window, lock the door. He wants to urinate, defecate, eat, drink, procreate. But having given himself a 50 percent dose, he is able to keep these surging desires in check.

The same cannot be said for Burgundy/Bree etc. etc. She was given the megadose, so what is a surfable wave to Dennis is a tsunami to her. She is helpless to resist. In fact, the word *she* might not even apply to her, since, grammatically speaking, it implies a certain specificity, and most of the traits, memories, and goals that form the core of who she is in the world and how she sees herself have been washed away as the Zoom courses through her like a marauding army of Visigoths charging through an undefended village, obliterating everything in its path.

"Hi, sweetie," she fairly shouts. She has no idea why she said this. It could be she is curious if she is still capable of human speech. She steps toward Dennis, cups his business, gives it a shake, and then, her eyes widening, she takes a deep, deep breath, squats on the floor, leans her shoulder against the arm of the sofa, hikes up her skirt, yanks her undies to one side, and lets loose a powerful stream of urine.

I'm going to pee-pee too! thinks Dennis. He is erect and it's something of a struggle to get his prick out of his pants but a moment or two later he is standing next to the woman and covering her urine with his own. The odor is amazing. It's like the best meal he's ever had combined with suddenly understanding exactly how everything in the world is connected.

He pushes himself into her mouth. She doesn't seem to mind, but she doesn't do what he would call a professional job. Her eyes momentarily roll back in her head and then reappear again, no more expressive than two blueberries in a slot machine.

She loses her balance and now she is on her back, oblivious

to the fact that her carefully lacquered hair, not to mention her head, is in the dark circle of wet the two of them left on the carpet. Dennis pushes her skirt up higher, until it is around her ample waist, like a thick carpenter's belt minus the tools. He attempts next to pull her underpants off, but she is twisting, perhaps writhing, from side to side, and it's too difficult, so he does what any God-fearing gentleman would do in his position—he tears them to shreds. The elastic band requires special effort, but soon she is fully available to him.

"In, in, in, in, in," she chants, and her tongue lolls out of her mouth and she pants like a dog waiting to be fed.

When Dennis was in high school, there was a student production of *Raisin in the Sun*—an all-white production, as it happened. He had a small role, but he took it to heart, and the poem from which the play took its title—*What happens to a dream deferred? Does it dry up like a raisin in the sun?*—has haunted him ever since. As someone whose life has been a series of frustrations, he has had to struggle not to lose heart. He has had many dreams deferred, but none of them, as far as he can tell, have dried up. And one of his deferred dreams—to have a woman begging for it, spreading her down-there lips and just completely fricking begging for it—is right now finally coming true. And it is no little desiccated raisin in the sun. It is a big juicy grape; it is, in fact, an entire vineyard at the peak of gushing ripeness...

That's the good news.

The bad news is everything that happens next.

CHAPTER 15

Below her is a pit of despair; she can smell it, she can taste it, and Cynthia hangs above it from a thin, fraying rope. And all that rope is made of is two brief text messages, one from Alice that says *We're okay,* and the other from Adam, typically more expressive, though in this case only marginally so, that says *See you soon, Mom.* The rope is tied around her ankle and she is upside down, turning slowly, facing and smelling the foul pit of hopelessness and grief, and everything else in life— eating, sleeping, shopping, thinking—is either undoable or ir- relevant.

I can't call the police, she writes in her journal. *What if the kids are up to some mischief—or worse? Those poor babies. What if they are taken away from me? Can they do that? I don't even know what my rights are. I don't know anything. Just this, these two things: Adam. Alice. I love them. And they need me.*

She sits in the middle of her bed. It is ten at night, and she is dressed, ready to leave at a moment's notice. The door to the bedroom is open wide. She scrambles up, pulls the door shut, and locks it.

She has been doing this for the past hour. Closing the door to the bedroom and locking it. Unlocking it and opening it.

Closing, opening, locking, unlocking. It is a state worse than indecision. One moment she feels safer locked away, and three minutes later it hits her that nothing could be more dangerous than a closed, locked door—she *must* be able to hear what (if anything) is happening in the rest of the house. But then the sight of that wide-open door and the thought of some beast, some intruder, a swarm of rats, a flying phalanx of bats pouring in   it's as if the person who left the door open must have been out of her mind, and she slams it shut, bolts it, only to open it again in a few minutes.

Now that the door is closed, the house emits more inexplicable noises. A thud. A creak. A bang. A squeak. She pictures the house. Why, oh why, oh why did she ever want to live in a large house? She remembers the first time she stepped foot in this place, not long after Leslie and Alex were engaged. How dazzled she was, how thrilled, moved as if by the sudden sound of overwhelmingly beautiful music—she had never been a guest in such a magnificent dwelling, let alone lived in such a place. Everything about it filled her with awe. Here was the source! For years she had been selling early American antiques, and walking through these rooms for the first time, she felt as if she were visiting the birthplace of all the fine furniture—the end tables, the paintings, the chairs, the sofas, the andirons, the pokers and tongs, the carpets, the lamps and chandeliers, the pewter serving trays, the immemorial gravy boats—all gathered together in their natural habitat. She had felt like a lover of animals who finally gets to see her beloved lions and giraffes on the Serengeti Plain.

But now. The bricks, the rafters, the beams, the window sashes, the glass—everything was pure hell. The house confounded her, mocked and tormented her. If you stood in one room, it seemed as if an evil presence was dancing happily in another. If you went to that room, the entity would have already moved on to another room, and another, and another, and another. If only she knew twenty-five people in New York City, twenty-five people who would help her, defend her, indulge her. She would have them here right now, one in every room.

But what about the cellar? What about the attic? The yard!

She scrambles off the bed again. Her journal slides to the floor. The noise of it turns her around. She laughs without joy, a *ha* and a *ha* no more merry than the sound of nails being hammered into the lid of a coffin. She races from room to room, switching on lights. A shadow—her own—terrifies her. A reflection in the window. The sound of her own breathing.

On the third floor of the once-magnificent mansion, now a brick box of dread, she stands in front of the twins' rooms, her chest heaving, her face contorted. The bedroom of a child is meant to be a cheerful, comforting place, brightly colored, sunny and safe, decorated with symbols of the innocent enthusiasms of youth—pictures of superheroes, beagles, kittens, pop stars, and dinosaurs. She has done her best to make the rooms right for the kids. Since their arrival, the twins themselves, however, have done nothing to make their bedrooms more theirs. Years in parental captivity, followed by the abrupt, powerless life of a child in the foster-care system, during which they were shuttled from family to family, house to house, room to room, have given them a permanent sense of impermanence. Wanting the children to make their rooms their own, Cynthia had deliberately left the walls empty, and they remain blank. The beds are tightly made, as if to pass inspection.

Cynthia enters Adam's room first. She turns on the overhead light, which shines brightly—too brightly for her nerves at this point. She switches it off, and the room settles down again, like a cobra retreating to its wicker basket. She crouches down and turns on the night-light, a winking, cheeky cartoon full moon plugged into the outlet and emitting a soft glow. The light— its kind intentions—breaks her heart. How we wish to make childhood a happy place and hope against all hope and against all evidence that if we love our children enough, we can keep them safe. Safe from the world. Safe from themselves.

Whoever it was who came to this room to take Adam's clothes left the dresser drawers hanging open, and now, going from the bottom to the top, she carefully slides them back into place. Next, Cynthia goes to his closet and picks up the hangers the intruder (or was it the twins themselves?) left on the floor. She returns them to the crossbar, steadies their swaying back and forth with her hand, and carefully closes the door. A part of her thinks that it might do some good to restore perfect order to the room.

She sits on the edge of his bed and strokes the soft down summer-weight comforter, encased in a pure silk French duvet cover, a ridiculous extravagance and one about as meaningful to a little boy as an honorary AARP membership, but, while furnishing the house in anticipation of the twins' becoming hers, Cynthia could not resist it. Now, however, she regrets it. She regrets...everything. She takes his pillow and holds it to her, as if it were a child. She buries her nose in it and there it is, mixed with the faintly lavender scent of the detergent, his soft, ever so slightly spicy smell, a combination of scalp and hair and skin and breath.

It is more than she can bear. The children were put into her care. She petitioned the court and said, *You must trust me.* She took them out of homes where they might not have been perfectly happy but where they were at least safe—not once in foster care did either of them go missing! But now it suddenly seems that keeping them in one place is more than she can accomplish.

She remembers how she used to feel selling antiques out of Gilty Pleasures, back in San Francisco about what now seems like fifty years ago. Sometimes, a wealthy customer would walk out of her shop with a delicate old painting or a fragile vase feeling that he or she had a right to the irreplaceable object because he or she had the money to pay for it. And Cynthia would watch the customer and the antique leave the store, mentally waving farewell to it and wondering if she were in fact sending the piece to its ruin and destruction. It was not enough to own a thing—you had to take care of it too. When you say, *This is mine,* you are signing a sacred contract that you will do it no harm.

And now, as far as she is concerned, she has committed acts of heedlessness and irresponsibility far, far beyond anything she imagined a few of her feckless customers capable of. She has failed to protect two beautiful, blameless, mysterious, and delicate little human beings.

She weeps into Adam's pillow and continues to do so as the darkness of the house closes in around her, slowly rising like a river, erasing everything in its path. Monster darkness, greedy, insatiable, implacable, pitiless darkness, the enemy of safety, the enemy of sanity.

Pay attention, pay attention, a part of her silently warns. Someone could be coming up the staircase right this very moment.

Oh, leave me alone, the rest of her answers. *I no longer care.*

*   *   *

Alice, fully dressed, slides out of Rodolfo's bed. All he asked of her is to sleep next to him, and maybe let him put his arm around her. She was happy to agree—it sounded like fun, beautiful fun—but now she cannot sleep, and tonight's meal moves restlessly in her stomach, like a dog pacing around for last outs. Someone brought in a sack of cooked chickens and gallons of mac and cheese and all kinds of sodas and energy drinks, and everyone was in pretty high spirits and it smelled unbelievably good. So Alice ended up eating more than her customary six well-masticated bites.

And now, with the house quiet, and her privacy (she thinks) assured, she slips into the wreck of the bathroom to get rid of tonight's meal and whatever other undigested calories might be dangerously lurking in there as well.

When she learned (this was in Cold Spring, New York, in her first foster home) that she might at least maneuver puberty into a stalemate by starving herself, it was amazingly difficult for her to get rid of her food. She used to stick the eraser end of a pencil as far down her throat as possible, until a muscle was touched, and she gagged, and suddenly the whole machinery of the body began urgently to run in reverse. Then she learned to use her finger. The entire process was painful, laborious, convulsive, and once she got herself to hurl, she would be sweaty and shaking from the effort. Now, it's easy-breezy. She can do it by swallowing a little bit of air, clenching the muscles of her stomach, and then forcing them out. It takes about two seconds, and bloop: she's empty and clean. It's really no more than an intestinal sneeze. It's not a big deal. She often wonders why everyone in the world doesn't do this, rather than letting themselves get gross. But she keeps it private. It's her secret, and like many secrets, it turns her life into a tiptoe journey over broken glass. Oh, well. She flushes the toilet as she empties herself, and no one is any the wiser.

Except that when she opens the bathroom door, Polly is standing there, fully dressed, holding a biology textbook, her dark brows raised and a crooked, superior smile on her face, like a schoolteacher who believes part of her job is to make sure your self-esteem is no higher than an ant's ass.

"Hi," Alice says. She covers her mouth, pretends to cough.

"Feel better?" Polly says. She is whispering.

"I'm okay," Alice whispers back.

"I know what you were doing in there," Polly says. She bends over, extends her tongue.

Alice feels her color rising, beginning with her cheeks and going all the way to her scalp. Saying nothing seems the best thing to do, the only thing.

"Right," Polly says.

"I wasn't," Alice manages to say.

"We don't do that," Polly announces in a way that implies there is a whole list of dos and don'ts that Alice knows nothing of. If Polly is trying to make Alice feel like an outsider, an un-welcome guest who might be booted out at any moment, she is succeeding.

Alice shrugs, as if the whole conversation is stupid. And with that, she starts to walk past her.

"Where are you going?" Polly asks, taking hold of Alice's arm.

"I'm tired," says Alice.

"Oh, look at her," says Polly. "She just can't wait to get back in bed with her boyfriend."

"He's not my boyfriend," Alice says.

"You better use protection. Safe sex, girl, you hear?"

"It's not like that."

"Kids like us, we give birth to things this world has never seen."

"I know. You don't need to tell me."

"Um…" Polly points at Alice. "You've got a little throw-up on your chin."

Nervously, Alice tries to wipe it away—but her chin is dry, and she realizes she has been tricked.

"Psych!" Polly says, grinning. Then, suddenly serious, her whisper marbled with apparent concern, she says, "You shouldn't do that. You could die from it. And it doesn't even work."

Alice shrugs. She cannot argue, but she refuses to confirm the fact that she has been tossing her food.

"Other kids tried it, you know," Polly says. She hasn't let go of Alice's arm; in fact, her grip tightens.

"Tried what?" Alice says, trying to shake loose.

"Stopping their bodies from changing. It only works for a while. We all know how annoying the body is. It does what it does, right? It wants what it wants. You think the body is some kind of car that the mind owns and drives around wherever it wants. But the mind is a passenger. It can't touch the gas, the brake, or the steering wheel."

"I know how to drive," Alice says. "For really. A Mazda. I had a foster brother in Cold Spring, he taught me."

"Yeah, for a blow job."

"Gross."

"Deal with it, Miss Perfect." Polly looks away for a moment. She is not stopping to think about what she says, and so far she has been pretty surprised at what's come out. In every back-and-forth in this house and with their friends out in the various parks, Polly has been the nice one, the reasonable one. Now she's acting like (what she would call) a total bitch—and it feels just fine.

Dylan suddenly appears. His hair is slicked back and he is holding a sandwich—peanut butter, from the smell of it.

"So?" he says to Polly. "We's leaving?"

"Yeah. You ready?"

"Me's born ready, all my life, sister."

"I'm bringing Dylan back to his pack," Polly says to Alice. "They're up near One Hundred and Tenth, West Side. Come with?"

"It's okay," Alice says.

"No, seriously. You have to. I can't walk back home all by myself."

"I'm so tired," Alice says.

"Come on," Polly says. At last, she relinquishes her hold on Alice, but only to throw her arm over Alice's shoulders. "You fucking owe me."

"I do?" But she has a feeling Polly has just offered to keep her secret and not tell anyone about her private weight-control program. It was insane, she thought. Even though these kids were living like animals, and selling their own blood, and sexing it up all over the place, and stealing, and some of them disappearing and some of them dying, Alice still didn't want anyone to know she sent most of her meals straight to the sewer.

A couple of minutes later, Alice, Polly, and Dylan are waiting for the elevator. The common hallway is tiled black and white, gloomily lit. The old elevator slowly rises, its cables shaking and rattling like shackles. Dylan cannot keep still. He is shrugging his shoulders, knocking his knees together, and the next moment, he somehow produces a hacky sack and is lifting it up with the toe of his sneaker and catching it on his forehead, humming tunelessly all the while. He basically makes most kids diagnosed with ADHD seem catatonic.

At last, the elevator doors open. The on-again, off-again elevator operator is at the controls, much to Polly's disappointment. (The rule of the house is to keep as low a profile as possible.) The elevator operates by push button, and Polly does not see why an elevator operator would ever be necessary, but here he is, old Dominick, with his basset-hound eyes and shiny shoes, and a blue-and-yellow uniform that looks like it came out of the 1980s or some other era of the past, an impossibly long time ago.

"Here we are," Dominick says as always, holding the door as if without his strength, it would cut Polly and her friends in half.

"Thanks, Dominick," Polly murmurs.

"Sort of late to be going out," Dominick observes.

"Not really," she says.

"So...is your mother back in town yet?" Dominick asks, as he has on so many other occasions.

"She called tonight, actually," Polly says, her voice confident, convincing. "Thanks for asking."

Alice and Dylan stare straight ahead, trying hard not to laugh.

"You take care of yourself," Dominick says as the elevator reaches the ground floor.

"You too!" Polly cheerfully calls out as the three of them clatter quickly over the lobby's marble floor. There is no doorman—an automated ID system has been installed—and now nothing separates the kids from the night. They enter it like fish poured from a bucket back into a lake.

They head east toward Broadway. Only Edible Broadway, which never closes, is open. The proprietor, a portly, pale greenish man whom everyone calls the Greek but who insists that he is, in fact, Portuguese, sits on a folding chair overseeing his display of grapes and plums, strawberries and oranges, as if without his constant vigilance, he would be bankrupted by marauding bands of fruit thieves. "Yo, Greek," Polly says as Dylan pockets a couple of plums without breaking stride. As for the Greek himself, he is mainly relieved the three kids didn't go into his store, where truffled olive oil and Kalamata figs and other pricey items are on display—he does not know what makes these kids special, but he can recognize these feral teenagers from twenty paces. He knows that until someone gets them under control, there is not a shopkeeper in the city who can consider his business safe.

They move east across Amsterdam and Columbus Avenues, go past the twinkling monoliths of Central Park West, and then scamper over the stone wall bordering New York's great green space, Central Park.

The three walk quickly, oblivious to sidewalks, tunnels, and the various paths ordinary citizens use when traversing the park. They have their own routes, direct and unmanicured. Dylan leads the way—he knows exactly where his pack will be, and he is also wired more tightly than the two girls and is constitutionally unable to proceed at anything resembling a leisurely pace. He jumps, skips, zigs, and zags.

"Me's wishing I's staying with Rodolfo!" he calls back to them, ten paces in front. "All's well when Rodolfo is here."

He lifts his hands in the air. In his excitement, his fingertips glow dark red.

"Look at him," Alice whispers to Polly.

"He's not the only one. All kinds of things are happening."

"It's sort of pretty," says Alice.

"I guess. We've got evolution on the run."

She suddenly stops, and Alice stops too. A look of concern crosses Polly's face. She tilts her head. She rests her finger on her lips, beseeching Alice's silence.

"Come on, you two!" Dylan cries out.

"I heard something," Polly says to Alice.

"Where?"

"In there." Polly points to a tangle of honeysuckle bushes thirty feet to the left.

"I once found a dog hiding in the bushes around here," says Alice. "A little white dog, he was so cute. When I was young." The memory of that time, the school she and Adam used to attend, their mother walking with them up Madison, the teacher, the other kids. It's been a long time since she's allowed herself to think about those days, and remembering them now feels ghostly and sad.

Polly looks at her, and her expression clearly states that whatever little white dog Alice is remembering is a hundred miles beside the point, and for her to even mention something so stupid and juvenile is proof that she has no idea what is happening.

Somebody is following us. Polly mouths the words silently.

Dylan has finally stopped twirling about and looks at them questioningly now, his glowing fingers darkening to a dull, dirty rust. Polly waves for him to come back.

The three of them, with utmost stealth, approach the bushes. They all have extraordinary hearing and they lean forward, turning their heads slightly to the left and then the right, aiming their auditory nerves the way you'd point a flashlight into a dark corner.

Polly lifts one finger. Then the second, and the third. On three, they converge on the bushes, plunging in through the resistant green maze without the slightest hesitation, as if they are starving canines who sense a helpless quivering chipmunk there, marinating in its own fear.

Rooting around in the dirt, they find nothing but condom wrappers and empty Snapple bottles.

Yet the rest of their journey is a nervous one. Polly is used to being constantly on guard, fearing the park police, who can be on bicycles, on horseback, in squad cars, or on foot. Dylan has also learned how to be basically invisible when he roams the park, though the lessons in caution he has been taught have to contend with the counterweight of his upbringing. His time in Gracie Mansion, his tenure as the mayor's son, in which he absorbed a kind of cellular certainty that he is privileged and protected, often interferes with the basic things the other feral kids have taught him about survival. (In fact, whenever Rodolfo thinks about the future of this new race of human over which he presides, that future does not normally include Dylan; he takes too many chances, and he is all over the map, and, worst of all, Dylan Morris is an extreme case of mutation—the ones who glow tend to be the craziest. One day, maybe next week, Rodolfo guesses, or maybe next year, Dylan Morris will be one of the Remembered.)

They head north past the reservoir, which tonight is full of sleeping ducks whose feathery frames bob up and down as they doze in the gently rippling water. With the approach of the three kids, a sense of alarm suddenly sweeps through the flock—there is first a rumble of nervous quacks, and then, like a crash of cymbals, the ducks explode into flight, racing over the threshold of moonlight into the dark palace of night.

"They hate us," Alice whispers.

"Who?" asks Dylan, who springs from his handstand back onto his feet.

"The ducks," says Alice. "When I was young we used to come here and feed them. The thing they liked best was Wheat Thins. They really liked them."

"Oh, me's memorying eating mad Pepperidge Farm Goldfish. 'Member them?"

"Cheddar-flavored," Polly says over her shoulder.

"Oh!" cries Dylan. "Me's want. From the yum to the tum to the gimme some more." He lifts his arms, and now the red glow extends from his fingertips to his palms to his wrists.

"Hands down, Dyl," Polly says, leading them away from the reservoir and into a thicket of trees.

They move in silence. Their steps are light, graceful, almost soundless. A park police cruiser goes by, its emergency light slowly revolving. It's not going anywhere in particular. It's just showing its colors.

At one point, Polly says to Alice, "So what do you think of Rodolfo? You think he likes you?"

"I don't know. I guess." Alice knows she must be careful around Polly, but she is not certain what being careful entails — should she tell the truth or refuse to talk? What does Polly want from her?

"You guess you like him?"

"I mean him liking me," says Alice. "I mean, it's not a big deal or anything. We're friends."

"How can you be friends? You've been away for a really insanely long time."

"I don't know. We just are."

Polly's laugh is not a real laugh—it's more a quick, toxic exhale.

"So what about you?" Polly asks. "You like him?"

"I guess."

"You guess?"

"I don't know what I'm supposed to say," says Alice, but with very little pleading in her voice. She says it as a statement of fact.

"Girl," Polly says. She puts her hand on her hip and juts it out. "I think you like him. You should just say." She tosses her head and then mutters, "Bitch," under her breath but certainly loud enough for Alice to hear it.

"Hey, guys! Guys! Me's here!" Dylan shouts as they reach 110th Street and he sees two members of his old pack. His hands are flashing and he is hopping up and down with excitement. His cohorts are pretending to fence, using skateboards as their swords. From a distance, it's difficult to determine their gender. They both have long hair, rising up in a frizzy nimbus on one, tied back in a ponytail on the other.

With a grateful glance over his shoulder, Dylan runs quickly toward his friends, pulsating with light.

"Yo, yo, yo, yo," calls out the one with the frizzy hair. He drops his skateboard to the ground and opens his arms wide.

Others emerge, as if from nowhere. There are ten altogether. Polly notices they are all wearing dark green T-shirts, as if they are a team, or a gang. Rodolfo stresses that it is not a good idea for packs living together to wear matching clothes. You want to be able to disperse quickly, blend in. As much as possible. But, really, no one on Riverside expects the 110th Street crew to last. They take too many chances; they're too exposed.

They've already lost two members to whoever is snatching the wild kids—and they don't even seem to know when someone goes missing, or maybe they don't care. They never look for the missing ones—they don't even mention it to anyone. When everyone meets at the Diana Ross, there's simply one or two less in the pack. Sooner or later, they'll all be gone; at least, that's what Rodolfo says, and Polly is inclined to agree with him.

"Let's go," Polly says.

Alice yawns, rubs her eye with the heel of her hand. A wave of hunger goes through her, sharp and urgent, but she has become expert in ignoring hunger pangs. When her body calls for food, she knows how to tell her body to shut up. And shut down.

They start back, but after a minute or so Polly stops, raises her hand. She looks worried, a little scared.

Alice tilts her head, knits her brow, as if to say, *What is it?*

Polly is looking intently at a cluster of bushes between the benches and the boundary wall. She takes a step toward them, stops, listens, and after a few moments, she shrugs and indicates with a wave that they might as well continue on their way home.

"Can you read?" Polly asks. Without talking it over, they are taking the sidewalk heading south, as if they were just two normal kids out for a very late stroll in Central Park.

"Yes."

"You don't have to say it like that."

"I'm just saying yes."

"A lot of us can't, you know," Polly says.

"I know. I guess it's not such a big deal."

"How about your brother?"

"He can read. We both can read. We go to school."

"But do you? Do you ever just, you know, start reading, just to do it? Not in school. Just for fun?"

Alice shrugs. She cannot say two words to Polly without feeling she has said the wrong thing or is about to and that she might even be letting herself be lured into a trap.

Polly slings her arm around Alice's shoulder. Her eyes widen. "Wow, you're really bony."

Alice wishes she could move away from Polly but worries that it would make everything worse. All she wants right now is to get back to the apartment, go to sleep. She knows that Polly is mad that Alice has shared Rodolfo's bed, and she knows that Polly thinks something sexy happened, which it did not. If it will make matters easier, Alice will gladly sleep on a sofa, or find where Adam is and sleep there, or sleep on the floor. She doesn't care.

"We have to put some meat on those bones, girl," Polly says. Her fingers creep down Alice's back and grab hold of her shoulder blade. "Is this what Rodolfo likes? Skin and bones?"

"I don't know and I don't care," Alice answers.

"You don't?" Polly is silent for a moment. When she speaks again, her tone has changed. It is no longer teasing and sharp, but soft and confiding. "We're a lot alike, you know, you and me."

"I guess."

"You guess? You do a lot of guessing."

"I'm pretty tired."

"We're not as messed up as a lot of them," Polly says. "We've got some of whatever that shit is our parents took, but not as much. Some of them are really bad. Some of them are like our parents, or worse."

"My mother says we didn't ask for this," Alice says.

"Your mother? I heard your mother killed herself."

"I'm adopted now. She's actually my aunt."

"You shouldn't call her your mother. It's disrespectful."

"I guess."

"I guess," Polly says simultaneously in a simpering voice, followed by openly cruel laughter.

They walk in silence for a full minute. The spires of the San Remo float into view.

Suddenly, Polly stops. She turns to face Alice.

"You need to go home to your new mommy," she says.

Alice returns Polly's stare. She waits for that familiar feeling of cringing and wanting to hide, what she has always felt when threatened or upset. But this time, for some reason, it doesn't come. She feels nothing. No. Not nothing. She feels calm. She feels ready.

"And you need to keep away from Rodolfo," Polly adds.

"I don't have to," Alice says. Her voice is small, but it is steady.

"Oh yes, you do, you little bitch," Polly says. Her breaths are rapid, and her face is flushed. She is trying to look as angry and as threatening as possible, but in fact, she looks frantic. She waits for Alice to back down, to start stuttering and promising and I-guessing and basically falling to pieces, but Alice looks calm. *Has the little bitch gone crazy?* wonders Polly.

In a moment of inspiration, she slaps Alice across the face. Not as hard as she could, but hard, definitely hard.

Alice is stunned. Her eyelids flutter. She steps back and places inquiring fingers on the spot where Polly's blow landed.

Polly interprets this as weakness and strikes again, this time planning to hit even harder and settle this once and for all. But Alice has quick reflexes and catches Polly by the wrist before the blow lands.

The little bony shrimp's grip is amazingly strong. Polly's hand is like a fox in a trap, crippled by pain, shit out of luck.

"Let me go," Polly demands.

"You were hitting," Alice says. Something is happening to her eyes. The brown of them is darkening, deepening. The pupils grow larger. She radiates a terrifying indifference. People who don't know any better talk about an animal being vicious when all the animal is is hungry. An animal cannot hate, any more than it can really love; at least, not love in the way humans want the word to mean. An animal won't burn a CD with seductive songs on it, and it won't lie to make you jealous. That story that gets told about the dog waiting for his owner patiently at the door years after the owner has fallen on the field of battle is either a myth or a story about a broken dog. Animals don't exact revenge, nor do they experience pleasure from the suffering of other creatures. What an animal can mostly do is want, and eat, and protect. An animal is designed to survive.

And yet, as Polly looks into Alice's eyes and feels the stubborn steely grip of Alice's fingers around her wrist, she does feel fear, a great, dizzying geyser of fear. She tries to yank free, and, failing that, she strikes out at Alice with her other hand. "Let me go, you little bitch, let me go," she shrieks furiously.

Alice feels a power spreading through her. It begins in her stomach and travels down to her legs and up to her throat, her hands, her face, and her scalp. Her mouth hangs open; her blood feels like warm honey. Phrases from childhood occur to her, and she repeats them now. "You need to learn some manners. What were you, raised in a barn?" Except when she heard these words, they were accompanied by a frown, a slow shake of the head. However, when she says these words, they

are accompanied by a physical fury that is sudden and absolute. It is as if she is being electrocuted by her own emerging
nature.

"All right," Polly says, as if anything were up to her anymore, "we better get going. We can talk later."

"Leave me alone," Alice manages to say.

"Yeah, right," Polly says, unable to concede more than that.

"Don't ever hit me again," Alice says. The muscles in her
neck are painfully tight. She strokes them with an open hand,
lifting her chin, grimacing.

"Then keep away from Rodolfo!" Polly says, her own
courage and energy suddenly resurfacing.

Alice cannot think of what to say next, so she growls, moving still closer to Polly, baring her teeth.

"Freak," says Polly. "You're the worst." Yet she takes a step
away. They are off the paved walk now; she feels the scratch of
a shrub of some sort on her back.

Who is this girl? Who is this new Alice who lowers her
head, stretches her lips so even more of her teeth can show,
and who charges at Polly now? Once, in Cold Spring, she
accidentally stepped on a little toad, camouflaged and practically invisible in the leaf litter on the front porch. The poor
thing popped beneath the weight of her foot, and when she
jumped back in horror and looked down, it was dying, its
tiny front feet pressed together as if in prayer, a look of dis-
gust and resignation on its little face. That night she wept
in her bed, mourning the life she had accidentally taken,
promising herself that one day when she was grown and
on her own and had money and freedom, she would buy a
ranch or a farm or a mountain somewhere and make a sanc-
tuary for animals of all kinds. Was that girl—so tender, so

humane, so human—still within her? Or has she been swallowed whole—like a little fish consumed by a big fish—by the self she has so abruptly become?

A self that grabs Polly by the shoulders and twists her left and twists her right and twists her left again—with such force that Polly wonders if the top half of her is going to be torn from the bottom half. "Stop it," she shrieks as her feet lose their purchase on the ground and she falls first to her knees and then flat on her back. She is exposed. Her stomach, with its treasure trove of guts, her throat, and the thin, utterly vulnerable coating of skin that shields the major arteries.

She makes a quick calculation of her chances and decides her best hope for survival is to beg.

"Okay, okay, I'm sorry."

Looking at Alice's face, Polly is not at all certain Alice heard or understood what Polly said. Or if she cared.

"I'm sorry, I'm sorry," Polly says, her voice rising.

As if to try it out, curious, tentative, Alice scratches Polly's right cheek. She steps back, peers down, waiting to see the effect of what she has done. Three red lanes of welts rise on Polly's face, a superhighway carrying pain from the corner of her eye to her upper lip.

Using her other hand, Alice strikes again, gouging the left cheek. Polly screams in pain. She knows now that adopting a posture of surrender will not save her. The animal courtesy of sparing the vanquished will not apply in this situation. Alice is not enough of an animal, or she is the wrong kind of animal. Whatever. Polly scrambles up, staggering backward as she regains her footing, whirling her arms to get her balance.

It takes Alice a moment to realize that Polly is going to get away. She is already running before Alice starts to chase after her. Polly is fast. She is a beautiful runner. Her long legs. Her long braid. Her arms hanging limply at her sides.

Alice is fast too. But not as fast as Polly. She runs hunched forward, her arms extended, her fingers pointing down. It briefly crosses her consciousness—like a shooting star, only half seen—that she might do better if she dropped to all fours and ran like that.

They reach the part of the park where they first entered. Alice does not want Polly to get back to the apartment before she does, though she is not sure why. She wants to catch Polly, and she is not sure why that is either. She wants to hurt her, and again she is not sure why. But she does. She does. She wants to hurt her. She really does.

And then, just as suddenly as it appeared, the desire to hurt Polly disappears, leaving no more trace of itself than a burst soap bubble. Alice slows down, letting the distance between herself and Polly lengthen.

Polly senses she is no longer being chased. She allows herself to look back over her shoulder, and sure enough, there is Alice, immobile in a yellow pool of lamplight. Polly stops, turns completely. Why has Alice stopped? Oh, well, no time to think about that now. She turns again to resume her journey back to the apartment on Riverside and finds she is face-to-face with a man in a black T-shirt, a grown-up with a pale face, dead eyes, a short greasy nose.

"Time for your see-ya juice," he says. Hot-dog-onion-and-coffee breath. He reaches for her. He is quick. He knows what he is doing. She feels a sharp pinch between her shoulder blades. She steels herself, prepared for hideous pain. But she feels nothing. Well…a little something. But not too bad.

Oh…a little more. Trouble thinking. Her brain like a radio with the dial stuck between stations.

"Polly!" Alice shouts.

The man picks up Polly and slings her over his shoulder as if she weighed no more than a jacket. With a few quick, efficient steps, he is out of the park.

Alice is running as fast as she can, but she is too late. A van is waiting for him, the engine coughing, a plume of black smoke wagging its way out of the tailpipe. The man opens the back of the van, tosses Polly in. Alice now is just a few steps away, but the van speeds off. She chases after it, but it's hopeless. There is a dripping faucet painted on the side of the van. The windows in back have been painted black.

CHAPTER 16

It's 4:30 in the morning, the very quietest time in the park. The wind is almost nonexistent; the squirrels and the birds are two hours from running their rounds; the homeless human foragers have gathered up every can and bottle from the trash bins, the lawns, and the bushes and wheeled them away in creaking shopping carts. The troublemaking humans have already made their trouble. The spooning lovers have put a fork in it. The night-shift cops are comatose, and the day-shift hard-asses have yet to punch in. It is the ideal time to converge the packs and have a general meeting, but even if it weren't the ideal time, Rodolfo would have had to send out the word, because what had been, up till now, an ongoing crisis has become a flat-out emergency.

"You's listen now, me's quick," Rodolfo says from his perch on top of the slide at the Diana Ross Playground. His opening words are repeated by those closest to him, and then are repeated again and again as his message spreads out like ripples on a pond.

"Three hours," he says, and then points over his shoulder to indicate the past. "Polly." He stops, collects himself. It hurts to say her name. He knew it would—but not this much. "The

207

snatcher. Ours Alice"—he points to her, in the front of the pack—"her sees it. One man." He holds up a finger. "One truck. White. Words on the side." He looks questioningly down at Alice.

"Watertight," she says.

"Watertight," Rodolfo repeats, and waits until the word makes its journey to those standing farthest away.

"We's finding the man. We's finding the truck. We's getting us brothers and us sisters back to freedom." He waits for the message to be transmitted through the network of feral boys and girls.

"We's not asking for this," Rodolfo proclaims, placing his hand, with its long shapely fingers, over his heart. "We's never asking to be born, we's not asking, no, to be the way us is." He lets this travel back, waits for it to sink in. "But we's proud. We's not bad. We's not broken. We's not worse. We's better!"

The crowd begins to cheer even before this last proclamation is relayed. They stand on the rise, on benches, on rocks. The smaller ones sit on the shoulders of the tall and the broad. Long hair, short hair, tattoos, and piercings, some dressed so raggedly it is almost comical, some in shorts, some in expensive jeans stolen from expensive stores, some still wearing the remains of their old school uniforms—blazers with the crests torn off, ties repurposed as headbands, regulation-length skirts filthy with food, grass, and all the other detritus of an ad hoc way of life.

"We's better!" they cry out.

"We's best!" Rodolfo shouts. He raises his fists above his head.

"We's best!" the gathered packs cry back—and now their voices are raised and there is a tumult of sound.

"We have to go home," Adam whispers to Alice. They stand together in the front of the crowd. On one side of them is Boy-Boy, and Little Man is on the other. All the crew from Riverside are front row; their faces show signs of the deepest distress, a collective grief.

"We can't," says Alice.

"Alice. We have to. It's not fair."

"Fair," says Alice, shaking her head.

"Alice." He tugs at her arm.

She doesn't want to fight back. She doesn't want to feel anything like that in herself. Ever again. She feels something rising within her, something frightening and shameful. It is like she has two kinds of blood, one normal and warm, the other fierce and hot. She has fought and fought to keep this bad blood at bay, but she is getting tired. The fight is too hard, too constant, and she is thinking about giving it up. Giving it up and letting nature take its course.

"After this," she says.

"We have to go. Now."

"Okay." She looks up at Rodolfo, but he is no longer making eye contact with her. He is transported. The sight of all the packs together and in harmony, the sound of their voices rising up in the most beautiful howl of courage and togetherness, the joy of all that mixed with the sorrow of knowing that somewhere Polly is in trouble and suffering and scared... it is more than he can absorb. His eyes are glazed with wonder and an ever-mounting sense of his own power. These wild boys, these wild girls: they are not just people with whom he shares a difficult genetic fate—they are all extensions of him. He has become a multitude.

Alice and Adam slowly make their way to the edge of the

gathering, and their movement catches Rodolfo's eye. He turns quickly toward Alice and makes an exaggerated shrug.

Alice holds up one finger, as if to say she and her brother are just stepping out for a minute and will be right back.

They walk quickly, but in silence, not wanting to attract any attention. When they are fifty feet away from the playground, they walk in a diagonal, heading north by northeast, toward the East Side, uptown, and home.

Adam is the first to speak. "You slept in his room."

"Not really," Alice says. "I think we should go back."

"We are going back."

"I mean back to the place. Back to the other kids."

"We can't."

"Why not?"

"Because it's mean." He pulls out his phone, shows it to her. "I already texted Mom and said we were coming home."

Alice is silent. At last, she says, "You call her Mom?"

Adam doesn't bother to answer.

A few steps later, Alice says, "And you call it home."

"She is our mother now. And it is our home. It's where we live. It's where we always have lived, just about. I don't like that apartment over there. It's noisy, it's dirty, you can't even dry yourself after you take a shower, and there's blood and needles everywhere. They're all going to get in trouble."

"That's baby talk," Alice says. "We're going to get in trouble," she says in a high mincing voice.

"You'll see," Adam says.

"You're not smarter than me," Alice says.

"I know."

"So don't act like you are."

There is a tremor of true irritation in her voice, and Adam

glances at her uneasily. After a few moments, he says, "I can hardly wait to get home."

"Then let's go," Alice says. She starts to run, and Adam keeps up with her. They are running side by side. Crocodile clouds glide by the moon, snapping idly at its fullness as they drift from west to east. A searchlight from somewhere arcs across the dark gray starless sky. Alice runs faster and faster, and Adam matches her step for step. A sense of relief fills both of them. It just feels so good to run, to feel their muscles warm, to have their lungs fill with the heavy summer air. Faster and faster. They are smiling now. Alice reaches out her hand, and Adam takes it. She bends a little at the waist, and he does too. She loosens her grip on his hand and reaches forward with both arms, bending lower as she does. He watches her and his own actions exactly mirror hers.

"You want to try it?" she asks.

"Okay," he says. "Just once."

A moment later, they are both running on all fours, racing their way home faster than they ever imagined.

Cynthia doesn't know what to do about the twins. She doesn't know what to do about her children. Her children. The more she repeats those two words, the less sense they make. Once, in San Francisco, in what now seems like a former incarnation, she had been seeing a man who was a corporate recruiter, and when he wanted to make her believe that she didn't know what she was talking about or when she was expressing what was to him an unacceptable opinion, he would say, "Uh, I think that's a bit above your pay grade." (It was the number two reason she stopped seeing him; number one being his strutting around her apartment naked except for his knee-high black socks.) But now, in her solitude and disorientation, she thinks that yes, when it comes to mothering Alice and Adam, she may be above her pay grade.

They have come home. She is sitting with them in the kitchen, watching them eat—which, today, basically means watching them not eat. Morning sun streams through the windows, igniting bursts of light on the handle of the Sub-Zero refrigerator, the dials of the stainless-steel La Cornue stove, and the backs of the spoons the twins idly move around and around and around their bowls of granola. They look tired. They are filthy. And, quite frankly, though Cynthia hates to think it, they don't smell very good. Actually, they stink. Of sweat. Of dirt. Of wildness, wind, and heat.

What to do? How to relate to the fact that they disappeared and cast her into a chaos of fright and despair? She wonders if she should scold them—they surely deserve to be scolded. They deserve to be put into a time machine and sent back a hundred years so they can be soundly spanked! And yet, they did come back on their own, and isn't positive reinforcement better? If they come to associate returning to their home with punishment or scolding or even dark looks, who is to say that they will return home the next time, or the time after that? Isn't it her job to teach them that this house is a place of safety (*Is it?* she wonders in passing), a place where it is cool in the summer and warm in the winter and where there is always good food and clean sheets and state-of-the-art televisions sucking in the signals of premium cable?

So no, she decides, no—she will not punish, she will not scold.

Should she even ask them where they have been? Surely, she has a right to know that—and a duty. She needs to know where they went, in case it is a place of danger or disease. And also it would be good to know in case they ever pull a disappearing act again—she will know where to start looking for them, at least, rather than having to wonder which of the city's five million doors to look behind. And yet—here comes that cursed *and yet* again—wouldn't it be a hundred times better if she were to wait it out a bit and let them volunteer the information? Wouldn't that really be the way to go? In the long run, isn't it more important to build trust than to maintain discipline? And a parent, she reminds herself, must in all situations think of the long run, because raising kids is not a sprint, not a dash, it's a marathon, a marathon plus a mountain climb plus a potato-sack race plus a rodeo plus a bungee jump plus a sail around the Cape of Good Hope in a little sea-battered skiff without a compass, without a map, and with only the stars to guide you. *Yes, that is what a parent does,* she thinks, *and apparently I am a parent.*

But ought she just sit there in silence? She worries. (Oh, if only the turbines of worry could be harnessed, she could generate enough power to light the city and have enough left over to send across the Palisades and into New Jersey!) She worries that her silence will be misinterpreted—though she is not sure what she means by *misinterpreted,* since she herself does not know what her silence means, or is meant to mean. More worries! She worries that they will take her silence for indifference. Or they may decide that an immense choking fury has rendered her unable to speak. Or they may decide that she is silent because she is afraid of them. Who knows what kinds of ideas get into the heads of twelve-year-olds? Especially twelve-year-olds who happen to be twins; twelve-year-olds who lost both of their parents within a week of each other; twelve-year-olds

213

who were raised in utter splendor and luxury and then, after living like rich kids, spent two years in foster care; twelve-year-olds—and let's not forget this last salient point—who spent years locked into bedrooms at night and who finally caught on to the unspeakable truth of their parents' forbidden appetites, appetites that, in the end, could only be satisfied by having the twins themselves as a midnight meal.

And then there is the thing she cannot bear to think. That they are beyond repair. That the fertility treatment that pushed their parents into a nightmare existence has left its rancid residue in Alice and Adam. She tries to push it away but it keeps coming back. And every hour the twins are away, it gets stronger—the only real explanation for the children's behavior is that slowly, inexorably, they are turning into their parents. All the love she has for them are just tears in the ocean...

No. She won't allow it. She knows that some of the offspring of the parents who went to Slovenia have gone...what? Feral? Is it fair to call a child a little wild animal? Some of them. But not all of them. Not. All. Of. Them. And she *knows* these two. She can feel their goodness, their sweetness. They may be drawn to wild kids but they are not wild themselves. Of this she is certain. Her task will be to make sure, as much as she can, that they steer clear of bad influences.

"Kids," she finally says. She doesn't know where to go with this, but she does know how to put one foot in front of the other and trust her heart to somehow keep her on the right path. "Kids, you know I love you, don't you?"

"We know," says Alice.

"And we love you too, Mom," says Adam.

Cynthia forces herself to maintain a calm maternal demeanor, though hearing Adam say that they love her makes her want to pitch forward, rest her head on her forearm, and sob. That, she feels, would not be helpful or good in any way—and to that, there is no *and yet.*

"Well, we need to keep working it out," Cynthia says. *Am I twelve-stepping them? "It works if you work it"?* "We're still getting used to each other. And we need to set some…rules."

"Why don't you just come out and say what you want to say," Alice says in an unpleasant voice. Not quite bratty, not quite mean—exasperated, as if she has been humoring Cynthia and now has reached her limit.

"She is," Adam interjects. He gives his sister an imploring look.

"Well, I'll tell you one thing," Cynthia says without quite considering it. "That trip to Mount Washington I was going to take us on? I don't really see that happening, not any time soon."

"Oh, wow," says Alice, holding her heart as if it were breaking.

"What I am saying is this." Cynthia hears her voice, calm and confident, and thinks: *Hey, this is me.* "You guys just absolutely, one hundred percent cannot leave the house without telling me you're leaving and telling me where you're going."

"So are we prisoners here?" Alice asks.

"Don't," Adam says.

"Maybe love is a little bit of a prison," Cynthia says. "When you're in a family—like we are, kids, right?—you get love and protection and all kinds of material things and things that just can't really be put into words. And in return, you give up some of your freedom. You're not just living for yourself. You're connected to other people. Is that really being in prison? I don't know. There's an old song called 'Chains of Love.' Maybe that's what you're talking about?" She regrets turning that last statement into a question, that fatal girlie-girlie interrogative lilt. And she particularly regrets referencing "Chains of Love." She doesn't want to be one of those mothers who are constantly trying to have their Cool Cards punched. She takes a breath. She feels a weird, destabilizing rush of anxiety. It's like being on a date and working yourself up into a frenzy over whether you are talking too much, making the person across the table from you like you either more or a great deal less.

"We won't do it again," Adam says.

Alice looks away. Her expression is contemptuous.

What is she thinking? Cynthia wonders.

Cynthia folds her hands, leans forward. Without having planned it, she has embarked on a line of inquiry that she is going to follow without regard to where it is heading, what it might accomplish. Will it do more harm than good? She really cannot say, but she will nevertheless go forward.

"Won't do what again, Adam? That's something I need to know—because right now, I don't know where you went, or why, or anything, really."

Alice is the one who speaks up, and she does so quickly. It's clear she doesn't want Adam to answer this question. She has lost faith in him. "We walked Dylan home."

"Dylan?" says Cynthia, her voice rising. She reins herself in, as if she were both horse and rider. "The whole city is looking for that boy. The police. Everyone."

"Oh?" says Alice. "Why?"

"Because he's the mayor's little boy."

Alice laughs. "Oh, that's just something he says. He's just a kid."

"Alice, come on."

"Well, how are we supposed to know?" Alice says. She acts as if she is being relentlessly questioned, as if out of nowhere and for no good reason, she is being persecuted and, even worse, even more hurtful and unjust, doubted.

"I guess he is," Adam says softly.

"You guess he is?" says Cynthia. The panicked horse she rides threatens to rear up and wave its front hooves in the air.

"I guess so," Adam says.

Alice breathes out a disgusted sigh and pushes her chair back from the table.

Is she getting ready to make a run for it? wonders Cynthia.

"His dad is mean," Adam says. "His parents are like ours used to be."

"Mayor Morris?" Cynthia is amazed. She is new in town, of course, and does not have strong feelings about any of the city's leaders, but the impression she has of the mayor is that he's a self-regarding but basically decent guy, not subject to short-man syndrome, like many of the pipsqueaks she has known in her life. To think of him and his seldom-seen wife, Claudia, herself a diminutive woman, half bouffant, half Italian heels, going through the same dreadful, filthy, insane fertility injections Leslie and that horrible Alex submitted to…

"You know half the city is looking for him," Cynthia says. "Right, kids? You know that, don't you?"

Alice picks up her spoon. She holds it as if it were a knife, something with which she was planning to harm…someone. She takes a deep, unsteady breath and plops it back into the bowl, upsetting the bowl and spilling milky granola across the table. It looks as if she is about to say she is sorry, but something stops her. She rises from her seat and glares at Cynthia.

"We went to the park with him, okay?"

"You weren't in the park all this time, Alice. I know it."

"So?"

"Come on, Alley-Oop," Cynthia says, her voice lowering.

"I hate that name," Alice says. "Don't ever call me that again."

"All right, I won't. But it's important to me—"

"It's always about what's important to you," cries Alice. "What about us? We have things that are important to us, you know."

"That's fine, Alice." *Now what do I say?* Cynthia wonders. She has been following a line of questioning like a path through the woods, but suddenly the path is gone, and all there is are trees, bushes, rocks, here and there a little patch of sky. "I'm not saying your stuff is unimportant." Her voice falters. "Your stuff is absolutely important."

"We met kids we knew from before," Alice says quietly. "We hung out with them."

"Are they your friends, Alice? Adam?"

"Kind of," Adam says.

"Did one of your friends come to this house and take clothing from your room?"

Alice just stares at Cynthia. Adam shrugs.

"What's happening here, kids?" Cynthia says. "Come on. Where are we going with all this? What will happen to us if this is how we're going to treat each other?"

"I don't know!" Alice almost screams the words. She turns and makes her way out of the kitchen.

Cynthia is not thinking of anything. There is no strategy, and there is no on-the-one-hand-this-and-on-the-other-hand-that. She bolts from her chair and reaches Alice before the frail little thing can get very far. She catches the child by the shoulders and turns her around. Alice struggles, but her strength is down; she is exhausted, hungry, frightened. She squirms, pushes, but Cynthia's grip on her is strong.

"Shhh, shhh," Cynthia says, as millennia of mothers before her have crooned to distraught children. She holds Alice, pets her, feels the child slowly relaxing.

At last, Cynthia relaxes her own hold, but as soon as the embrace lessens, Alice burrows deeper into her, grasping at her with sudden fervor.

"Don't," the child says. "Tighter. Hold me tighter. Please don't let me go."

CHAPTER 17

The woman who called herself Bree, and sometimes Tracy, and sometimes Submissive Sara had a real name, of course, and that was Jeanette Tomczak. She was born thirty-one years ago in Harrisburg, Pennsylvania, the third daughter of a ruddy-faced postal worker named Kathy who thought something was wrong with you if you weren't grinning from ear to ear, and a livestock auctioneer named Henry who could say 315 words a minute when it came to raising the price of a calf or a set of tractor tires but who barely uttered a sound once he was home and parked in his chair. Jeanette will never make it out of Dennis Keswick's apartment, and certain details of her life are noted here out of respect. She loved music. She had a collection of eight-track tapes, cassettes, and CDs. She held on to them all, as best she could within her disordered life. Even when a kind of media became obsolete, she kept it because she could not bear to throw away something upon which music was recorded. (She had no way of playing her eight-track tapes, but how in the world could she consign the Pointer Sisters to the garbage can?) She loved Chinese food, especially sweet-and-sour chicken. She was afraid of dogs. She wrote down her dreams in a large spiral notebook and often at the end of a working day would go over them, years' worth, and discern patterns in them, patterns that edged up to the very cusp of revelation and then slowly backed away into obscurity. She was tough. She didn't save her money—it's tricky to hold on to dough when it's all in cash. She didn't take particularly good care of herself. She gained weight. Her face became ruddy, like her mother's. Still, she had a long run, compared to others, but by the time she went out to Dennis's apartment, she was on the downward slope, professionally speaking. The escort service kept her on for old times' sake and sent her out if a client called and wanted someone right away and no one else was available or if some low-roller in one of the outer boroughs needed to get off. The thousand-dollar gigs at the Plaza Hotel were not for her; she was doing the thirty-minute mercy calls in Sunnyside, Queens. She didn't sweat it. She knew she was on her way out, and it was just as well. Since she couldn't quit the Life, the Life would quit her. She had an optimistic nature. She never stopped believing that one day she would move back to Pennsylvania, marry, and have children.

Jeanette had under three hundred dollars in the bank and, aside from clothing, very few possessions. But she did have the gift of friendship, and of her many friends, none was more loyal than Portia Ramirez, who also went by the names Taco Belle, Karmen, Chiquita, and, on busy weekends, Submissive Sara—there were actually four Submissive Saras at Nite Movz, the escort service for which Jeanette and Portia worked. In the pecking order of Nite Movz, Portia was roughly halfway between the high-priced girls who were quite young, many of them just starting off their lives as prostitutes, and the older women like Jeanette.

On the night Jeanette disappeared, she and Portia were to meet at three in the morning at a diner on the corner of 107th and Broadway. Portia's cousin Seny had suddenly left New York, taking with her only a few precious things and leaving behind two closets filled with clothes. Seny was always on a diet and had in the past five years weighed anywhere from 120 to 200 pounds. What this meant for someone going through her hundreds of pieces of abandoned clothing was this: There was sure to be something in the right size.

Portia was on time for their rendezvous. She took a booth with a view of Broadway, looked at what was left of humanity at this hour, and slowly nursed an iced tea and an order of fries. Twenty minutes passed, and no Jeanette. (She was still technically alive; Dennis was crouched over her, naked and tumescent, trying to get his mind to work in a rational way while he figured out what to do next.) Portia broke her French fries in half to make them last longer—a trick learned in poverty and maintained as a way of keeping in reasonable shape. Thirty minutes, forty. It was not unusual for people in the Life to run late. You'd never want to try to go to the movies with any of them, or catch a train. The shelter and security of an everyday, straight-edge, nine-to-five-house-in-the-suburbs-picket-fence-401(k) life was not available to any of them, so why pay the price that all the good little boys and girls willingly forked over for a life of no worries? Why make a big deal about being punctual if life was not going to keep its side of the bargain? Talk about being played; talk about sucker punches. And so when a full hour passed and Jeanette did not show, and when Portia called Jeanette's cell and it went straight to voice mail, Portia was not particularly concerned. And she was not in the least bit angry. Maybe, Portia thought, she got another booking. Maybe she was tired and went straight home and went to sleep. Jeanette was an epic sleeper; once she was out, it took a bomb to awaken her.

The next day was a busy one for Portia and she more or less forgot about Jeanette. The day after was busy too, but not as bad, and Portia remembered to call Jeanette's cell, and once again it went straight to voice mail. She texted her, waited. She was in a taxi on her way downtown to see a regular customer on Tenth Street, and she rode with the phone in her hand, resting on her knees, staring down at it, willing Jeanette to answer. Of course there was no answer. Portia finished up with Tenth Street—rushed service, to say the least—and as soon as she could called Carol, who managed Nite Movz from four to four, working the phones and matching the johns to the girls and, as they say, vice versa. Carol had been working at Movz for five years. Salary, commissions, and bonuses appeared in cash in an envelope every Friday morning. She didn't know who owned the operation. No one did. When she had a problem or a question, she dealt with a Korean named David Kwan, but he wasn't in charge of things any more than she was. He was just a spoke at a different part of the wheel.

Now, two days after that, Portia and three other Nite Movz employees, Doris (Dee, Dee-lite, Deirdre), Sue (Samantha, Sindy, Submissive Sara), and Luis, are deep in Brooklyn's back pocket, standing in front of a pitiful apartment house on Ocean Parkway, home to Carl Ravenswood. Portia had to break her ass to get this address. Carol had gone from "I don't know where Jeanette is," to "We had to let Jeanette go," to "I'm furious with her, she can't treat people this way," to "Okay, here was her last appointment," to "You want to talk to him, then talk to him, but be nice and don't make trouble because he's sort of a regular."

Hundreds of people live in that apartment building, its bricks the color of thoroughly chewed gum. Portia and the others stand in the lobby. Smells of disinfectant, someone's last-minute cig. Buzzer system, countless nipple-y buttons like the left side of the world's largest accordion. Portia runs her finger up and down, looking for the name. Ravenswood, Ravenswood. People coming and going, mostly old, sneaky-looking, even the guys in yarmulkes skulking around like illegal immigrants. After a while, a good-looking young lesbian with a dachshund comes out, wearing cargo pants, tank top, earbuds, and carrying a shit bag—she takes one look at Portia and her friends and makes them, no questions asked, none needed. Drugs, robbery, or prostitution. Whatever. Isn't that what they say? Whatever? Whatevs?

"Here he is," Portia says, finally locating Ravenswood, way up there on the ninth floor.

"Let's do this thing," says Luis.

Portia buzzes, waits. Nothing. Buzzes again. More nothing, but even more nothing-y the second time around. She pretends to know Morse code and gives his intercom nine floors up a lengthy series of short and long buzzes, buzzes that say, she imagines, *Open up and meet your Maker!*

A middle-aged woman, chunky and tan, shameless in shorts and a skimpy shirt, comes into the lobby eating from a big bag of Golden Spring organic potato chips. She lets herself in with a key, and before the glass-and-metal door can close behind her, Sue (who is quick, with reflexes like a mousetrap) slips in behind her and holds the door open for the rest of them.

They ride up with the potato-chip lady, who seems nervous in their company. Each time she takes a handful of chips, she rolls the bag tightly closed, as if this were it, her last potato-chip indulgence of the day. But as soon as she swallows one haul, she unrolls the bag and dips her hand in for the next. She gets out on the seventh floor, and Portia and her friends have a good laugh at her expense. Portia knows it's low to laugh at fat people, or at anyone, really, but it always strikes her as funny that you can be any kind of freak, greasy and fat and a fright to the eyes, and still you're more respectable than a well-toned, clean, nicely dressed person who makes her living giving people sex.

The elevator door opens on the ninth floor. Ravenswood's apartment is two doors away. Portia stops Luis from knocking. She puts her ear to the door.

Sure enough, the little *maricón* is in there. She can hear him singing along to some crazy song on the radio. "Ooo, e, ooh ah ah, ting tang, walla walla bing bang."

She gestures to the door, looking up quizzically at Luis. He frowns and strokes his chin like a doctor considering the symptoms of a hard-to-diagnose patient. He crouches, looks more intently at the door handle, gives it a gentle turn, another. He stands up, a look of mastery on his face.

"Ridiculous," he says, pulling an old Macy's credit card out of his back pocket.

"Wait," says Doris. "We can't just—"

Portia lays a silencing finger across her lips, her eyes sternly narrowing.

"I'm out of here," whispers Sue. "This is nuts."

Portia waves them over to a spot farther from the door.

"She's in there," Portia says. Her passion is such that even whispering, she seems to be shouting. "Tied up, maybe. Who the fuck knows? Something. What if it was you, Doris? Or you, Sue? Or any of us? Wouldn't you want someone to do something? Or would you just want everyone sitting around with their thumbs up their asses?"

"That costs extra," Doris says, and they all laugh, breaking the tension.

"Ready?" Luis says, twirling his Macy's card on his fingertips, making it travel from thumb to pinkie, like a magician with the ace of hearts.

"Arthur?" Cynthia says, grasping the phone, leaning forward, amazed that he has taken her call. "Look, I'm sorry about—"

"It's okay," Arthur says. "What's the situation?"

"They're back. They're here." She is sitting in the main parlor; she gestures vaguely up to the third floor, where the twins are resting. Or so she hopes.

"Well, then," Arthur says, his tone adding: *Then let's hear no more about it.*

"Don't ask me where they were."

"I wasn't planning to."

Cynthia knows she is being insulted, but she is not in a position to take offense. Best to breeze right past it.

"I need to ask you a question."

"Go on."

"A legal question."

"So I would assume."

"I want to put the house on the market."

"The house? What house?"

"This house." She takes a breath. "My house."

There is a silence as he takes this in.

"Well, of course you understand that that is complicated. Do you understand that, Cynthia?"

Oh my God, you condescending prick. But she again feigns tone-deafness and speaks to him as if he were decent and well-meaning.

"I believe I do. It's complicated. And to be honest, I didn't pay too much attention to the clauses and subclauses. I never for a moment dreamed I would want to leave this place, or live anywhere else, or take the children away."

"The house belongs to them, Cynthia."

"I realize that."

"Their mother's will was quite explicit."

"I'm their mother, Arthur."

"Yes. Of course. Their previous mother. Their birth mother."

"So what are we talking about here, Arthur? The house has to have some liquidity." Yes: take that! *Liquidity.* She slapped the word onto the table like a trump card. Did he think she knew nothing, that running an antiques business in San Francisco—with all that competition—for fourteen years had taught her zilch?

"Of course it does, Cynthia." She can hear it in his voice. Her saying *liquidity* has lanced the boil of sarcasm. "I'm just saying it's complicated."

"Well, complicated doesn't bother me, Arthur. Complicated is like a lovely massage and a box of strawberries compared to what's been going on. I have to get them out of here. It's something I must do, I simply must. I want to sell this place, find somewhere to live, and get these kids out of this city as soon as possible. It's not safe here, Arthur."

"In New York? I'm surprised to hear you say that. Mayor Morris—"

"Don't get me started on Mayor Morris. I mean here, in this house." She stops, listens. What is that sound?

Breathing?

A carpenter someplace or other, sawing away at a two-by-four?

No. It's the rats in the cellar. Maybe in the walls. Working. Working.

She checks her watch. She has called the exterminators twice already. They keep promising to come. She's afraid to call again, afraid of alienating them and having them dilly-dally even more blatantly as a way of putting her in her place.

She taps her fingers on the phone. A feeling has taken hold of her—she is not alone. *Stop being stupid, you've got enough problems.* She sits straighter in her chair and peeks around its winged back.

Alice.

Standing there. Her eyes burning with indignation. She has visited the kitchen; she holds a roast beef sandwich in one hand, fantastically overstuffed, the edge of the meat bright red, as if the poor cow had just been butchered.

Without knowing what she is doing, operating on a fusion of fear and instinct, Cynthia hangs up the phone.

"Your frightened me," she says to her daughter. "You can't go sneaking up on people like that."

"We're not moving," Alice says. Her voice is foggy.

"I'm glad you're getting something to eat, honey. You need to eat."

"We're not moving," Alice repeats.

"Just eat slowly. And...you know. Give yourself time to di-gest."

"This is our home," Alice says. "You can't make us leave." And with that, she turns to leave. As she is making her way to the main staircase, she opens her hand and lets the sandwich fall to the floor.

This is hopeless, thinks Cynthia, knowing that hopelessness is the greatest, the least forgivable, sin.

*   *   *

Getting into Ravenswood's apartment was the easy part. Now Portia, Luis, Doris, and Sue have to find a way of getting out. He was completely ready for them when they entered his apartment, greeted them with a handgun pointed directly at them, and, moving quickly, he stuck each of them with a big dose of see-ya juice. And then the little bastard just stood there with a cockeyed smile, scratching his chin with the barrel of his .44, his toe tapping, watching them like they were something on TV as first one and then the next and the next and the next buckled at the knees and hit the floor, like apples falling out of the bottom of a wet paper bag.

Now they are coming to in roughly the order in which they were stuck. He didn't use a syringe. He just slapped them on the back, touched them on the upper arms; Doris got hers in the ass. He was a blur of action. He was good at this. A needle the size of the business end of a thumbtack pricked their skin, and that was all she wrote; it was good night and good luck, it was welcome to the darkness, darling, it was Nite Movz to the nth degree.

But the worst part was waking up. Not one of them has an idea of how long they've been out. Dennis has handcuffed them all together, wrist to ankle, turning them into a sixteen-limbed pile of We're fucked. One can't move without hurting another—those cuffs are steely and stern and seem to hate skin and bone with a passion—and one can't be hurt without moving. It doesn't take them long to learn they must be absolutely still, even though none of them are in position's that are in any way comfortable—or even tolerable.

"And to what do I owe this pleasure?" Dennis asks, addressing them all. He is seated comfortably in his one good chair, which he has dragged into the center of the room in front of the human pile he has created. At his feet are two duffel bags, brightly colored, one orange, the other yellow, both stuffed to bursting.

He waits for an answer, and when none is forthcoming, he points to Portia, randomly.

"We're looking for our friend," Portia says. The only way she knows how to make her voice meek and cooperative is to speak very softly.

"Your friend?" says Dennis as if the concept were somewhat new to him, full of delicious comic possibilities.

"She came here," says Portia.

"Oh, did she?" He stands up, grabs the bags. His T-shirt rises, showing a bit of belly and the gun tucked into the waistband of his pants. "Well," he says, "I can't say I have any memory of that."

"Her name was Bree," Portia says, her courage returning.

Dennis laughs.

"What is so funny?" Portia says. Her anger forces her to move, and there is a chorus of complaint from the people to whom she has been chained.

"Oh, nothing, really," Dennis says. "It's just…I don't know. Bree. It's such a cheesy name." His laugh is hearty now. Like a mad devil, he tilts his head and roars with merriment.

He shifts his duffel bags and gazes around the apartment, bidding it a fond farewell. *What a shitbox,* he thinks. It's good to be leaving it behind. The long commute. The cramped quarters. The idiotic neighbors. The kitchen in name only. The constant whine of traffic from Ocean Parkway. Ocean Parkway! Where was the goddamned ocean? He could not see it; he could not smell it; it gave absolutely no evidence of itself.

His new place, once found, would have at least a river view. The mighty Hudson! Or maybe down there on the South Street Seaport. Or in one of those big shiny buildings on Third Avenue within eyeshot of the East River. In the meantime, he'll be staying in a hotel. Let the landlord of this place, the classless place, so insanely beneath him, let the greedy old fuck beat the bushes in search of Mr. Ravenswood, who, ladies and gentlemen, is about to—before your very eyes!—disappear into thin air.

"Be good, guys," Dennis says, heading for the door. "Don't do anything I wouldn't do. Oh, and if anyone needs to use the facilities, they're right over there, second door to the right. Try not to look in the tub!"

CHAPTER 18

Rodolfo is beset with worries. So many worries! He cannot organize his mind and figure out which of his worries is most pressing, which worry to worry about first, which is second, third, which can safely be put aside for some future time. The worries are like huge waves that come from all directions, and his mind is a little ship constructed out of Popsicle sticks, out of paper, out of dreams.

He is not stupid. No one who oversees a band of outcasts, finding actual indoor shelter for some, reminding the others of their responsibility toward one another; who keeps the peace among boys and girls who nearly 100 percent of health-care, educational, social work, and psychiatric professionals would deem incorrigible and unreachable, untreatable and undeserving of a minute's freedom; who is basically president of a nation of outcasts, with some disappearing and some reproducing (and what is being reproduced is not really a reproduction in the strictest sense but a furtherance, another rung up or down the evolutionary ladder); who runs an underground enterprise with an ever-increasing cash flow, who oversees the quality of the product they sell and who, unlike many CEOs whose pictures are snapped at celebrity balls or on their yachts bobbing sunnily off some Greek isle, never allows greed and the pursuit of profit to get in the way of quality control or any other good business practice—no, no sixteen-year-old boy with Rodolfo's cares and responsibilities can be called stupid.

He is merely overwhelmed.

The disappearance of Polly has destabilized his household.

The defection of Alice has destabilized *him*.

Central Park, 8:00 p.m. The summer sky is blue and purple on the east side. To the west, however, the light still lingers, smoky pastels and a sinking red sun—it looks like a blanket hanging in some tourist shop in Arizona. Every once in a while, one of the windows in the big Fifth Avenue apartments will flash red as the sun reflects way across the park to the east side. One by one, the trees dissolve into the darkness.

The police are still maintaining the fiction that the two cops were mauled by a pack of wild dogs, and there are signs posted on the trees, yellow plastic with black lettering, warning people: Park Closed—Wild Dogs—Danger. Yellow tape and sawhorses block the roads going in and out of the park, east and west, north and south, around and around: all blocked, forbidden; what a laugh it is for the wild children. The dogs who once pranced through the park with their proud owners can now only look longingly at the deserted acres of hill and dale while they are leash-walked along the park's periphery. They whimper, they strain; the squirrels look down on them from the sycamores, oaks, and maples, safe at last from constant harassment by these well-fed beasts when they, the bushy rodents, are only trying to do their *job*. But the dog owners know that dogs do not make good decisions. Word is that the police will shoot to kill any dog they see in Central Park— border terriers, borzois, dogs in booties, dogs with rhinestone collars; none will be spared. What's next? Rodolfo and his kind wonder. Open season on cats? Peregrine falcons? The police are lying and Rodolfo knows why, they all know, all the crews, every last one of them. The powers that run the town don't want to say that two of New York's Finest succumbed to a pack of teenagers. They don't want to say that some of the wealthier citizens of the greatest city on earth shot themselves up with a mix of ingredients that jump-started their reproductive engines and that in quite a few of the cases things took an unexpected turn. (Talk about dogs making bad decisions; couples longing to be pregnant can make some doozies as well.) They don't want to say that each and every one of the wild children living in the park and in a few other of the city's nooks and crannies—some of them not quite children anymore, a few even with children of their own—are there because they were not safe at home. Not safe! That's putting it mildly. At home, under the roofs of their loving parents, they would have perished. And the cops will definitely not say (Rodolfo is not certain if they even *know*) that in that pack of outcast children is Dylan Morris, who, if anyone bothered to ask him (the other wild children don't have to make inquiries; they know), would burn the ears off the average listener with tales of his life at Gracie Mansion, the city's official home for its mayors. In that mansion, where his parents managed to create an aura of privacy where other mayors and their families had submitted to the public nature of the place, with its security guards and CCTV and aides at all hours and always a repair or a renovation under way, here in these rooms, he learned to dread the hour growing later, dread the inevitable moment when his parents' desire reached critical mass, and they started in on each other, acknowledging his existence only inasmuch as they hollered, *Leave us alone for a while.* They were intermittently aware of Dylan's presence but never of his proximity. If he was in the next room hearing every grunt, hearing the squish and thump of their hideous union, they seemed none the wiser. He compulsively wandered into his mother's bath, as if in a trance, and saw the evidence of her desperate depilatory efforts—the heaps of Lady Schick razors, the pots of bleach, the strips of waxing adhesive with her dark hair clinging to the amber gum, like insects infesting the rinds of a melon—but if she was in any way aware that he witnessed what she had to do to make herself presentable, if she had of any knowledge of his invasion of her most tragic privacy, she gave no indication. There was a lack of consistency, not unheard-of in most households, but here it was more costly. He would be hurried out of the room if his parents felt a quarrel coming on or if they wanted to show their affection for each other by wrestling on the floor. But somehow, it did not occur to them that little Dylan ought to be protected from watching them eat—the less said about this, the better: The man *is* the mayor of New York City, and the woman *is* the city's First Lady.

But Dylan did not join Rodolfo and the feral boys and girls because he was repelled by his parents. He ran because he was frightened. He ran because he feared for his life. Like so many of the others who quickly became his friends, his new family, the human levee that protected him from the rising waters of oblivion, Dylan ran because he overheard his parents, Mommy, Daddy, his havens in a heartless world, heard them agonizing over how terrible they felt about wanting to devour him. We've all heard parents *kvelling* over their offspring, saying, *You're so cute, I could eat you up.* Well, Mayor and Mrs. Morris meant it.

They were not dealing in metaphor or hyperbole. This was not a figure of speech. And Dylan knew it. And most of his new friends knew it about their parents too.

Rodolfo has slipped into the park undetected by anyone, even around the perimeter, all along the wall separating Central Park West (and its apartment buildings with a thousand eyes) from the park itself. Wherever he goes, he looks for that Watertight truck. He has already figured out what he will do when he finally finds it—he will follow it and discover where it takes the kids it collects. He will run behind it at an easy lope. Upright all the way.

He will find them. He will save them. How? Here, he's not so sure. But it can be done.

It may be time to arm the troops. Rodolfo has secreted quite a bit of money away. Real money, a serious sum. Some of it right here in Central Park. Several months organizing Zoom sales around the city—it gives a boy access to other illegal activities. Oh, the things he knows. Where the brothels are, the loft on Watt Street where rich men and women watch kickboxers from Southeast Asia fight to the death—though Rodolfo has also heard complaints, bitter complaints, that the deaths are faked. He knows who sells passports and for how much. He knows who will buy a kidney, a chunk of liver, the promise of a heart. And he knows where he can buy weapons: automatic rifles, handguns. There is even a Zoom customer, a skinny little guy with a long waxed mustache like two question marks, who can hook Rodolfo up with a flamethrower, not new, but still functional.

He walks through the park, from shadow to shadow. All of a sudden—it is like an abrupt shift in the weather, when the wind changes and the temperature plunges ten degrees—

he is beset with the most terrible sense of loneliness. The darkness, the caution, the underlying sense of fear: It reminds him of home. Home! He is now the head of a vast, mad, endangered family — Boy-Boy, Dee-Dee, Little Man, on and on — but every now and then comes the taste of the purest, most unendurable longing for his old house, his old room, the sights from his bedroom window, the smell of the carpets, the urgent sound of the telephone in the hall, its echoing ring, and even for his parents, who were so mad, and so dangerous. He forgives them. He realizes that they were as screwed as he was, realizes that they could not help themselves, they were blitzed, they were blotto, they were as gone as gone can be, they were the original Zoom heads before there was Zoom. He can still recall their touch, the way they petted him, coddled him. His father used to put him right on top of his head, walk around like that, with little Rodolfo balanced there, hanging on to Daddy's ears. *How do you like my new hat?* Sometimes it was just too much. *Get away, get away,* Rodolfo would squeal, a little two-year-old touch-me-not. Oh, he wishes he could have a shot at those paternal caresses now. Before biochemistry had its ruthless way with his parents, before nature, dormant for a while after the injections, came roaring back. Back then, in that gauzy, barely remembered paradise called *before.*

Rodolfo stops, startled. His cheeks are wet. He did not realize it straight off — he's crying! He thinks he should slap some sense into himself. But then he thinks better of it. Just let it out. Don't keep it bottled up. Lighten the load. Where's the harm?

But there is most certainly harm, because what he lets out is not just a little sniffle of sadness. This is no common cold of teenage angst. This is a raging malaria of grief. This is a sadness that twists the guts and weakens the knees. He sees a bench and realizes that, whatever the risks, he must sit.

It is not only that he is sitting on a bench, which is a dicey enough thing to do in this locked-down park where cops and who knows who else are on the lookout for lawless boys whose description Rodolfo fits to a proverbial T, but, to make matters worse, he is sitting on a bench right next to a streetlamp. He sits there, dramatically lit, as if this were a play and a stage set, and for this scene of sadness and regret, Rodolfo is lit like an actor.

He is leaning forward. His elbows are on his knees, his hands are molded to his face as he weeps into them. His tears follow the pathways of the lines in his palms. It has been nearly six years since he saw his mother and father. He refuses now to call them his family. That would be too much. It's hard enough: Mom, Dad. But *family* means something different now, something that has taken the place of his former life on Seventy-Seventh Street. Family is on Riverside Drive. Family is in this very park, or Washington Square, or Carl Schurz Park. Family is selling Zoom down in Gramercy. Riding the elevator with a backpack full of the red. So no, he does not, will not, cannot think of them as family, or even say the word. But he does manage those two old words, *Mom, Dad.* And they take him by surprise. It's an ambush, a self-ambush. And it's really too much for him. He is wired to run, to hide, to take, to lead, but not for this: He is not wired to feel. He is not wired to grieve. *Mom. Dad.*

He misses them. There. The thing is thought. The admission is blinding. It is like staring into a house on fire. *Me's turning into little bitch,* he thinks, punishingly. But the cold water of it does nothing—except maybe make him feel a little bit worse. Yet what does he miss—what can he miss? These two, old to be parents in the first place, soon beset by one medical complaint after the other. First loving, yes, but then so stern, and finally so deadly. Yet there it is: He misses his father's reedy voice, the gap between his front teeth, the way he cleaned his eyeglasses on his necktie until one day he didn't need glasses anymore, and there was no reason to wear a tie...

Wait.

Rodolfo sits up straight, holds his breath. He has heard... something. A twig snap? Maybe...

He looks up and realizes he is directly in the glow of the streetlamp; he is at the end of the yellow cone of light like a note coming out of the bell of a trumpet. He rises up on his hands like a gymnast, then flips backward off the bench, into the humid grass and a measure of darkness. He backs up, looking left, right.

He sees nothing. But he is certain someone is near.

He sniffs the air. He smells human skin, the perfumed stink of an adult. Smoke too. Detergent. Leather. Oil. Oh yes, yes. Someone is near. More than one person. More than two.

If he were fully human, Rodolfo might spend another moment or two standing there, cocking his head left and right, trying to figure out just what he is hearing, trying to make a reasonable evaluation before deciding what, if anything, he ought to do next. But he's not fully human. He is evolution's next step—or evolution's sidestep, at least. A menagerie of DNA courses through him, with several species waging a constant struggle with one another for dominance. His last thought before he runs—and it's not really a thought at all, it's just a sudden knowing—*horses.*

He's off! A lesser creature would not make it ten steps in this murk. A lesser creature would be tripped up in a tangle of vines, blocked by boulders, stymied by chain-link fences, lost and even panicked in the park's elegant undulations. But Rodolfo is not only swift, he is graceful, guided by the invisible cartography of a creature's deepest sense of the world, and even those parts of the park he doesn't know from experience he knows by instinct; the map is in there, and always was.

He is heading vaguely south, vaguely east.

He hears a man's voice, a thick voice, a heavy, bellyish bellow. "Tallyho!" The call goes up, and suddenly Central Park is horribly alive with lights—lights propped up on the roofs of squad cars, enormous klieg lights on tripods as if to illuminate a theater before a world premiere. The darkness of the park turns bright silver. The privacy of night is stripped away—it is like tearing the clothes off a helpless person.

Rodolfo runs. Cops on foot, cops in cars, cops on BMX bikes, and cops on horseback chase after him—all that is lacking is the bugler in a red cutaway coat and the hounds. Instead of crops, they carry clubs. He hears their engines. Hears the frantic clop of hooves. How many are there? He cannot say. But there must be at least twenty in the field, all in hot pursuit, plus a couple of hilltoppers watching from a distance, keeping track of the hunters and their quarry.

He keeps away from the ribbons of roadway, rendering the squad cars useless. He resists climbing any of the trees that go whizzing past him as he runs. In a tree, he will be trapped. In a tree, he will be killed.

The ground behind him shakes as the cops on horseback draw closer.

"Tallyho, tallyho!" an enormous cop on a very small bicycle shouts.

"Halt," shouts another.

One particularly fit young officer is making the chase on

foot. He runs with his arms at his side, and his hands, hanging limply, paddle back and forth. Has he learned something new about the physics of foot speed? He is coming at Rodolfo at a vertical. His path will intersect with Rodolfo's in ten more paces. Beyond that, the corridors of brightness created by the lights the police brought begin fading, dimming—if he can only get to the darkness, his chances of survival will increase.

"Don't shoot, don't shoot," the speeding young officer says as he bears down on his quarry. His piston gait is tireless, robotic.

Rodolfo can feel the heat of the horses like sunlight on his back. It is difficult to put space between himself and his pursuers because he will not, must not, run in a straight line. He must weave, he must cut a path as unpredictable as possible. He does not fool himself into believing that the cops want to take him alive. He does not comfort himself with the sweet story that they would never snuff out the life of a minor.

Their own blood has been spilled. There is nothing they will not do.

Rodolfo is on the Great Lawn now. The ground is soft. It is far too open. He might as well be running on the moon.

He thinks about going on all fours, but there are two or three seconds in the transition from biped to quadra-, and right now he cannot afford them. He is running as fast as he has ever run, and now it is clear that he must run faster.

The young cop on foot makes his move, and Rodolfo powers himself forward toward the lawn's border.

"Aaaar," the cop grunts as he prepares to tackle Rodolfo.

The tires of the squad cars behind him are digging up long black and green curls of lawn. The sirens let out little whoops—there is something strangled, almost involuntary in the sound, which makes it somehow all the more nerve-racking. Rodolfo leaps over the benches on the lawn's border, and the young cop slams into the wooden slats.

Rodolfo's leap has taken him six feet over the benches and when he lands, he staggers for a second, almost falls.

Now he has the moment and the momentum to go on all fours. The bag of Skittles he was carrying in his front pocket falls out; the hard little candies bounce and disappear.

Rodolfo tries not to think. Thinking is not what nature wants, not at a time like this. But he cannot stop himself. He wonders what they will do to him if they catch him. If he were a fox, the hounds in their frenzy might tear him to shreds, but here the hounds are the hunters. He knew this day would come. The man in the white truck is picking them off one by one. And now here come the cops—two of their own are gone and they want justice. No, they want revenge. Of this Rodolfo is certain: He will be beaten, he will be hurt, humiliated. His dread of capture and punishment is so acute, he can almost feel the blows raining down on him, smell the breath of the hunters, see their smiles of swinish satisfaction…

One of the squad cars drives right through the barricade of benches. Of the four mounted cops, two coax their horses to leap over the benches, and two pull their horses up short, causing them to rear up, paw at the air with their front hooves.

A shot is fired. Rodolfo holds his breath, waiting for the pain. But maybe it was just a warning shot. Whatever it was, it missed.

A dark geyser of dirt rises up where the bullet strikes the earth.

The park has always been a place of safety, his refuge, all of the wild children's. But now his only chance of remaining free, remaining *alive,* is to get out of there. He wills himself to go faster and faster. The ground moves beneath him as swift as water roaring out of a tap. He had no idea this kind of speed was in him. He runs left, and right, and left again. He does not dare look over his shoulder, but he can feel himself putting distance between them and him.

He has reached Eighty-Fifth Street. The Metropolitan Museum of Art floats into sight. It is massive, heavy, definitive, a stone-and-marble crypt for everything from prehistoric tools to recent masterpieces. The extension on its west flank, a pyramidal glass enclosure for its tons of Egyptian bounty, looks milky white. He doesn't know why (nor does he question it), but Rodolfo runs toward the glass pyramid, unsure what he will do once he reaches it. Sprinting, leaping, he makes it up the slope leading to the museum. By now, he has left most of his pursuers behind, but the two on horseback are still hunting him, still close.

He allows himself a brief glance back. The mounted police are twenty feet away, maybe closer. One of the cops has his club drawn. The other, a woman, her trousers clinging to her powerful thighs, her blond hair streaming from beneath her uniform's cap, has drawn her weapon. Both horses are winded. Their eyes are wild, showing a great deal of white. Their nostrils palpitate like beating black hearts.

Rodolfo's leaps become a kind of flying. In moments, he is at the base of the Egyptian wing. He looks up, surveys what he must do. Closer and closer the mounted police come. And...

He's up. He catches the lowest edge of the roof, lifts himself up easily, and scrambles across the steep glass slant to its apex.

"Halt! Halt!" the man on horseback hollers.

Yeah, me's doin' a lot of that, thinks Rodolfo, his first actual thought since the chase began. He stands atop the Egyptian wing, looks down at the police and their horses. How little they look. The man is telling the woman to put her gun away.

Rodolfo raises his arms in triumph. He takes careful steps as he makes his way along the rooftop.

Some of the other hunters are catching up. A string of flashing blue and red lights is closing in.

Who knows what is on the other side of the museum? Fifth Avenue. More hunters?

He has one thing to say to them: "Mother. Fuckers."

That said, he scrambles over the very top of the roof. He loses his footing for a moment and starts to slide down the roof's eastern slope. Waving his arms and vocalizing little grunts of fear and distress, he manages to turn his feet in a way that brakes him. He sits for a moment.

There is a breeze up here. But it feels warm, recycled, like breath.

Next he scrambles up the museum itself, higher and higher, until he has scaled the slate roof and looks down at the city. A couple of buses idle in front of the Met. From this height, they look no bigger than a vial of Zoom. Taxis, limos, and the occasional private car stream southward on Fifth as the traffic lights turn green.

There are no police, he sees, but moments later, eight squad cars arrive, their emergency lights dancing crazily around and around, their sirens silent.

Rodolfo squats and looks down, hoping not to be seen. He thought that by now they would have been discouraged, would have given up. But no, it seems clear they will hunt him and hunt him until they can kill him or take him away.

He hears something. A scuffling sound. He turns toward it—but too late. A hand clasps his ankle.

Terrified, he looks down and sees a pair of large eyes staring up at him. He tries to pull his leg away, but he is gripped too strongly. Trapped! He pulls again but it throws his balance off and he starts to tip.

"Whoa, Rodolfo, you's slippin'," a voice says.

Whoever has caught him by the ankle has a flashlight, a small one, three inches long, but with a powerful glow. He shines it in his own face.

"Globe!" Rodolfo cries, amazed and relieved.

Globe is one of the original wild children. He was on the scene when there were no more than ten of them eking out an existence in Central Park, skateboarding eighteen hours a day, chasing and eating squirrels, bathing in the reservoir. As the population of cast-off and runaway kids grew, relations between Rodolfo and Globe deteriorated. As Rodolfo took more control of the lives of the castoffs, Globe resented his growing power—though, in fact, he had no desire to be leader of the brood. What he wanted was to be left alone and to have no authority to answer to, especially when it came to his all-important, all-consuming sex life. He and Lily-Lou mated three years ago; their child was wingless, but strange in other ways. After that, he mated with Casino; their child *was* winged but died shortly after birth.

"Why you's up here?" Rodolfo asks.

"We's living high, my brother," Globe says.

He sweeps the shining arc of his flashlight, illuminating his pack, nine in all, crouched prehistorically, with hungry, wild faces, unkempt, grinning. Two small children, naked, hover a couple of feet above the roof, their rapidly beating wings like the shuffle of cards.

Globe jabs his thumb down toward Fifth Avenue. More police have come. They are dragging sawhorses onto the street, detouring traffic east.

"Troubles?" he asks.

"Me's carrying a million woes," answers Rodolfo.

One of Globe's crew, a girl with braids pinned to the top of her head, catches one of the hovering babies by the foot. She lifts her T-shirt and brings the child to her breast. The baby's wings continue to flap, but more slowly as he latches onto his mother.

"Ow!" she says. "Take it easy, Icona, you's got teeths."

"Me's need to go," Rodolfo says.

"You's welcome twenty-four-seven," Globe says. He points his flashlight at the others, letting the light linger on a girl dressed in a white T-shirt and black shorts, with short blond hair, several tattoos on her face. She smiles at Rodolfo.

"How me's go?"

"No problemo, my brother. You's hundred percent?"

"Me's gotta go."

"No problemo."

"We's not say *problemo,* Globe. We's *say worries.*"

"Life goes different up high," Globe says. He winks at Rodolfo. "Us's knowing all the things about this picture house no other bodies know. We's having you long gone in no time."

"All right. Go now?"

"Sure. Where?"

"Me's got a visit," Rodolfo says.

Globe grins a grin far too knowing for a boy his age—but there it is. "Sure now?" he says. "Soft company here." He shines his light back toward the blond girl. She raises a hand to shield her eyes, but she does not stop smiling.

"Sure now," Rodolfo says.

"Okay, then." Globe claps Rodolfo on the shoulder. "We's here, you's gone. No problemo."

No problemo turns out to be a bit of an overstatement. There *are* problemos, and worries too. But in the broad stroke of the promise, Globe is as good as his word. Using rope ladders, treetops, ledges, and their own dexterity and guile, Globe and his trusted sidekick Stash have Rodolfo on the ground and on his way in about ten minutes. His final descent is at the south end of the Met's parking garage, and from there, unmolested, he makes his way south and east.

To Sixty-Ninth Street. Out of nowhere, a summer rain. The drunken roll of thunder. Couples running for cover. A homeless man rising groggily from his tormented sleep. Rodolfo walks with his head down. Hands in pockets. Looking at no one and hoping no one looks at him.

The rain awakens Alice in her bed. She has been sleeping with her window open and now she sits up, presses the heels of her hands into her eyes, shakes her head. Rain is blowing in and she gets out of bed to shut the window.

When she reaches the window, she sees a face. She lets out a yelp of shock and covers her mouth.

It's him. Her pulse races. She can hardly breathe.

"Rodolfo!" she whispers.

He is standing on the fire escape. He doesn't wait to be asked in. He climbs through the window. He is drenched. His long hair is shiny and dark. His shirt is soaked, transparent. She forces herself not to look at his muscles, the dark scribble in the hollow of his chest. A zigzag of blood runs along the skin from his wrist to his elbow, but he seems unaware of it. He stands now in her girlish room, rain dripping off him, wetting the carpet as if he were a cloud.

"What happened?" She points to his arm.

He looks, noticing it for the first time. He makes certain it's nothing serious. He wipes the blood clean with his hand and then attempts to dry his hand against his jeans, but his jeans are soaked.

"Me's okay."

"Look at you!"

"Look at *you,*" Rodolfo says, and the tone of it, and her perception of its meaning, silences Alice; the tone carves a trapdoor in the moment, and Alice falls through it as if through the opening in a hangman's scaffold.

But rather than being afraid, she chooses to be brave. She takes Rodolfo's hand and leads him into her bathroom. She runs the water until it's hot—it's a long journey from the water heater in the rat-infested cellar to her bathroom on the house's third floor—and soaks one of her fluffy taupe towels. Gently, she cleans the blood off his arm. Now she can see the extent of the gash.

"Oh, Rodolfo," she says.

"Me's okay."

"What happened?"

He doesn't answer right away. He looks deeply into her eyes. She is still holding his arm with one hand, and the towel—now bloody—with the other.

"You left without saying good-bye," he whispers.

He hears them. Adam turns over in his bed, checks the clock. It's 2:14 a.m. He hears his sister's sweet alto, as familiar to Adam as his own breath. He hears another voice. It's Rodolfo.

He hears the occasional car going down Sixty-Ninth Street, the sibilance of deep treads over wet pavement.

He hears the hot water thudding in the pipes.

He hears the rats in the walls.

From one floor below, he hears his mother getting out of bed, opening the door to her room, stepping out into the hallway.

He wraps his pillow so that it covers his ears. His squeezes his eyes shut. The world recedes but now he hears his own blood going around and around on its innocent errands. Nervously, he puts his hand down his pajamas, feels himself. Oh God: a hair. He yanks it out.

Slowly, reluctantly, Cynthia makes her way up the stairs to the third floor of the house. She knows she is embarking on a lose-lose proposition. Either nothing is going on, in which case she will be trumpeting her mistrust, or something is going on, in which case she will have to face it and do something about it. She pauses, listens.

The gnawing of rodents in the walls. Ceaseless.

Fucking exterminators, she thinks. *What do you have to do in this town to get someone to come over and kill a rat?*

She gathers her resolve. She is the parent. She needs to do her job. If she suspects something is wrong upstairs, she needs to go and investigate it. End of story.

She corrects her posture. She straightens her robe. Rubs and gently slaps her face so she won't look like death warmed over.

She hears Alice. A high-pitched, wordless…what? Is she crying? Laughing?

It occurs to Cynthia that she has heard neither laughing nor crying from the tightly wound little girl.

She raps on the door, rather vigorously. She doesn't want to make a tentative little knock, a little timid *tap-tap* that basically says *It's up to you whether or not you open the door.* Those days are gone, maybe forever.

The knock stops the laughter, or the crying, cold. A brief silence. Then Alice says, "What?"

Cynthia chooses to take this as an invitation to enter, and she quickly opens the door.

Alice is there with…a boy. A boy half a head taller. With long wild hair, the eyes of a panther…and he is naked.

No. He's not. Her optic nerves jumped to conclusions. He is almost naked. His chest is bare, his legs and feet. However, he has had the decency to wrap a bath towel around his middle.

He turns slowly to look at Cynthia. In her day, if a mother caught a boy in a girl's room, the boy would be all over himself trying to escape, he'd be frantic. He'd be hopping up and down, or the blood would be draining from his face. But this boy looks relaxed, amused.

"You can't come in here!" Alice shouts. Her pajamas are wet. The bone of her sternum is visible through the fabric. There is blood on the cuffs of her shirt.

"I'm already in, Alley-Oop," Cynthia says.

"Stop calling me that! You have no right!"

"Of course I do. I'm your mother and you're still a little girl."

"Best if you's taking another looks, Moms," the boy intruder says.

"Who is this?" Cynthia asks, directing her question to Alice.

"He's my *friend*."

"He's your friend. And what is your 'friend' doing in your room at two in the morning?"

Alice is silent. Her face hardens, and she folds her arms across her chest. "You never trust me, do you?"

"That's not an answer, Alice. I was about to call the police."

"I'm like a prisoner here."

"A prisoner? A prisoner? I don't even know where you *are* half the time."

"He's my friend. He came to visit. What is the big deal?"

Rodolfo, perhaps wanting to drive home the point, pats Alice's arm. But she shakes him off.

Encouraged by this, Cynthia calms herself. "All right, let's just be reasonable here. Shall we? Let's start with you," she says, pointing to Rodolfo. "What's your name?"

"His name is Rodolfo," Alice says in a crudely sarcastic voice, as if reminding someone that two plus two is four. She even rolls her eyes after saying his name.

"Why don't you let your friend answer for himself, Allie. Okay? Okay, Rodolfo. And where do you live?"

But rather than answer her questions, he leaps upon her. He springs eight feet through the air. His towel unknots itself and he is naked. Cynthia, taken by surprise, cast into terror, falls backward, and Rodolfo is on top of her. His body odor is very, very strong. His penis is long and tawny, his testicles small and black. She is quite sure he is going to kill her—the only question is *how*. He places his hand on her neck and squeezes. It doesn't hurt. She feels something between a kind of inner thud and a dull electric shock. And a moment later, she is plunged into darkness, a deep unanimous blackness without a dissenting quiver of light.

When she awakens, she is alone. She is woozy, but basically all right. She gets up, looks at the clock. Only seven minutes have passed. Adam!

She races to his room. Adam is gone too. They're both out there—somewhere. She has no idea where, and cannot bring herself to fully and explicitly ask herself this, but in some wordless, inchoate way she wonders if this is it, the final disappearance, and now they are gone forever.

CHAPTER 19

Well, to be honest with you, Dennis, you couldn't have chosen a worse day to come asking for a raise." Cal Rogers folds his large, meaty hands and thuds them onto the desk. His steely hair has just had a fresh crew cut, but that's the only thing that looks fresh about him. He looks, in fact, haggard. Back in the day, when he was a grad student at UC Berkeley, Cal could work seventy-two hours straight and hardly be fazed by it. But now, just one all-nighter leaves him feeling like his eyelids are made of Velcro, his tongue is a scarf, and inside his small intestine lives a swarm of hornets. Things are not going well at the lab. Another subject has perished, and, even more distressing, the results of all the tests have been rubbish. The Borman and Davis researchers are no closer today than they were two months ago to isolating just what it is that makes the wild children so supernaturally vigorous and their blood able to restore potency, desire, and, to an extent, even youth itself. Taken in small doses, of course.

"Well, Cal, I must say that is not good news, not good news at all." Keswick looks around Rogers's office—the framed picture of his family (standard-issue wife, overachieving son, grumpy daughter), the good-natured trophy engraved *Cal Rogers, Thirty-Ninth Place, New Hampshire Goofy Golf Tournament,* the framed degrees—and he thinks that this could have been *his* life, *his* office, *his, his,* if only a few things had gone differently. If someone had believed in him, set a fire under him, so to speak, made sure he worked hard and didn't give up, kicked his heinie a bit, if that's what was necessary, which it was...now look at him! A glorified dogcatcher.

Rogers looks Dennis over and thinks with some small satisfaction, *This guy looks in worse shape than me. Might be time to flush him.*

"I'm a scientist, Dennis. I don't make salary decisions."

"I'm in trouble, Cal."

You can say that again, you lunatic.

"I'm sorry to hear that, Dennis."

"I've had to move out of Brooklyn. I'm living in a hotel and I'm having a heck of a hard time finding a new place. I'm priced out of the market."

"New York can be very expensive, Dennis."

"I need money, Cal. A substantial amount. Not this bullcrap I get at the end of the week. Money. Real money. We're friends, you and I. Aren't we? We understand each other. Am I right?"

"Dennis, this really isn't a good time for a heart-to-heart. Corporate's down my throat like a tongue depressor. If we don't start getting results, my bosses are going to shut us down."

"People are looking for me," Keswick says in an unstable whisper.

"What people, Dennis?"

"Never mind. Private business."

Cal thinks for a moment, and suddenly he sees a path that

might be beneficial—it might be a perfect solution: The experiments can go forward with an increased chance of success, and Dennis can have his stupid money. (And Dennis, Cal is quite certain, *is* a child when it comes to finance; Borman and Davis has a net worth nearing a trillion, and this idiot thinks five thousand dollars is a fortune.)

"How'd you like to make five thousand dollars all in one shot, Dennis? Would that be helpful to you?"

"Every little bit helps, Cal." Dennis feels a stirring within, unpleasant. Complaining and feeling poorly treated are common for him, and they are oddly relaxing in their familiarity. Being offered something, however, destabilizes him. Being drawn into a confidence. Being offered a deal. He worries about being tricked and worries he will agree on a price that he will look back on with regret. "What do you have in mind?"

"Do you have your guidebook with you, Dennis?"

"Aye, laddie, you mean me Bible, then, don'tcha now?" He says this with his cartoonish approximation of an old Irish priest—it was a routine he used to do to amuse his mother when she went into one of her moods. The book of photographs is on his lap and he gives it a thump.

"Okay, good. Here's who we need. I'm sure they are in there."

Dennis opens his book and looks at Rogers expectantly.

"We'd like to take a look at those twins. Sired by Alex Twisden, yes? And the dam was Leslie Kramer, who made our life quite difficult by her insane attacks on our Slovenian friend. You have them in there, I assume."

Dennis places the open book in front of Rogers. There are two pages of their photos: Alice and Adam in their school uniforms taken five years ago; a grainy shot of Alice getting off a school bus, taken two years ago, while she was in foster care in Cold Spring, New York; Adam in a Cub Scout uniform, his hair wet-combed, a frightened, beseeching smile on his face; and three pictures of the house on Sixty-Ninth Street, of the surveillance variety, showing the front, back, and cellar doors.

"Well, that's your five thousand dollars, Dennis."

"So you really think these two might have the right balance? Is that the plan? Get in there, have a chance to test them on an ongoing basis so we can replicate the exact mixture of dominant human strain and the recessive tincture of the nonhuman?"

"Dennis. Take it easy. Even a lot of the experienced chemists are struggling to keep up with this. Just do your job, okay? This isn't an audition. We need you to get those two and bring them in. Do you think you can handle this?"

"Handle it? Why wouldn't I be able to handle it? I've handled everything else, haven't I?"

"You've been terrific, Dennis. No complaints here."

"You said I have a much higher capture rate than anyone else working here."

"Did I? I actually don't remember saying that."

"Oh, you said it. You definitely said that."

"Well," Rogers says. "It doesn't matter. You're a valued member of the team, that's what counts."

"So, five thousand dollars," Dennis says.

"That's right. I've got the authorization."

Dennis sits back in his chair, crosses his legs. In his view, this is going exactly as he wants it to.

"And that's ten for them both," he says.

Rogers is silent. In truth, he has been authorized to pay twice this, but he feels it will be safer if this idiot believes he has won some great battle for his measly 10K.

"I don't know, Dennis…" Rogers says, as if worried, nervous.

"It's what you said."

"You keep on telling me I said things I know I did not say."

"Well, you said. And even if you didn't—it's what I want. It's what I deserve. And I'll tell you another thing. We're going to go back, you and me, and see the lab. All I see of this place is the loading dock, shipping and receiving, one hallway, and your office. I'm tired of being treated as less-than."

"Less-than? Are you in psychotherapy?"

"No way."

"So, Dennis. You want to see the lab."

"Yes. I bring those little beasts to you. I want to see what you do with them. I'm not a glorified dogcatcher, you know. I want to understand what you're doing with all this flesh I'm throwing at you."

"You want a lot of things, don't you, Dennis. You want money, you want access. My grandmother used to say this thing: You've got a handful of *gimme* and a mouthful of *much obliged.*"

"A man does what a man must do, Cal."

"All right. I'll tell you what. I'm going to okay a double payment on those twins. Bring them in, unbruised, preferably not flailing around and half crazed—the real emotional ones have been hell to work with. Bring them in, and you'll have your fucking ten K. How's that? Make you happy? But as to the other thing—bringing you back so you can get a look at our facilities, see those little fuckers being put through their trials? That's not going to happen."

"Why not? Why can't I see?"

"Dennis, my friend. You don't want to see. If you had a look, you might not be able to do your job. Trust me on this. You do not want to see."

"How bad can it be?"

Rogers's answer is a long, silent stare.

"Are you killing them?"

Silence.

"What do you do with them when the trials are over?"

"Dennis..."

"All right. That's it. Right now, you need to tell me. What are you guys doing to them?" Dennis asks. A wave of queasiness breaks within him, a weak, dirty tide of misgivings.

"What did you do that you need money so badly all of a sudden?" Rogers counters. "You're getting ready to leave town too. Aren't you? What did you do? I need to know if it will affect our company, if we have anything to worry about."

"If I tell you, will you tell me what you're doing to those kids?"

Rogers answers with an after-you gesture.

"I accidentally hurt a woman."

Rogers's blood quickens. This will have to be dealt with. "What woman?"

"A woman. A prostitute."

"Hurt her how?"

"Badly."

"How badly?"

"Very badly."

"Is she dead?"

"Now that you mention it."

"Oh..."

"Now take me to see."

"I can't do that, Dennis. I'm not authorized."

"But we made a deal."

"You made a deal. I didn't say anything." He sees that Dennis is about to object and he raises a hand, a cop stopping traffic while a wreck is cleared off the road. "My advice—and I do think you should take it—is to do your job, bring us those twins, take your money, and get as far away from here as possible. There's a lot at stake here, Dennis. Trillions of dollars. You and I are old friends, of course, but believe me, the people who run this thing—they don't screw around. If they think you've done anything to bring undue attention to our operations, they will…" He rubs his hands together and opens them up, like a birthday-party magician who has just made a dime disappear.

Cynthia knows this much. Wherever those kids have taken off to—with that awful Rodolfo, to be sure—they are going to be in danger. Whatever aspect of their nature prevails, they are kids, and kids court danger. They are magnets for oddballs, marginal types, creeps. Kids need to be watched. Protected. They could end up smoking pot. Shoplifting. And this is the best-case scenario. The very best case. Alice is just restless and angry enough to be lured into having sex—which (and this is another certainty of Cynthia's) she is in no way ready for. And then it occurs to her: Underage sex is also a best-case scenario. In fact, anything short of replicating the vicious, uncontrollable behavior of their biological parents would have to constitute a best-case scenario.

She waits on the ground floor. As soon as the door opens— when and if—she will see them, and she will grab them. They will be punished. There is no way around that. But how do you punish children who ran for their lives because they believed the people who gave birth to them and were pledged by all the laws of nature to nurture and protect them were, instead, planning to eat them? How do you punish children whose father's body burst like a balloon full of blood when he was plowed into by a bus? How do you say to children, "Okay, you're grounded," when their own mother was ground to a spray of blood and bone by the implacable, insatiable whirling turbine of a jet engine?

Okay, no punishment, then. So? What are the magic words to ensure that they will come home and stay home? Is she somehow, Cynthia wonders, not communicating to them how loved they are? What are the magic words that will make them trust her? What are the magic words that will keep them off the streets, out of the park, not on the run, not sprinting into God knows what kind of danger? Will someone please tell her: What are the magic words?

The sun has come up. It is already hot in the city and it is only eight o'clock. She turns on the central air-conditioning; its frigid whisper is no match for the gnawing of the rats. She fishes for the TV's remote, finds it in its familiar resting spot between the middle cushions of the sofa, and turns on the too-big Toshiba. She doesn't care what channel comes up; she only wants something to compete with and, if possible, mask the infernal *nyyahh-nyyahh* of the rodents' auto-dentistry. She'd gotten the big TV for the kids, thinking, what child doesn't love a large television? But they are indifferent to it.

Those exterminators! What kind of city is this? As the TV comes on, Cynthia grabs for the phone. By now, she knows by heart the numbers of three separate exterminators. She calls the one that has been the most apologetic. Better to have a bit of blue sky blown up her behind than be overtly insulted.

As she waits for her call to be answered, she sees a familiar face on the TV. It's that glowing little boy the twins had with them. Dylan! He is standing in front of a beautiful old mansion, flanked by Mayor Morris and his wife. The words *Happy Ending, Mayor's Son Found, Little Dylan Safe and Sound* march across the bottom of the screen.

Cynthia aims the remote at the set, turns up the volume.

"We are a family reunited," Mayor Morris is saying. He looks stern, sleepless. It's odd to see him without his signature outfit: the blue blazer, white shirt, shiny necktie. Here he is without a jacket, and the top button of his shirt has not been fastened. At first, Cynthia thinks he has taken foppishness to a whole new level and is wearing an ascot. But she realizes a moment later that it is not an ascot but body hair, rising like thick smoke.

At the same time, the exterminator's voice mail has been activated and she is instructed to leave a message and assured that someone will call her back "just as soon as possible."

"As soon as possible isn't going to do it, guys," Cynthia says. "I am living with a fuck-ton of rats!" She leaves her numbers once again and emphatically breaks the connection, though pressing an Off button makes her long for the days when you could slam a receiver down into its cradle and really let your feelings be known.

"Thanks to the efforts of the entire NYPD," the mayor is saying, "and in particular the tireless work done by our stalwart Central Park Precinct, the story of this one New York City family has an extraordinarily happy ending." He looks down at Dylan—who is pulling faces at the phalanx of cameras—and pats his head.

Did I imagine that? Cynthia wonders, because to her exhausted eyes, it looked as if the mayor's hand was trembling as he performed the paternal pat for the media.

Now one of the newscasters is on-screen, a lovely woman with a strident tone to her voice. She looks to be about twenty-five, but her manner is that of a woman who has been cheated and deceived and has made a personal promise to be ever vigilant from that day forward.

"On the heels of Dylan Morris's rescue and return to Gracie Mansion, the questions surrounding his disappearance continue to circle Mayor Morris and his closest advisers. There is no doubt that the very real human drama accompanying Dylan's disappearance—indeed, the disappearance of any child in this great city—is a riveting event that plays on the emotions of anyone who has been a parent or a child; in other words, every single human being not terminally hard of heart. Nevertheless, speculations as to what really happened the night of Dylan Morris's disappearance continue to surround the event, and the sudden, somewhat puzzling nature of his return will do little to quiet those who say, for instance, that the boy was in a rehab of some sort, or that the entire incident was staged as a way of bolstering Morris's flat polling numbers as he approaches re-election, or that Dylan was not abducted or held against his will but was a runaway. And those who hold with the runaway theory are quick to ask the question: From what was Dylan fleeing?

"Meanwhile, the fabled Central Park Precinct, which was, by all reports, spearheading the search for little Dylan, has been remarkably quiet about the search and his so-called rescue. All we could get from a precinct spokeswoman was the following statement: 'The New York Police Department continues in its commitment to make our Central Park safe and fun for all the people of New York, as well as the millions of visitors to our city. To best further that aim, we are closing the park in order to deal with security risks and make the park a place where all New Yorkers can go without worry. I won't be taking questions at this time. If you see something, say something. And be safe. Thank you.' "

With Dylan no longer on the streets with them, there is nothing to prevent or forestall open season on the brood.

Rodolfo knows it's time to move—not just for him, and not just for the few select friends he has with him on Riverside Drive, but for each and every one of the wild boys and girls. Over the past few years, they have been managing to live safely and even thrive on the outskirts of the city's life. They have even managed to make money. But now it's over. This much he knows. And he has a responsibility, not only to his own genes, but to all of them. Even the ones who he knows grouse about him and shoot him the bird when his back is turned, even the ones who have openly challenged his authority—they need him, and their safety is his sacred duty.

He has sent out the word. The place where all the packs have been gathering—the Diana Ross Playground—is no longer safe. It is out of the question. And as for the wild ones living around Tompkins Square Park, the message is the same—get out. City Hall Park, Washington Square Park, Inwood Hill, and Van Cortlandt—begone, begone, begone, begone. Of late there has been a migration to Brooklyn's Prospect Park—easier hunting, fewer hassles—but Prospect Park is no longer safe, nor is Fort Greene.

"We's scatter now," Rodolfo says. He is getting everything valuable out of the apartment, starting with thousands upon thousands of dollars in cash and then going on to enough vials of Zoom to plunge a hospice into an orgiastic frenzy.

Alice is following him as he winds through the apartment. She holds a striped-green-and-yellow laundry sack wide open and he drops the money into it. There is money under cushions, behind books, in the back of the closet, in the inside pockets of old overcoats. After the cash is collected, the fridge is emptied of product—for this part of the operation, Rodolfo has Adam's assistance; he holds a duffel bag lined with towels, to keep the vials safe in transport.

"What are you going to do with all this?" Adam says, peering into the bag. A strange coppery smell rises from it. A part of him is repelled by it, but he is also intrigued.

Rodolfo shrugs. "We's never know," he says. "It's money. Us's making a whole new life, far away, brother. We's got a hundred and thirty-five thousand dollars. Maybe it's enough, maybe not. Maybe us's needing a little top-off. What do we do? Zoom. Oldies who want to be young, they going to be there too."

"Are we going to meet here?" Alice asks. She is on one side of Rodolfo, Adam is on the other. They walk the apartment's long central corridor to the front room, where Boy-Boy, Bump, Suzie, Captain Blood, Lola, and Little Man have been making calls, letting everybody know that today's meeting is important—the most important they have ever had.

"We's going to Pelham Bay Park," Rodolfo says. "Separate ways. *Cho-cho número seis.*" He snaps his fingers, grins. He is trying to make the best of it. Optimism has always been his style, personally and administratively. Positive reinforcement is how he and his kind best learn. Dark looks, worried body language—it all does more harm than good.

"What about Polly?" Alice asks.

She and Rodolfo lock eyes for a long moment until, finally, he shakes his head sadly.

A couple of the crew make the run to Broadway and come back with pizzas and bottles of Mountain Dew. Before setting out for Pelham Bay, they all gather in the front room for a final meal together. It does not look particularly ceremonial—some sit, some stand; they are eating right out of the boxes and drinking straight from the bottles. But the mood is somber, final, and apprehensive. Boy-Boy has his arm around Lola, and Bump gazes at Rodolfo with adoration, as if the wiry sixteen-year-old were a vision. The infants have been propped up on the sofa, and they play languidly with one another, a barely coordinated tangle of arms, legs, and wings.

"Tell us's what me's said, okay?" Rodolfo whispers to Alice. He purses his lips, shakes his head, letting her know that he doesn't trust himself to keep his emotions in check were he to speak to them all.

"Okay," Alice says. She notices Adam looking questioningly at her, but she turns her eyes away from his.

"Rodolfo wants us to take the number six train uptown. The stop says Pelham Bay Park. Go up the stairs where it says Bruckner Street."

"Bruckner Boulevard," Rodolfo says.

"Right. Bruckner Boulevard." Alice takes a deep breath. A kind of happiness goes through her. It feels as if she has just quickly drunk a cup of warm tea. She feels the rush of it in her throat, her stomach, her arms, hands, legs, feet. She wonders: *Is this the thing you hear about? Is this love?*

"We can't all go at once. Okay? So three at a time. Starting at…" She glances at the American Girl wristwatch Cynthia gave them. Way back when, in the car. After court. When was that? It feels like years ago…

She furrows her brow. It's 9:17. But that's not the source of her consternation. The wispy silver down that used to lie flat against her skin near the face of the watch has darkened, and even slightly coarsened. *That's* the source of her consternation. *That* is what freaks her out.

Cynthia has decided: When—if?—the twins return, they cannot live in this house one day longer than absolutely necessary. Whatever legal hoops need to be leaped through, she will deal with them—even if the hoops are on fire! When she thinks of how she had once (let's face it!) *lusted* after these rooms, how weak in the knees she had been at the pedigree in every sconce and every floorboard, how lovely the world had looked through the slightly purple waviness of the old windows, how ridiculously impressed she had been by the sheer craftsmanship of the house, she wants to somehow reach back in time and take that deluded self by the shoulders and shake and shake and shake until it comes to its senses. The fact is now painfully apparent: For years, this house has been bad news. No. Worse. Hideous news. No, worse than that too. What comes after hideous? Oh, it doesn't matter. What matters is this: She has to dump this place and take whatever money she can pull out of it and buy another house. Or an apartment. Out of the city. A suburb, perhaps. A lovely little town by the sea. Cape Cod! She has never been to Cape Cod, but she knows it's lovely. Who doesn't like foggy beaches? Who doesn't like cod? Who doesn't like pumpkin-scented candles and clothes bought from Talbots? Anyhow, anything would be better than this.

She needs to take them from whatever is luring them away. That boy—Rodolfo! Surely, he is part of it.

Away. A condo maybe. A place where, if you stand in the middle of it, you can see every room.

A doorman.

A superintendent.

A neighbor whose music you can hear through the walls. And who can hear you should you scream...

She realizes that selling a town house is not an easy proposition. It will take time. What is it worth now? Thirty million? Screw it. She'll take twenty-five.

She paces the house, holding her cordless phone in one hand, her cell phone in the other, every few steps shaking them both as if they can be rattled into ringing.

Back in San Francisco—just the merest beckoning of memory, the slightest recollection of her past makes her dizzy with wonder and grief—back then, in California, in the chill and the fog and the scent of eucalyptus as ubiquitous as the smell of gasoline is in New York—back then...She has lost her train of thought. Oh, yes—now she recalls. In San Francisco, when she had her shop (oh! her shop, her shop, how she misses Gilty Pleasures), sometimes a very special piece, expensive, unusual, might sit around for months, even a couple of years, before the exact right person appeared, the person who was meant to buy it. Conceivably, selling this house will take a year—though you never knew; it could go in a heartbeat.

She does a bit of research on the Internet and decides that the most high-end real estate company right now in New York is an outfit calling itself Oberman and Lewis. Of the past twenty-five big sales Cynthia could track, Oberman and Lewis agents were involved in nine of them. She calls them on the cordless, with the cell on her lap lest the kids call in. She is put through the tumbler of their phone system, pressing numbers to answer the various inane recorded questions until, at last, she is connected to a real estate agent.

Cynthia gets it: She's probably been connected to someone not so very high on the Oberman and Lewis food chain, someone who is available to take random calls. But the voice on the other end of the phone is elegant, melodious, and confident. Her name is Katie Henderson. She sounds young—she has that pajama-party voice, what linguists have called a vocal fry, a languid way of talking meant to impress upon the person to whom you are speaking that you are extremely relaxed and will not put out an extra ounce of effort.

But Katie Henderson *is* willing to put out effort. In fact, upon hearing what property Cynthia wants to place on the market, she sounds like she wants to fax herself to East Sixty-Ninth Street. She doesn't even bother to be coy. "Well, this is very, very exciting, I must tell you," she says, several times over, in fact.

"It's not without its complexities," Cynthia feels obliged to say.

"Properties this important never are," Katie Henderson says, her voice a reassuring croon, as if she were settling an agitated child down for the night with a bedtime song.

And her enthusiasm is not just a phone manner. Less than thirty minutes later, Katie Henderson is seated in the front parlor, looking eagerly and appraisingly at everything in sight. She is not as young as her voice; she is probably forty, maybe even a little older—there are streaks of gray in her abundant black hair, lines around her piercing blue eyes, and her skin looks a bit raw, as if she has recently undergone some fierce dermabrasion.

She is dressed as if for a brisk autumn evening. The heat is already pressing against the windows, and Katie sits there, visibly warm in her black pantsuit and copper-colored ruffled blouse, buttoned to the neck and accessorized by a black silk scarf. Cynthia watches, fascinated, mesmerized, really, as beads of perspiration emerge from Katie's hairline and roll down her forehead, where Katie blots them with the back of her hand, right before they can trickle saltily into her eyes.

"Feel free to take off your jacket," Cynthia says.

"Oh, that's all right, thank you," Katie says. Sensing that that is not quite enough, she adds, "I guess I'm just a slave to fashion." She sits up straighter, brushes her hand against her jacket's fabric.

"I could turn the air-conditioning up, if you'd like," Cynthia offers.

"Oh. Would you mind?" Katie smiles enormously.

"Of course not," Cynthia says. The thermostat is on the other side of the room. It's complicatedly digital, and she has yet to fully get the hang of it. As she fusses with the controls, she glances in the mirror hanging over the black marble fireplace. She sees that Katie has opened her briefcase and taken out a notebook and a sleek little digital camera.

"It'll take a few minutes for the place to cool down," Cynthia says, sitting again. She looks closely at her visitor. Cynthia can't say exactly what it is, but something seems odd about this woman. And though there is no particular physical similarity, something about her puts Cynthia in mind of Leslie. Starting with her refusal to take off her jacket.

"So…how many bedrooms are there altogether?" Katie asks.

"I've got it all right here," says Cynthia. She hands the real estate woman a sheet with all the basic information about the house: year built, square footage, number of bedrooms, number of baths, fireplaces.

"Oh, this is great," Katie says, giving the spec sheet a cursory glance. She tugs at the sleeve of her jacket so that the hem is touching the heel of her hand. Leaning back, she adjusts her pants, pulling at the fabric.

"It's a great house," Cynthia says, narrowing her eyes.

"Oh my God, it's spectacular," Katie says. "Shall we do a walk-through?"

"But I'm curious," Cynthia says. "Are things like this selling these days?"

"A house like this? It's like it's never quite the right time, and it's always the right time. Obviously, it awaits a very special buyer. Luckily, I am working right now with a number of international clients who would be thrilled to death to have a chance at a house like this, with this location and history. And most important, they have the means to move quickly, without winga..." She clears her throat. "Without...witta..."

Cynthia looks away, embarrassed by the real estate broker's momentary difficulties. She knows how these things can happen; sometimes when she is exhausted, her tongue feels as stiff and cumbersome as a Ping-Pong paddle. And God knows that on boozy afternoons she had to scale each sentence as if it were a glass mountain. And yet...this little verbal breakdown Katie is undergoing reminds Cynthia of something, something else, something she has pushed deep into her unconscious, filed away in a drawer she had hoped she would never have occasion to open.

But sometimes these drawers where we stuff our memories move of their own accord. And this one slowly creaks open, revealing a memory that has been not only stored but kept crisper-fresh: Cynthia's sister, Leslie, as the balance slowly but inexorably shifted within her, away from the strictly human and toward the creaturely, started having more and more trouble remembering words. Sometimes her sentences had blanks within them, and sometimes wholly inappropriate or even nonexistent words would crop up. It was like Tourette's syndrome in its explosive unexpectedness, and like early-onset Alzheimer's in its pitifulness.

Katie, however, finds her way through the verbal thicket and emerges relatively unscathed on the other side of her sentence.

"Without waiting for a mortgage or anything." She laughs her bright, professional laugh. "My, oh my, this is what happens when I leave home without my third cup of coffee. Anyhow, many of my clients are capable of doing an all-cash deal."

"But what kind of money are we talking about?" Cynthia asks.

"Did you have a figure in mind?" Katie asks.

"I was thinking of something in the neighborhood of thirty-five million," Cynthia says. She feels her pulse quicken—she actually *loves* doing business.

"That's an excellent neighborhood," Katie says.

"I should tell you," Cynthia says. "Or perhaps you know. This house. It has a history."

"What piece of really important real estate in this town doesn't have a history?" Katie says. " 'Behind every great fortune lies a…' " Her face goes blank. " 'Lies a'…something."

" 'A great crime,' " Cynthia says.

"A French guy," Katie says. "I used to know this stuff."

"Balzac," Cynthia says. Her heart is pounding. With every

moment, she is more certain that this woman has undergone the same treatment that destroyed everything mild and sweet in Leslie, and she is also afraid that at any second this pantsuited stranger will come hurtling across the room and start ripping at her flesh.

"So," Katie says, standing up. "Let me look around, take some…" She moves her finger up and down, as if pressing the button on a camera.

Did she forget the word camera? "Well, we can start here," Cynthia says, her voice breaking. "Do you want me to show you around?"

"Oh, that won't be necessary. I actually like to go on my self thing and you know. You know?"

"Uh…I guess."

"I'll start in the cellar and work my way up."

"Um…the cellar is the one problem in this house." Cynthia tries to say this nonchalantly. "We have a bit of a mouse problem down there. I have a call in to a couple of exterminators, and I do believe the whole thing will be cleared up in a few days."

"Mice?"

"I think so," Cynthia says.

"Have you tried those whatchamacallits?"

Cynthia shakes her head.

"You *know*," Katie says with good-natured insistence. "Those…" She wiggles her fingers in the air. "Glue traps! The mousie steps on the sticky part, and then his feet get stuck in the glue. And then all you have to do is…well, you can do whatever you want."

"Why don't you check on the cellar at some other time? After I get a good exterminator in here."

"Oh, that could take a week or two. Anyhow, not to worry. Nothing bothers me."

"Well, I'll take you to it."

With some reluctance, Cynthia escorts Katie to the cellar door. Just looking at it brings back the horrible experiences Cynthia had down those steep wooden steps. And she knows that if the floor below is covered with what is in effect a turbulent lake of rodents, Oberman and Lewis will definitely not be representing this house on the market. Oh, well, she's not certain she'd like to do business with Katie Henderson anyhow…

"I'll get you a flashlight," Cynthia says. She herself will not venture down even one step.

"You know what?" Katie says. "I think I'll leave the cellar for…you know…for last!"

"Okay." Cynthia stretches out the word.

"I'll be fast," Katie says. "I may not look it, but I am known for my foot speed!"

I'll bet you are, thinks Cynthia.

As Katie scampers up the stairs, Cynthia goes back to the sofa and makes calls. First, she calls Arthur, wanting to let him know that she has decided to put the house on the market. But he doesn't pick up, and she leaves a peevish message on his voice mail. After that, she re-calls the exterminators; she is so infuriated with them that she hints darkly—to an answering service, and to someone who sounds as if she has just been awakened by the call—that if someone doesn't come to the house right away, she may have to begin a lawsuit. It doesn't make much sense, but someone once told her—she can't remember who it was—that threatening to sue is the one surefire way to get the attention of your average New Yorker. While she is ranting away, she sees out of the corner of her eye that Katie has opened the cellar door and is on her way to inspect downstairs. She leaves the door open behind her. Cynthia doesn't dare close it, but the sight of it wide open paralyzes her with fear.

She turns off the phone, lets it fall from her hand.

A few minutes later, Katie emerges from the cellar, and she considerately closes the door behind her. She drops her little silver camera into her impressive Louis Vuitton bag.

"I love your house," she declares. "It's going to sell in two seconds."

"There are some legal issues, unfortunately," Cynthia says.

"I just love it." Katie is weaving; her head lolls lazily, and she is running her tongue along her bottom lip. She is, in fact, acting as if she'd just pounded down a pint of vodka.

Suddenly, her eyes open wide. Her hand goes up and her fingers tap nervously on the side of her throat. She coughs, while pursing her lips.

"Are...are you okay?" Cynthia asks.

Katie nervously nods yes.

"Can I get you something? Maybe a glass of water?"

"I'm all right. I'm diabetic. I have to watch my blood-sugar levels."

Cynthia nods. "So...do you have children?" she asks.

"Do I have children?" Katie says this as if the question were fantastically inappropriate.

"Yes, I'm wondering."

"I have a daughter," the real estate agent says with sudden primness.

"A daughter. Oh. How old is she?"

"She's almost twelve. She's my precious angel. I just love her to death."

I'm sure you do, thinks Cynthia.

"She's such a good kid. Really, it took me forever to get preggers, maybe that's why I'm so crazy about her. I could just...I don't know." Katie smiles, shows her exceedingly prominent teeth. "I could just eat her up."

"Well, I'm glad you like the house," Cynthia says. "I have a few...other appointments."

"With other real estate firms?" Katie inquires. "I'm sure you'll find our commission rates very competitive. And in terms of access to qualified buyers, no one can compare with us."

"Yes. Of course," Cynthia says. She can feel the drip of her own perspiration trickling down her spine. Her armpits are humid; her mouth completely dry.

"I'm going to need you to sign a couple of agreements. You'll be giving us an exclusive on this property."

"You can just leave the papers here. I'll look them over."

"There's nothing to look over. It's standard stuff, okay?"

"I need to look them over, Katie. Okay?"

"I see," Katie says.

Cynthia can feel the rage in the real estate agent's body, and she wonders, Will she strike now? She looks around the room for something with which to defend herself. All that seems feasible is a heavy, clear glass vase filled with pale yellow irises. She picks the vase up by the rim.

"I think you'd better leave. Now."

"Excuse me?" The real estate agent's eyes register profound shock—or is it fury?

"I know what you are," Cynthia says. "My sister was just like you. You went to the doctor, didn't you? That's where your 'precious angel' comes from."

"My daughter?" Katie asks. "What doctor? I don't know what you're talking about." Thinking Cynthia is making a move toward her, Katie flinches, brings her hand up as if to protect her face.

A moment later, the real estate agent darts around Cynthia, grabs her things from the sofa, and heads out the front door—though not before leaving an agreement giving Oberman and Lewis a six-month exclusive on the house on Sixty-Ninth Street.

CHAPTER 20

Cal Rogers strolls through the corridor at Borman and Davis, slapping a clipboard against the side of his leg and whistling what he believes to be "Anchors Aweigh," though others might not be so sure. He is approaching the double doors separating the executive portion of the facility from the labs. The doors are locked and usually manned on either side by a uniformed guard. Cal does not quite register the fact that on his side of the doors, the chair where the guard normally sits is empty.

As he nears the doors, they swing open. It's one of the ferals, the least altered of the crop—the one named Polly. She is wearing the clothes she was in when Keswick snatched her, but they have been laundered, and she looks freshly showered—she looks like a fifteen-year-old girl on her way to a music lesson.

When she sees Rogers, she smiles. "Hi there," she calls.

He snaps out of his semi-reverie.

"What are you doing?" he asks, reaching for his phone.

"Nothing," Polly says.

"You're not supposed to be just walking around."

"It's okay." She continues walking, and now she is practically flush against him, ignoring the most basic rules of personal space.

"You're supposed to be in your quarters, young lady," Rogers says. He has already dialed security. He holds the phone away from his ear, listens to the *ring-ring-ring*.

"Yeah, I guess." She puts her hand on his shoulder. "But here's the thing. You want to hear the thing?"

Fucking security! Where is everyone? Rogers realizes he must take matters into his own hands. He removes this horrible girl's hand from his shoulder but holds on to her wrist. He rarely has direct contact with the subjects of his investigations—it's strictly a blood-and-tissue-sample relationship. But now he grasps her tightly, so she will know who is in power here.

He knows it's crazy thinking, but he can't help noticing how attractive this young girl is.

"Your hands are cold," she says, tugging away from him, but without much force or purpose.

"I'm taking you back," Rogers says.

"Okay, but before you do?" She stops. She has strong legs and it's hard to budge her when she digs in.

"What?"

"You guys are supposed to be—what? Doctors? Scientists?"

"Yeah? What's your point?"

"Well, you're hurting us. These are our *bodies,* you know? Doing all kinds of personal shit too. It's not right. We didn't do anything."

"Think of it like this: You're making a contribution."

"We didn't ask to be born. And we didn't ask to be different."

"You're out of the rain. Right? You're fed. Place to sleep. Three hots and a cot. You've got nothing to complain about."

"The stuff hurts. The needles. The scraping."

"We do our best, honey. No one wants to hurt anyone. Hurting is the furthest thing from our minds."

"Two of us have died here."

"No one feels worse about that than I do."

"Really?"

"Come on, it's back to quarters for you, young lady."

She shrugs. "It's up to you." She relaxes her legs and allows Rogers to lead her through the double doors.

"Do you have children yourself?" she asks.

Cal Rogers is swiping his ID card through the door's reader, but the reader seems not to be working—or necessary. The doors swing open to his touch.

Separated as he has been from the grim business of imprisonment and the forced extraction of genetic data, Rogers is slow to recognize just how insanely out of control the situation is— he actually thinks that those bodies slumped against the wall are part of some kind of game. Or exercise? A drill?

Those two seconds of fantasy will be the last time he is not in agony. But the agony will not be without its end point. He is slammed against the wall. He feels the impossible pain of teeth in flesh. His final thought: *It's going for my liver.*

All of the surviving wild children are out—instinctively obeying the call to quit the city. The doors to their enclosures are open wide. The stench of their imprisonment comes off them in waves. Their excited, raucous voices fill the air like a rain of coins. *Hurry, hurry.*

There is no time for further retribution. Some of the bodies against the wall are dead, others...maybe not. But time is what matters now. Time. Revenge does not matter, nor does justice. All that matters is freedom, and freedom is theirs. Some upright and some on all fours, evolution's errors streak down the hall toward the loading dock.

*   *   *

Is it just New Yorkers, or do the residents of all the great and complicated cities of the world — London, Singapore, Istanbul, Rio — learn to live without entirely seeing what is happening right before their eyes? In the multitudes, all manner of human variation exists, unseen. And when something odd *is* noted, there is rarely time or space to take it in and evaluate its meaning. Hoodlums, mystics, the terminally ill pass city dwellers by like little bursts of light, apprehended and then gone, leaving no trace. Here comes a man dragging his useless leg, making his way forward on the pavement on one hardworking leg, like a gondolier poling up a concrete river. Here comes a nun with a shiner. Here is a couple in their forties on their way to see a charlatan who runs a so-called fertility clinic. Here is a cop who has just learned that a man whom he crookedly sent to prison is being released. Here comes a father and his two young daughters whom he shepherds quickly, as they are on their way to the hospital where the girls' mother, dying of cancer, wanly awaits them. It's summer, and more than any other season, there are children among the urbanites. Children of all stations, children bearing destinies as light as spun sugar or burdens too massive to be borne. Boys afraid to go home. Girls in terror of their mothers' new boyfriends. Children who have not had breakfast today. Children who have not had breakfast since school let out. Children with bruises under their shirts. Children on meds administered by those in charge of their well-being. Children on speed. Children dizzy, sleepy, and growing fat from their drugs, dragged through the psychoactive alphabet from Abilify to Zoloft. Children with weapons in their pockets.

Are they invisible? They might as well be. They are flesh,

but they come and go in a flash. How can anyone be expected to notice, much less care? Too many, too fast. And who doesn't have plenty of problems of his or her own?

And so the feral boys and girls of the parks make their way through the city in twos and threes, safely unnoticed. Some glow; a few will spawn more winged babies. We are at only the beginning of the breathtaking dance between science and nature. What has been done with the atom will be done with the gene.

To Pelham Bay Park! Those with money—and who can stand the confinement and the noise—take the subway. Others, with Zoom dollars in their pockets, share taxis. Still others go on foot, some straight up Broadway, some on the bike paths along the Hudson.

Mayor Morris and his wife are having the windows of Gracie Mansion soundproofed. Once the work is complete, it is their fondest hope that passersby will no longer stop and cock their heads curiously toward the windows, wondering if what they are hearing is the howl of a dog or the wild cries of a caged child.

Alice, Adam, and Rodolfo wait for the number 6. They are the last ones from the Upper West Side pack to make their way north. The air in the subway is filthy and hot. The other people waiting for the train look as if they are hovering in some imperiled state between life and death. A strong wind could blow them in either direction—but no wind can enter this tunnel several feet beneath the stinking sidewalk. The electronic message board promises that the next uptown 6 will arrive in four minutes. But it has been saying that for a while...

"You's okay?" Rodolfo asks Alice.

She shrugs, then poses the same question to Adam.

"I miss Mom," says Adam.

"Our mother's dead. We watched it happen."

"I mean Aunt Cynthia. She *is* our mother. Now."

"We don't have a mother, Adam. We never did and we never will. When you have a mother, you're *like* her. Do you actually think we're like Aunt Cynthia?"

"In some ways," Adam says, looking away. He's afraid he is going to cry, and he doesn't want his sister to see his eyes.

Alice glances over at Rodolfo. He is staring at her. She can't discern if he is furious or if it's just his usual over-the-top intensity. She moves closer to him, her fingers wiggling in the air. She plucks at the shoulder of his T-shirt.

"Hi," she whispers.

"Don't leave," Rodolfo says. "Please."

Alice doesn't say anything.

The arrival board is suddenly functioning again. The northbound 6, it says, is approaching the station. Alice cranes her neck, looks down the long sooty tunnel. The distant light of the oncoming train shines in the darkness.

The Hotel Hedley on East Twenty-Sixth Street is not luxurious, to say the least. There are a few hipsters who have a special affection for the place because it reminds them of what New York was like in the 1970s and early 1980s, when the city teetered on the brink of collapse and the stink of empty municipal coffers was everywhere, like the smell of mildew on a scarf. Now it seems as if the addicts and scammers and unshaven German documentary filmmakers from that era have found a permanent home at the Hedley. The rooms are tiny, the beds are penitential, and any windows that don't look directly at a brick wall have views of an air shaft. But at the Hedley, it is not only the ambience that recalls the 1970s; the prices are old-fashioned too, and it is here that Dennis has been staying since leaving his apartment and the mess therein on Ocean Parkway.

He cannot stop dosing himself with his ever-dwindling stash of Zoom, even now as he walks through the Hedley lobby with his phone to his ear. The Borman and Davis line rings and rings—no answer, no voice mail, nothing. Screw it.

It's gotten to the point where he actually *knows* people lurking in this lobby, this dank repository of dozens of fake ficus trees. The furniture looks as if it's been dragged out of the world's most melancholy Hopper painting; the bellman looks as if he has done freelance work as a hit man; and the desk clerk stands rigidly tall with an oxygen cannula clipped to his nose and a large No Smoking sign in front of him—the clerk is legitimately worried about exploding.

Oh yes, yes, yes. Dennis has to upgrade his situation, and today he aims to pick up those twins, get his bonus money, and start looking in earnest for a decent place to live. Getting them should be, he thinks, relatively easy. He knows where they live. It'll just be a matter of needling them, putting them in the van.

How many times has the phone at Borman and Davis rung? Thirty?

Dennis's face is gray and moist, like wet clay. He walks with a bowlegged gait, maneuvering one of those fabled eight-hour erections the hawkers of ED medicine brag/warn about. Dennis very much doubts there is anything on the market that can turn a noodle into a battering ram, but yesterday's gulp of Zoom is still working its mysterious way through him. He is half mad with desire. As determined as he is to capture those twins and get his reward, he is nearly as focused on putting his stiff prick inside a woman—in his imagination, it will be like a blacksmith cooling his red-hot tongs by plunging them into a bucket of water: the sizzle, the steam, the relief.

His Watertight van is parked on the street, a block from the hotel. As he gets in, he sees, to his surprise, that a parking ticket has been placed under the windshield wiper—usually the cops are good sports about his van, figuring he's on a job somewhere and cutting him some slack. Oh, well. The van is not registered in his name and he couldn't care less about parking fines. It's Borman and Davis's baby to rock.

He is dressed in loose-fitting clothes. The weather is beastly. Even in the raspy, slightly rancid air-conditioning of the van, he is pouring perspiration. Sweat drips from his armpits, from the tip of his nose. His underwear feels like a slur of wet cardboard. His ankles are wet. He knows this profusion of perspiration is in all likelihood a side effect of the Zoom—but hey, you've got to pay to play, right?

Traffic is not too bad. At least, not by Manhattan standards. (If cars were moving in such a molasses ooze in any other city, you'd think there'd been an explosion somewhere or that a sci-fi monster was loose on the streets, hurling buses and breathing sulfur.) He travels north on Madison. The sidewalks are filled with shockingly good-looking people. The shops display their legendary brands.

There is a vial of Zoom in his breast pocket. He pulls it out, looks at it, tilts it back and forth; the blood leaves a smudgy trace of itself along the glass. Then, feeling kind of "what the heck," he pops the cork out of it (using his thumbnail) and downs his second Zoom hit of the day.

Soon enough, he arrives at the house. There is a parking space (saved especially for him by a fire hydrant) close to the front door. The twins are not very big; he can fling one over each shoulder, toss them in the back, and have them in Flushing by one o'clock, where for all he cares the researchers can scoop out their DNA like the gooey web of seeds in a cantaloupe.

He kills the engine and sits there for a moment. *Think,* he orders himself. But he's not completely certain what he is supposed to be thinking about. He opens the glove compartment. A few used needles fall out. He doesn't bother to retrieve them. They sink into the litter on the van's floor, the PayDay wrappers, the Red Bull cans, the sucked-pale Stim-U-Dents. He closes the glove compartment and thinks: *The English call it a glove box. That is so stupid.*

What he has not thought about is how to gain entrance to the twins' house. He wants those freaking twins so badly, he would even consider just hurtling himself through the window of their fancy house and grabbing them. That obviously is not a good plan, not smart, not even viable. He is aware that he is not thinking clearly. Desire, sheer carnality—which he is used to experiencing as a kind of distant thunder, a warning of sexual weather that seems to be rolling in but that never quite lives up to its rumbling fanfare—desire is now, as Van Morrison would have it, a full-force gale. He is pelted by it, drenched. He is caught on the vast open prairie of his aloneness and there is nothing to shelter him from this storm of desire. All he can do to protect himself is remember that he is not thinking very clearly…

There is another working van parked near the house, this one beige and red. An exterminating company called The Ver-minators. Bingo! That's his way in.

He bounds up to the porch, presses his thumb against the doorbell.

Cynthia is making a call to yet another real estate company when she hears the doorbell ring. Her heart accelerates. With the twins on the loose, every sound in the world triggers either hope or dread. She quickly breaks the connection and hurries to the door, forgetting the New York procedure and failing to look through the fish-eye peephole to see who it is.

It's a sweaty, rather frantic-looking man in loose-fitting clothes who's shifting his weight from his left foot to his right and back again. He looks vaguely familiar, but there is too much going on in Cynthia's mind for her to spend more than a moment on this particular thought.

"I'm with Verminators," the man says, stepping quickly into the house, not even giving her a moment to consider.

"Oh," she says. "The others are already here. I think they're starting off in the cellar. It's really bad."

"Well, that's what we're here for," the man says. He reeks. His distressed humanity oozes from every pore.

"I'll take you to where—"

"That's okay," he says. His voice is webbed with phlegm. "I got it covered." He breezes past her—a foul breeze—and the phone in her pocket starts its chapel-bell chimes. Sunday! God is in His Heaven! All is right with the world! Except it is Wednesday. God, if He exists, has surely left New York for Martha's Vineyard or Sag Harbor. And not a thing is right with the world.

Except! The display on her phone says *Alley-Oop*.

Welcome home, God!

"Alice?" Cynthia breathlessly says into her phone. "Where

are you?" (The greeting that has replaced "How are you?" since the advent of the mobile phone.)

But what is that sound? A dragon chewing a tin roof? People trapped underwater struggling to get out?

"Alice? Alice?"

Now Cynthia can make it out: It's the noise of a subway. She can hear the amplified voice of the conductor announcing one thing or another—these squawking bulletins are usually impossible to understand even if you are physically *on* the train, so whatever is being communicated is completely unintelligible in this incarnation.

"Honey? Honey, can you hear me? Are you there?"

Cynthia realizes she has been ass-dialed—Alice obviously sat on her cell phone and accidentally called home.

Or is it so obvious? Maybe the call was not an accident. Maybe Alice deliberately called but is not in a position to safely say anything. Maybe this call is like a roadside flare set off to mark the location of a disabled vehicle.

Cynthia paces around with the phone to her ear in case, against all odds and expectations, Alice's voice comes through, but the call is disconnected. She goes to the window, looks out at the street in the stark summer light, the leaves of the tree silvery and parched, the passersby immodestly dressed. She hears the exterminators clumping around in the cellar, hears their voices, manly and monotonal, all information, no emotion.

"Nest," one says.

"Where?" asks another.

"Here we go," the first one says.

"Gimme that, uh…" a third voice says, the indefinite *uh* sizzling like a strip of bacon on a hot griddle.

From somewhere up above: footsteps. At first heavy, then

quieter, as if whoever is up there suddenly wished to go unnoticed. Cynthia's brow furrows; she looks up. Why are the exterminators up there? They are supposed to be concentrating on the cellar, where inside the walls—she is sure of this—there is a veritable honeycomb of rodents. And didn't they already agree that she would show them through the upstairs rooms herself before they started setting traps, chipping away plaster, rummaging through closets, putting out poison pellets?

"Hello?" she calls out, looking up at the ceiling.

Of course there is no answer. What is she thinking? They're exterminators, for crying out loud. They are not here to talk.

Maybe she should just sign off on this whole project and leave them to it, give them the run of the house. Maybe she should leave the house, go to a coffee shop—iced tea and fries! But no. How could she even consider leaving? What if the kids came home and found the place empty save for three—now four—strange men carrying rat traps and canisters of whatever rodenticide they are using? (The head rat assassin—an elegant man with a Spanish accent, bald except for a swoop of hair on either side of his head, the hair black and glossy like the fenders of a hearse—was very hocus-pocus about what kind of poison they were going to use, calling it only "our secret potion.")

Cynthia sits on the sofa, pulls her phone out, and stares at it, as if to intimidate it into ringing. Fat chance. She stands after a few moments and returns to the windows, where she hopelessly scours the street for signs of the twins.

She hears a door slam shut. It's coming from the second floor—possibly the third. The house is tricky in how it transmits sound. But what in the hell is that exterminator doing up there? He belongs down in the cellar with the rest of them.

Cynthia goes to the foot of the stairs, cocks her head, listens.

She can hear the expensive whoosh of the air conditioners push-ing cool air out of the house's forty-two vents. Silence from upstairs. Until...

Footsteps. Running. Fast. And then stopping.

"Hello?" she calls up. Hearing her own voice infuriates her. *"Hello"? What is that supposed to mean? Why do I say "Hello" when I mean "Come down here this instant"?*

Holding on to her anger, a lifesaver in a sea of confusion, she walks loudly up the steps, hoping the soles of her shoes will communicate her irritation and her seriousness. Three-quarters of the way up, just as the staircase takes its gentle westward swoop, she stops, listens again. Silence. Her heart begins to beat harder. Something is not right about all this...

She makes her way to the second-floor hallway and goes from room to room, looking for the solitary rogue exterminator. She steps inside her bedroom. The walk-in closet door is open—she is certain she did not leave it like that; she never has and never would. She is afraid to approach it. Maybe it would be better—wiser, safer, *saner*—to just go downstairs and pretend none of this is happening. Or, better yet, register her concern with the Spanish man with the polished fenders of hair and let him deal with it.

Yet something compels her to see for herself. She looks around her bedroom for something with which to arm herself, but everything here is soft, useless—blouses, pillows, shawls, skirts, scarves. It is as if, despite all the evidence, mountains of it, centuries' worth, she still fundamentally believes a woman is safe in her own boudoir. Wait. There *is* something. A silver candlestick — an old one, with a Colonial provenance, possibly forged by Paul Revere himself, now holding a handmade taper and standing on Cynthia's bedside table.

She wraps her hand around the candlestick's cool silver shaft, draping one finger over the node so as to give her downward blow a bit more force should she find this creep in her closet. With her free hand—though, strictly speaking, no part of her body is "free," all of her has been colonized by fear, dread, and confusion—she opens the closet door to its fullest and stands there for a moment, her heart shuddering, her bowels watery, waiting for the fiend to emerge.

But all is stillness. She reaches in, groping for the light switch. Ready for something unseen and unspeakable to touch her. At last, she locates the switch, and the closet light blinks on. The closet itself was built for someone with four hundred changes of clothes and is now largely empty. At the very back of it, however, there is a darkness, a lump of…something. Slowly, she approaches it, the candlestick raised above her head should she need to strike. The closer she gets to the mass, the less light she has. Her heart is climbing a ladder made of fear on its way to her throat.

She hears a voice, a squeak, a whimper, saying, "Mommy." It takes her a moment to realize the voice is hers.

The mass at the back of the closet is a painter's drop cloth, left behind when the workers were getting the place spick-and-span for Cynthia and the twins' new lives. Impatiently, she kicks the drop cloth to one side. Beneath it, to her horror, is a nesting mother rat and her ten little thumb-size kittens, or pups, or whatever the fuck you're supposed to call those fetal little creatures that are somehow able to project both utter helplessness and insatiable carnivorous mayhem. She is too sickened to scream. Her fear of rats is starting to dull—she supposes that's a good thing. Maybe the only good thing that has come from this whole ordeal. She toes the canvas back over the rat family and retreats from the closet.

By the time she is back on the main floor, the men are emerging from the cellar.

The foreman approaches her, wiping cobwebs and dust from his forearms with a beige-and-blue handkerchief. "We will return tomorrow to check on the traps," he says.

There is something regal in his Spanish accent, and it lends a sense of dignity and even some pageantry to everything he says. Ah! Tomorrow! The fabled ceremonial checking of the traps! Flanking him are younger exterminators, one rotund with a failed mustache, the other lanky, wearing round, rimless eyeglasses. These were the three men who arrived originally—but where is the fourth?

"Are you leaving now?" Cynthia asks.

"Yes," the foreman says, his *Y* a *J*. In fact, he is striding quickly toward the front door, his crew in tow.

"There's someone else here," Cynthia says.

But the foreman is already on his phone to the home office, informing them he is done here and is on his way to a fast-food restaurant near Times Square.

"Excuse me?" Cynthia calls out.

The foreman turns, looks at her, his brows knotted, his head cocked to one side.

"You're leaving someone behind," she says. "There's someone still here."

"No, madame. Three come in, and one, two, three, we leave."

CHAPTER 21

The rains come suddenly and with furious force, startling and overwhelming. The sky is a vast suppurating wound. Thunder pounds out its chaotic rhythms. Pedestrians, most of them, scurry for cover as if in mortal terror—though a few seem to take this deluge as a relief from the oppressive New York summer heat.

But to Cynthia, the tumult of the storm is primarily an impediment to hearing possible footsteps in her house. Even when she moves away from the windows, the noise from the thunder and rain overwhelms her.

She walks toward the kitchen, passing on her way the door to the cellar. She opens it a crack, moves her ear close, and listens. *Snap! Snap!*

It's the sound of rat traps tripping, the sound of rat necks breaking.

Shivering with revulsion, she closes the door, locks it. If that fourth exterminator is lurking down there, he can stay there until his pals return in the morning.

Except this: She knows he's not down there.

He's upstairs. In one of a dozen rooms.

There's only one thing to do. Call the police. She pulls out her phone, notices the battery is waning. She dials a 9, a 1...and that is as far as she can get without second thoughts. (The road to ruin is paved with second thoughts.) Is she really going to call the cops and tell them there's a rogue exterminator somewhere inside her house? The cops are probably getting sick of her. And if anyone ever wants to make a case for taking the kids away from her—legal adoption or not, she nevertheless feels her right to parent them, to adore and protect them, is subject to question, subject even to sudden intervention—having the police arrive and incidentally note that once again Adam and Alice are on the loose and once again Cynthia has no idea where they are, that will surely be entered into a ledger somewhere.

Nevertheless, her finger hovers over that final 1. She waits, waits. And turns the phone off to preserve the battery. In the kitchen, the German knives are stored in a wedge of butcher block, with slots cut out for a dozen knives, a perfect fit for each, from the paring knife to the cleaver. She pulls out a black-handled Wüsthof carving knife with an eight-inch blade. She grips it so tightly, her hand aches from the pressure. After all these years in her own skin, she is learning something brand-new about herself: She is capable of true violence. There is a limit, and she has hit it. Morality, compassion, even cowardice—they have all been rendered obsolete by the sheer unadorned animal instinct to survive. She will not run and she will not beg. There is a crazy man in her house. Her house! Her children's house! And she will kill this guy if he is here and makes even the slightest approach toward her. She will stab him in the chest, and if that does not kill him, she will pull the knife out and stab him a second time.

But meanwhile: Where is he?

*   *   *

In fact, Dennis is on the third floor, sitting on the edge of Adam's bed. He glances around the boy's room, trying to somehow guess from the look of things where he might be.

Think. Think. He rubs his forehead, closes his eyes. His brain is broken. He can think about sex, food, water, the temperature in the room; he can listen for sounds. But anything other than the most immediate and needful things is beyond him right now. Dimly, he knows it's the Zoom. Or is it? He's not sure. He's not sure if he's even taken any today. Or when. Or...wait. If. When. Isn't there another category? Something not *if* and not *when*. Oh, heck, it eludes him. His thoughts are starlight upon dark water. He tries to scoop them up and they disappear.

While he tries to remember if he's already taken his dose, he pops open another vial and downs it. This little batch is particularly salty, with a flabby kind of undertaste. Maybe it's gone bad. He has a dim memory of someone at the lab mentioning something or other about those things, the square things, you plug them in and whatever you put inside of them gets cold. Refrigerators! He has a dim memory of someone, one of the smocks, saying that samples from the feral urchins were meant to be refrigerated. And Dennis is pretty sure that refrigerators are what you use to refrigerate. In fact, he is sure of it. A shiver of pleasure goes through him, a long ripple of well-being. He grabs Adam's pillow and presses it against his face, breathes in the scalpy scent of the little boy. He parts his knees, wider and wider, and rubs himself, gently at first and then with real vigor. Holy moly, does that ever feel good!

*   *   *

Cynthia has turned the lights on downstairs and she stands now at the window, holding the knife, the point down, watching the rain lashing the roofs of parked cars. The wind is outrageous. Puddles have formed, and as the rain pounds into the standing water, drops like ball bearings rise up and fall again. Those who have umbrellas have mostly seen them turned inside out, and they try to hold on to them, staggering sideways.

Oh, please, oh, please, let them come home.

The windows are clouding over and she rubs a circle clear, turning the world outside into a Renaissance tondo. The rain falls on the wicked and the innocent, the rich and the poor, the old and the young. In seconds, the cleared circle starts to shrink, and she rubs her open hand on the glass again, convinced that any moment she will see them, her darlings. With the darkness on one side of the window and the lamps bright on the other, she can see the room she's in reflected in the glass. The fireplace, the chandelier, the paintings, the corridor…

But wait. A flash of something.

Someone.

Moving.

Gasping, she turns around, holds the knife in front of her as if to begin a fencing match. But the fear—which she thought she had completely under control—comes back with such an-nihilating force that her hands shake and she drops the knife. It falls point down and sticks into the fringe of the red-and-blue Sarouk on the floor. Quickly, she crouches, pulls the knife up, grips it again, and surveys everything she can see from that posi-tion, hunched over like a desperate creature, breathing through her mouth, daring whoever is there to make a move and hoping against all hope that her eyes were somehow playing tricks on her and that no one is there.

Wouldn't that be something? If this was all simply a matter of confusion? And that last exterminator, whoever he was, had come by simply to have a quick look around and was finished and gone before the other three emerged from the cellar? Why is that not possible? Doesn't it make more sense than what she has been thinking—that there is a man lurking somewhere in this house, this too-big house with too many rooms, too many doors, too many staircases, and far too many bad memories?

Slowly, she gets up. The change displaces her blood and she feels a sudden inchoate alarm, as if she were in an elevator whose cable has snapped. "Whoa," she says. She shakes her head, rights herself.

She walks down the center hall, past the cellar door. She makes it a point not to even glance at it. She walks through the dining room, with its dark yellow walls, it's soft beige carpet, its oval mahogany table large enough for a dinner party of eighteen, though she has only four chairs.

Oh, this house used to have such exquisite furnishings, every detail just so, back in the day, before Alex Twisden and poor Leslie went mad…Most everything they owned was either destroyed or hastily put to auction. Heartbreaking, irretrievable loss.

So Cynthia has been waiting for the right chairs. She has extremely refined and specific taste re chairs.

It all seems so foolish now…

She stops, looks at the chairs, shakes her head.

And at that very instant, a hand wraps around her ankle.

She manages one word, a sound, really: "Hey!"

*   *   *

It's a piece of good luck, and those children of the wild who were given religious instruction while they still lived with their parents go so far as to think it's more than luck—it's divine intervention. The storm has emptied Pelham Bay Park. The wild children don't mind getting wet—in fact, some of them are energized by the rain. They clown around. They chase each other. They dash, climb, wrestle, and wait for the pack to be complete. They come in twos, threes, fours, and fives. Rodolfo has climbed a tree; he can see who is arriving and can scan the park for dangers.

And then there is the greatest moment they have ever known. Four of the wild ones who have been in captivity appear. They are bandaged and look weak, unhappy, exhausted, and pale. But they are here—against all odds, they are here. A huge wild cheer goes up at the sight of them, and they rise to the occasion by joining hands and lifting their entwined fists high in the air, like a circus act absorbing the hurrahs under the big top.

"Bless us!" Rodolfo hollers from his perch in a sycamore.

"And them's like us!" shout the others.

Cynthia hits the floor, and she hits it hard—so hard that her head bounces up a few inches, comes to the limit of what the neck will allow, and crashes down a second time. Consciousness has not vanished but it is severely compromised, and she tries to blink the world back into focus—reality bulges and deflates like the throat of a croaking bullfrog. A presence…something looms above her.

It is the fourth exterminator. She knew it. She knew all along he was still in the house. But it's strange; having her worst fear confirmed fills her not so much with terror as with an awful, crushing *sadness*. The end of life, once a distant speck on the far horizon, once an abstraction, is all of a sudden hard upon her. And all her love of life, of the sweet world we live in, with its ten thousand pleasures and boundless beauty, all of it comes surging forward in a maelstrom of love and regret. It's over. Her flicker of light on the river of time. No time to say good-bye, no time to sum it up. Oh—after all this, to have to end it in pain! She no longer has it in her to fight. Or to take flight. In all of the most sudden of suddens, she is at the very end of what she can do. She raises her hands, not to defend herself, not to fight, but merely to cover her eyes.

She feels his hands on her. They are clammy, cold. His breath comes in excited little bursts and he is grabbing at her legs, her feet. He tears her shoes off. Even the noise of her shoes hitting the floor fills her with the pain of departure—it's another thing she will never experience again. Who knew that life in its every plangent detail could be so precious?

Oh no. She feels his tongue on the bottom of her foot. And then she feels the tip of it exploring the concave of her instep.

"Oh, boy, oh, boy," the man burbles.

Though her mind has surrendered, her body rebels, and she tries to yank her foot out of his grasp. But he has her. His grip is sure and tight. This is not how she wants to end. Not writhing. *Be still,* she tells herself. *Breathe . . .*

She hears the front door open.

"Mom?" a voice calls out.

Alley-Oop?

"We're home!"

Adam.

"*Kids!*" Cynthia hollers as loudly as she can. "*Kids!*"

They are running, and the man who is assaulting her does

not have even a moment to tell them, Stay back! Nor does he have a moment to protect himself. Or run.

The world again is something she wants to see. Cynthia uncovers her eyes, turns her head. And there they are: her children! Racing toward her. Adam upright.

Alice on all fours.

And now they are airborne.

And now the man has dropped her leg and is raising his arms to cover his face.

And now he is screaming in terror.

And now they land on him, Alice striking at his neck, Adam barreling into him from below.

And now the exterminator is being exterminated.

Cynthia rolls away from them and scrambles to her feet. *I'm alive!*

But it does not take long for her relief to turn to revulsion.

"Kids!" she screams. "Stop, stop, enough. *Enough!*"

They are eviscerating him. The exterminator is no longer struggling, no longer shouting and screaming or waving his arms, no longer kicking, no longer doing anything to save his life or even to extend it another moment.

There is blood on the floor.

Cynthia continues to scream at the twins, continues to beg them. But they do not listen to her. They cannot really hear her. They are utterly—and tragically—keyed into a higher authority. They are obeying the commands of their own deepest, truest nature.

Cynthia falls to her knees.

"Please, please," she cries. "Oh, please…"

For a moment, she seems to have gotten Adam's attention. He turns toward her, his head cocked, his eyes curious, a piece of Dennis Keswick's flesh hanging from his mouth, blood coursing down his chin.

"Adam. Baby. Please. You have to stop."

When she thinks back on it—and she will, many times over, often in the middle of the day, sometimes, punishingly, in the middle of the night—she will recall the look on Adam's face just then, as if for that moment, there was a chance that he could be called back from going over the precipice of his own nature. But really, it was just a moment. It might not have been real. She might have merely imagined it. The proof was right there before her eyes. And in her ears, in the snarl and the slurp, as the twins made a meal of the man—a man who might have deserved to die, it seemed to Cynthia, but no, not like this. Not like this. His moist gray face, what is left of it, is expressionless. His eyes have lost their cunning, and now they are losing their color, their luster, the slightest hint of animation. They are just two blobs of vile jelly.

EPILOGUE

She trusts them this much—she allows them to ride in the back of the rented car. They are sound asleep anyhow, sprawled and snoring, entwined with each other. What harm could they do?

And what she saw them do...they did it for her.

They have already tried to make their case to be dropped at Pelham Bay. Their friends are there—or at least nearby. Cynthia did not give it a moment's thought. She just kept driving north. She has about four hundred miles to go. If she drives hard, she can make it in about seven hours. When a little bit of light will still be lingering.

Soon she is out of the city. Over the RFK, onto the thruway, onto I-95. Connecticut. All those dear Yankee towns, like picture postcards pinned to the bulletin board, right through the tall steeple that stands in the center of each of them.

At one point, Adam awakens. "Where are we going now?" he asks.

"You just rest," she says. "Leave this to me."

"We're sorry, Mom," he says. "But he was hurting you."

"He was going to rape you," Alice adds. She is still lying

301

down; her eyes are still closed. Her stomach is distended with her awful meal.

"I know, kids. I know." She sees a cop car pulled off on the right side of the road, half hidden by a cluster of blue spruce. Looking for speeders. What a laugh…

Through Connecticut, angling through Massachusetts, slicing through Vermont, and now they are in New Hampshire. She stops for gas, bathroom breaks, snacks—granola bars for her, and the kids want beef jerky and energy drinks.

They stink of blood.

She refuses to tell them where they are going. All she will say is "Someplace you can be safe from the world, and the world can be safe from you."

"What is that supposed to mean?" Alice demands, her voice rising, turning dark red.

"From now on," Cynthia says, "if there are any questions being asked, I will do the asking. You understand me? I am your mother, and your job is to listen to me."

"I'll kill you," Alice says rather casually.

It terrifies Cynthia, but she manages not to let it show.

The evening is a dark royal blue. A quarter moon rocks gently in a sea of stars. They are in the middle of New Hampshire, climbing Mount Washington. The headlights of the rented car sweep over a sign that reads Use Low Gear, Stop Occasionally to Cool Brakes. Her heart is pounding—it may be caused by the thin air, though she doubts it.

"Where are you taking us, Mom," Adam says.

"Remember when I told you about this place? How one day we'd go see it?"

"Where the wind is?" asks Adam.

"That's right. Where the wind blows nearly three hundred miles an hour."

"What's so great about that?" asks Alice.

"I don't know, honey," Cynthia says. "It just is."

Even in the depths of summer, the landscape looks chilly, almost barren. Of the few trees, half of them have already begun to change color.

She hasn't seen another car or a sign of human life in half an hour. Without warning, Cynthia suddenly pulls the car off to the side of the road.

She reaches down into the well of the front seat and pulls up their backpacks. She has filled them both with changes of clothes, snacks, matches. She tosses one to Adam, the other to Alice.

"Okay, kids," she says. She hopes her voice has an element of encouragement in it. "Hop out."

She gets out herself, taking the car keys with her, just in case.

She waits for them, and eventually they open the back doors, first Adam and then Alice. There is a wind—it's not three hundred miles per hour, but it's considerably more than a sweet summer breeze.

"Mom?" Adam says, his voice trembling.

"I don't have a good choice here, Adam."

"You never seem to," says Alice.

"That's true, Alley-Oop. I never seem to. But what am I going to do? Turn you in to the police? Let you roam the city? The best I can do here is put you someplace where maybe, maybe maybe maybe, you can make lives for yourself in the wild and stay out of trouble and live whatever kind of life you are able to live."

Oh, shit. This is the last thing she wanted. She has started to cry.

"Maybe you've got a shot, huh?" Cynthia says, trying to force her voice through the web of tears. "I have to give you that chance. I want to. I couldn't bear to see you locked up. Or hunted down. And I couldn't bear your hurting another person."

"Did you *want* that guy to rape you?" Alice asks, her mouth twisted defiantly.

"I want you to understand something, kids—"

"Mom, please," Adam says. "You're not going to leave us *here*?"

"Fuck she's not," says Alice.

"Mom, come on, really," says Adam. "It was so totally not our fault."

"I know that, Braveheart," Cynthia says, suppressing a sob. "I really do. And I want you to understand that I don't blame you. You didn't ask for this. Not any of it."

"We're going to die out here," Alice says. "You know that, don't you?"

"I don't think you will, Alley-Oop. You're strong and you're swift and you're very, very smart. If you leave the humans alone, no one will bother you. And right now, no one knows you're here and no one's nearby. You just have to keep it that way."

"Sounds like you've got it all figured out."

"We just have to do the best we can."

"What about the house?" Alice says. "It's ours."

"The state will probably seize it. If I can sell it, I'll get you the money. I'll put it in an account under your names and send you the information. Every year on New Year's Day, look in the *New York Times,* and if I can sell the place, I will put a little ad in the real estate section. It'll say 'Wanted, House for Three People in Sargeants, New Hampshire.' If you see that, you call me. And I'll tell you how to get the money."

"This is not happening," Alice announces. She makes a move to get back into the car, but Cynthia clicks the remote, and the doors are locked.

The three of them stand there in silence.

"I'm sorry," Cynthia finally says.

"We're sorry too," says Adam.

"We didn't do anything," says Alice. "We saved you."

"It's just too dangerous," Cynthia says.

"For who?" asks Alice.

"For all of us," says Cynthia. "For everyone." She opens her arms. First Adam and then Alice slowly enter her embrace. She kisses the tops of their heads, their soft, silky hair. She feels their hands on her. It's no use. She does not have the strength to hold back her tears. And they do not have the strength to hold back theirs.

With a suddenness that catches the twins unawares, Cynthia disengages the locks of the car and gets in, quickly locking the doors behind her. She starts the engine and puts the transmission in gear. Slowly, she starts to roll away.

The twins frantically beat their little hands against the car's windows.

"It's not our fault!" Alice cries.

"Mom, come on, please," cries Adam.

Cynthia presses her lips tightly together and grips the steering wheel so hard, it feels as if her hands will break. The road curves before her, leading down and down into the darkness below. She glances in the rearview mirror. The twins are standing there, watching her leave. And then one of them—from this distance, she can't tell if it's Adam or Alice—sees something off to the left. An animal. A deer, perhaps. Maybe something larger. Cynthia looks straight ahead for a second to make sure she does not steer herself off the side of the mountain, and when she looks back in the rearview to check on the twins, they are already gone. Gone, gone, like a cool breeze, gone.

ACKNOWLEDGMENTS

I am glad to have this opportunity to gratefully acknowledge New York attorney Emily Goodman for her generous and patient explanations of certain questions regarding the law that arose while I was working on this story.

ABOUT THE AUTHOR

Chase Novak is the pseudonym for Scott Spencer. Spencer is the author of eleven novels, including *Endless Love,* which has sold more than two million copies to date, and the National Book Award finalist *A Ship Made of Paper.* He has written for *Rolling Stone,* the *New York Times, The New Yorker, GQ,* and *Harper's. Brood* is his second novel as Chase Novak.